Charles Davis

ANGEL'S REST

MIRA®

ISBN-13: 978-0-7783-2304-4
ISBN-10:   0-7783-2304-8

ANGEL'S REST

www.MIRABooks.com

Printed in U.S.A.

To my wife, Jennifer.

ACKNOWLEDGMENTS

To my wife, Jennifer Cole Davis, my son, Jackson, and the little one on the way, thanks for all of your help and inspiration. And to my parents, Thomas J. Davis and Linda L. Davis (thanks, Mom), my sister, Sheri L. Bailey, and my brothers, Jake, Fred and Ken, thanks for being such a loud, supportive bunch.

I'd also like to thank Marc Puckett, Warren Gillespie, Gary and Becky Alderman, Michael Smith, Joe and Lori McGraw, Phil Alexakos, Gary Tinder and, two great dogs, Chucky and Benny. Chucky was with me from the get-go of this writing journey. You're surely missed, old pard. I'd also like to thank Larry and Elaine Cole, who somehow stood by their daughter for five years as she somehow believed in a struggling writer.

Last but not least, I'd like to thank my agent, Lucienne Diver, and my editor, Ann Leslie Tuttle. Both have given so much of their time and talents in the making of this book. And this list wouldn't be complete if I didn't give a sincere thanks to Jerry Gross. Thanks, Jerry.

Chapter One

People said he was crazy. He'd come down from Angel's Rest a couple times a week and folks cleared the sidewalks when he passed. Hollis lived alone in a tar-papered plywood shack halfway up the mountain next to the reservoir. Most of the town was scared of him. I was, too, even before Daddy died and rumors started floating all over town. For as long as I can remember, my mother told me to stay away from Hollis Thrasher. I asked why, she gave me her most severe look and said nothing. I once asked Dad about Hollis, too, got the same look, and he said I'd better leave that poor feller alone.

I'd occasionally see Dad speak to Hollis or give him a ride from here to there. I remember seeing him almost every Tuesday night when our small library stayed open past seven o'clock. Mom worked there in the evenings to help kids read and I'd walk down there with her sometimes.

Hollis would barricade himself in a corner with a fort of stacked books. He had a look about him that said stay away and his face looked hard as a split chunk of firewood behind that brushy beard. He couldn't hide his eyes though. They were shiny and black and looked like the eyes an animal that hunted at night would have. I guess that's why some called him Wolf.

I was maybe seven or eight when I got the nerve to walk by Hollis Thrasher as he sat on the floor in the far corner of the library. Most people thought it better to walk to the other end of the long bookcase rather than disturb Hollis. I did, too, but I'd become curious as to what kind of books a man like him would read and besides, I got dared to do it.

I paused going by to take a look, he caught me staring and I wanted to run, wishing I'd taken my Mom's advice. But I couldn't move. He looked like a wax museum monster sitting there so big and still with dead eyes that never blinked.

I finally ran and found Momma in the back storage room, and I locked the door behind me when she wasn't looking. She was fixing old books people had borrowed but not taken good care of. When it was time for her to tell everybody the library was closed, I looked down every row and Hollis was gone. I was glad he was and we never saw him on our walk home, either. I was even gladder of that.

The next day I told and retold my tale of courage at school. I still had friends back then. It was one of those moments of glory everyone has.

About the time I was finishing fifth grade, I noticed that

I hardly saw Hollis anymore. He didn't come to the library much and he'd quit thumbing on the corner of Main Street. Every now and then I'd see him trying to sell a sack of firewood he'd tote over a shoulder, or he'd be sitting on the bench in front of the Piggly Wiggly. Once I saw him swinging an axe one-handed behind the hardware store where Dad said he'd bust up pallets for bean money, but that was about all. Hollis only had the one good arm because the other one got shot up in a war, Daddy said.

Like most people in Sunnyside, Virginia, I grew up on the side of Angel's Rest, too. It was a big, blue-green wave that met the sky and went on forever with ridges that blocked out the sun in the afternoon. Mom told me folks named it Angel's Rest because it was so high the earth's caretakers took breaks on the peaks before they came down to help those in need of God's assistance. I'd never been all the way to the top. Mom said it was always cold and windy up there. I didn't mind the cold and wind, but I wasn't in a hurry to meet a resting angel.

Our town had one stoplight, a grocery store and two filling stations that hoped to catch people with empty gas tanks on either side of the town limits. There were lots of gravel and dirt side streets, most of them dead ends, but one road with paint on it would take someone in or out of that narrow valley.

Sunnyside could have been a pleasant place to grow up. In 1967 that small town was slow as drying dew, but there was plenty for young boys who didn't know anything different.

Some new people moved up near the reservoir the spring

that Daddy got killed. Out of the seven kids they had, I eventually became best friends with one of the middle ones, named Jimmy.

Jimmy Peyton was my best friend. The Peyton family was poor or near it like the rest of us in Sunnyside, so they immediately fit in and I became friends with Jimmy one day after Sunday school when he asked where the good fishing holes were on Catawba Creek.

Jimmy was one of those tall, raw-boned boys who'd be good in school sports if he ever played them. He had a birthmark the size of a Sunday-school coat button on the center of his forehead and everyone in his family called him Spot or Bulls-eye, but Jimmy didn't like either of those names so I called him Jimmy.

Some folks just don't talk much, and Jimmy was that way but when he did people tended to listen. He was a couple years older than me, but we were in the same grade.

Jimmy and me ran the creek banks and ridges of that rural, green county. His mom didn't seem to care that he was gone all the time and after a while Jimmy started sleeping at my house a lot. We played war and built lookouts and lean-tos and started our own Boy Scout troop. We didn't have any uniforms or any adult leaders. We did have a ragged scout book that I'd swiped from the library, and one day after Jimmy and me swam in Miller's Pond, I flipped a lucky penny squashed on a southbound train track to see who the troop leader would be. He won but I wanted him to anyway.

We tried to get some of my old friends into our troop

but after a day of recruiting, we could only muster up Jimmy's brother, Alvin, and the Wilson twins.

Alvin was with us all the time anyway because Jimmy always had to take his kid brother along. I made up the secret initiation oath—Jimmy said I had a talent for that sort of thing—and he poked the holes in everyone's finger with a pocketknife he'd stolen from Barton's store once when he found the knife case unlocked.

Alvin was the first to enlist by taking the blood oath. He almost flunked the test when he started crying and had a hard time swearing his loyalty while sucking on his finger at the same time. The Wilson boys didn't have any friends and we didn't, either, so we let them join, too. I can remember them being pretty excited when we told them about our troop.

Harry and George Wilson were strange from day one. About the only thing I can remember about first grade is those two boys showing up on the first day wearing matching red capes that their mom had sewn a big letter "S" on. The teacher told the class not to make fun of Harry and George because they both wore masks and stuttered something fierce, and we didn't until they both locked themselves in a closet and stayed there all afternoon until the teacher finally convinced them to come out.

They quit wearing those capes before they joined our troop or we wouldn't have let them in.

Once the whole troop had taken the sacred oath, Jimmy and me went up on the mountain to find a spot for our fortress. The Wilson twins were sent home to fetch hammers, saws and nails, and Alvin went home to steal a tin of snuff from his grandmother.

We all met a couple hours later at the reservoir, and it wasn't long before we found the perfect site. The five of us stood, kicked dirt and looked for treasure when I walked down to the stream and took a cool drink. "It's paradise," I said.

The name stuck.

Paradise was located on a flat spot in a hollow off an old grown-over path. It was beside a small mountain spring and was about a fifteen-minute hike from the end of the town road. The best thing about Paradise was there had been a house there at one time, because there was a burned-out chimney and some old, charred boards we could use to build our fortress.

We worked all day, me and the rest of the boys, building walls while Jimmy carved a big chair out of an old stump. By afternoon, Jimmy had made a lopsided table where we could talk troop business.

I'd been camping with Dad a few times but was surprised that evening when I asked my mom if I could camp on the mountain with just my friends. I found her in bed like she was so much of the day since Daddy was killed. She had an arm covering her eyes. I hated the way she stayed in that dark room so much and couldn't hardly stand going in there for any reason anymore but I had to.

"Hi, Angel," she said real quiet.

I'd planned what I was gonna say and started telling her who all was going and how careful I'd be with matches and stuff like that, figuring she wouldn't be in a mind to let me go unless I put it to her right.

She interrupted me and said, "It'll get chilly tonight so take a couple of blankets from the hall closet. And you may want to take a tarp—"

"I know what to take camping, Momma."

"Okay, baby."

For the first time that I could remember, I felt like a grown-up and it scared me for a minute. I would have sworn she'd have said no.

I didn't dare say anything else, figuring I needed to get out of the house quick before she changed her mind. I threw a can of soup, a big hunk of corn bread, two blankets and book matches in a sack and headed out the door for Jimmy's house, where he and Alvin were waiting ready to go. The three of us waited at the reservoir until almost dark for the Wilson twins, then figured their mom had said no, and headed up to Paradise without them.

When we got there, Jimmy didn't want to build a fire in the burned-out fireplace because he said we should make a fire like the Indians and trappers used to make. Right in the middle of that flat spot, we made our first big fire and hung our cans of soup using wire and propped sticks and put our toes as close to the flames as we could until we had to pull away. We all agreed how good it was to be in a troop. After everybody ate their supper and it started getting quiet, I thought about telling a ghost story but it had already gotten dark and I didn't want to scare myself, so I didn't. I wondered if everyone else had the same thought because nobody told any stories about women in white dresses floating above the fields or places in the forest that the devil has claimed. It was unusual on a camping trip not to hear something that keeps you up half the night. I did make the motion that we should take turns as lookouts to keep the fire going until morning. Jimmy agreed, so everybody else did, too, and I volunteered for the first shift 'cause I couldn't sleep anyway.

None of us had a watch but I guess it was around midnight when I heard the far-off sounds of breaking branches. It got quiet for a spell after that except for the normal sorts of strange utterances a mountain says at night. I couldn't see or hear nothing, but a feeling came over me slow and all over—like what happens when you get too cold—that something was out in the darkness watching me. I tried to tell myself I was imagining things until leaves started crunching way down in the hollow.

The sound of those leaves got closer and then the breeze shifted and it seemed like what was mashing them was miles away. Then it got completely still until I heard something breathing. I knew I wasn't scared half to death for no good reason.

I could see a good ten yards with the fire and full moon and the knot in my throat got tighter by the second. I stood up with my guard stick, couldn't get out any words to wake up Jimmy so I kicked him and he jumped up all addled because I kicked him a lot harder than I meant to. Alvin crawled out of his blanket, threw more wood on the fire and we waited as the noise got even louder. It got to where I couldn't hear from my heart beating in my ears and I looked at Jimmy and saw the back of his dungarees shaking.

I got really scared then.

The large form of something appeared and it stopped. Alvin screamed and I may have, too. I thought it was a bear until the huge, dark shape got closer and I saw the overalls and looked into the black eyes of Hollis Thrasher.

Everybody saw the chunk of lumber in his right hand except for me. I stared at those eyes. Tiny flickers of flames began reflecting back at me.

"Boys, I own this piece of ground and it's special to me," he said.

Hollis kept looking at us and nobody could say anything. Then his eyes leveled on me and he took a step closer to the edge of the fire.

"Stay tonight, just move your camp a ways down the hollow or up on the ridge next time."

As soon as he turned to leave, Alvin'd already wet his britches.

"What're we gonna do, Jimmy?" Alvin said, crying. "He might come back and kill us."

Jimmy turned and peed on the fire, I threw a jug of spring water on what was still alit, and in one motion, we all looked at each other, took off running and yelling like our butts were a-blazing and didn't stop until we got to the reservoir.

I got home that night and the door was unlocked. It surprised me 'cause Mom had gotten real serious about locking the door after Daddy was shot. I walked in and there was a note on the kitchen table. It said that a lot of boys come home early on their first camping trip and there was rhubarb pie in the refrigerator.

I lay in bed the rest of that night awake because every time I closed my eyes, I saw a huge man-wolf standing alone on a windy mountain ridge with fire in his eyes. And if I weren't seeing that, I found myself in the middle of that awful nightmare where I was standing in the kitchen as my mother screamed and screamed and screamed wearing a bloody apron.

I guess I did eventually get to sleep because Mom shook me the next morning to go to Dad's old shop. I jumped out of bed and was glad I didn't have to sleep or try to sleep for another whole day. I liked daytime a whole lot better than nighttime after Daddy was buried. I only dreamed in the dark, you see.

Chapter Two

When Dad was still alive he ran our town's only radio and TV shop and I had to work there in the mornings during the summer. It was divided into the front showroom, the back service area and his small office. The back of the store was where men from all over the county gathered throughout the day, huddled around a coffee percolator or the woodstove, where you could usually find a pot of beans of some sort or a cast-iron skillet of fried potatoes and onions.

Between the jokes and stories told back there, you could usually find out about everything that was going on in Sunnyside if you listened hard enough to what nobody was saying.

The back of the store had a smell of men who worked for a living and whatever was simmering on the wood stove. Dad's office, heaped with bills and statements, smelled of aged paper and old spice and the front showroom had a pipe tobacco mixed with furniture polish smell.

Dad used to keep me busy…sweeping up, chopping wood and learning here and there how to fix broken things. One of the jobs I loved best was going on service calls. Being that there weren't many people living in that part of Virginia, there weren't many people who could fix TVs, either. Dad spent half his days riding the winding mountain roads in his beat-up paneled truck, and I got to ride with him. I felt pretty big riding in my father's work truck, sharing a bottle of RC and a pack of nabs.

My job in those days was to be his technical assistant, a title Dad always said with a big grin to his customers and then they'd look down and grin at me, and then I'd grin so we'd all be grinning.

Most of the places we went to on service calls were small, white, clapboard houses sitting on hills with dirt driveways. They all smelled the same and were all too warm inside. The little, gray-haired ladies that usually opened the doors always looked a little different in size or shape, but they seemed pretty much the same to me, too. They'd rub my curly hair, tell me how much I'd grown since they'd last seen me and would offer me something to eat. I could never eat until I did my technical chores, though.

I can remember many times getting antsy because I'd have my technical work completed and would be waiting on Dad to leave the kitchen and fix the TV.

Sometimes it seemed he'd sit for hours drinking coffee and talking with those old ladies. I'd overhear him saying how her husband had been such a fine man and I'd hear them laughing about a story he told. I found out people tended to die a lot in wars and coal mines, or they got some kind of cough that got worse and worse, or they just keeled over dead for no reason anyone could explain except God said it was time to go to heaven.

It seemed Dad knew everyone in the whole world and they all wanted him to sit and talk about the old times and people dying. Maybe they wanted to talk and talk because he was the only man who could fix TVs, and he was also the town mayor. Dad told me once that most people always have a few words to say to the mayor. Or maybe it was because he was never in a big rush like I always was. I'm not sure about why there was all the quiet talking around kitchen tables, but there was a lot of it.

I noticed, too, when we'd leave those small houses on hilly ground that Dad never had as much money in his hand as when we left some of the bigger houses in town. Sometimes there was no money or promise of payment to record in the brown book he kept above the visor in his truck. He usually did get a sack of green tomatoes or put up beans or sometimes a mason jar of corn liquor that he always told me was for grown-ups unless I had the night fevers.

I can remember a few times we'd go into a home and notice the TV was unplugged when we tried to turn it on. All the while, the gray-haired lady in the apron would be fretting how it just quit working and she and Dad would go into the kitchen for coffee. I'd plug it in, go ahead with my technical chores and they'd sit. It seemed like on the service calls where the only thing wrong with the TV was that it was unplugged, he'd end up sitting a lot longer. I asked him once about the unplugged TVs and he told me sometimes older folks get lonely. I didn't understand what loneliness had to do with an unplugged TV, but he told me I would one day.

Before I was old enough to start school, I'd sometimes spend the whole day at Dad's store and at closing time, I'd usually end up in the same spot. I'd end up asleep on the leg of an old feller who worked for Dad named Lacy Albert Coe. Black folks called Lacy "Storyteller" and white folks in town called him "Slim." I guess they called him that 'cause he was slim, but I just called him Lacy.

Dad claimed Lacy worked for him, but I never actually saw Lacy do anything.

I can remember we'd pick him up first thing in the morning in front of his cinderblock house on Old Tannery Road and once a week he'd leave a feed sack of clothes in the paneled truck for my mom to wash. I asked Dad why he hired an old colored man to just sit all day. He said he just liked having him around.

Every morning, I don't care how cold it was or how late we'd be to pick him up, Lacy would be standing at the end of his dirt driveway leaning on his cane with a blue ball cap pulled low on his head. It would take him a while to get in the truck, but I remember Dad never would offer to help Lacy like I'd seen him help other old people whether they were colored or not.

His one-room house sat crammed beside a bunch of other cinderblock houses and trailers on a bluff overlooking the river and the tannery. A lot of people in Sunnyside called that part of town Niggerville, but they never called it that name if coloreds were in hearing distance. I called it Niggerville once to Mom and she grabbed me by the arm and whacked me a bunch of times on the backside. She told me that I knew better than to use that word and I did, especially around her, but at the same time, I knew other people used it in jokes and stuff so I didn't see the harm in it as long as you didn't say the word nigger around a nigger. She told me I wasn't "everybody else" and that they were black people, not niggers or any other bad names and the proper name of their neighborhood was Town Heights.

Lacy was someone I kept an eye on but didn't take to immediately. First of all, the palms of his hands were pink-looking compared to the rest of his wrinkled, dark skin. I couldn't figure why one side of his hand would look so different than the other. And he was so old. He had a long nose that matched his long ears and hair poked out from both, and he kept a close-cropped, white mustache. I always thought he wore the same clothes every day because I never saw him in anything but blue work pants, a heavy, button-down white shirt, white socks and black shoes that looked too big for him. He always kept his collar buttoned even when it was really hot, and he had a silver chain that ran from one button into his front pants pocket.

The routine when we'd get to the shop was usually the same. Dad would walk around, turning on lights and feeding the stove while I'd get into something until I was told to stop. Lacy would slowly walk to the service area, hang his cane on something, get the coffee percolator going, look around for wherever he'd hung his cane, find it eventually, and would walk three-legged back to the front and look at the occasional car or trailer truck going by. That was usually the only time I'd see him stand up all day, except around noon when he washed up and ate the dinner my mother made for him.

As I was heading here and there, Lacy would be in his straight-back chair in the corner of the showroom next to Dad's office. He'd occasionally say something to people milling around but I noticed that most people pretty much ignored him altogether, even other coloreds who'd stop in occasionally to look at the TVs. Dad said Lacy didn't see or hear so good was why he sometimes missed the few who addressed him but I couldn't figure out why white folks and black folks sort of treated him like a stick of furniture and hardly never said howdy or nothing. And Lacy never went in the back room with the other men to talk around the woodstove. Mostly, Lacy just sat and looked straight out at nothing in particular.

I once asked Dad why Lacy didn't have to work and he told me Lacy was working. I figured Lacy must be a lot higher up the ladder than me or the other technical assistants to be able to just sit and smoke his pipe and get paid a wage, until Dad told me that he didn't pay Lacy, he'd just give him the dinner Mom would fix him or he'd buy Lacy two slaw dogs and something to wash them down with at the Tastee-Freez on Wednesdays when they sold dogs two for a quarter.

Some of the other men who worked for Dad would wrestle with me, give me magnets or do card tricks and stuff, but Lacy never did. I never saw Lacy talk to anyone for too long, unless it was Dad, and the two thought they were alone.

I can't remember exactly how we became friends, but it had to do with a brown stone shaped like a cross that hung from his pocket-watch chain. I never had the guts to ask him about it because he always looked like one of those tough sea captains when he sat in his straight-back chair and smoked his pipe. I didn't know if there were colored sea captains but that's what he looked like.

I had to know what that brown stone was and I wanted to look at his pocket watch up close because I had seen there was some kind of picture in there. I don't know how I finally asked, but I remember he told me the brown stone was a special rock he'd found with Mrs. Coe at a lake just after their nuptials.

A fairy stone, he called it.

Lacy eventually let me hold the fairy stone and showed me his watch, too, and let me look at the faded black-and-white photo of him and his wife, who'd passed a long time ago he told me. I didn't believe the young man in the picture was him, but he said it was.

I started ending my workdays sitting on the floor next to Lacy. I'd have my last soda pop and would ask him to tell me a story. At first, I'd sit cross-legged on the floor, holding the heavy pocket watch as he'd carefully light his pipe, rubbing his chin to think of another story.

One day I climbed up on one of his knees to try and figure out what he looked at all day. After a while, I just liked sitting up there. I can remember Dad occasionally waking me, pulling me off his lap while a raspy voice would say, "It's all right, Mr. York. Child's not hurting nothing."

Over the course of two or three years, Lacy must've told me a hundred tales. A few he had to tell many times because I would want to hear them again and again, but they were always a little different and a couple times I had to retell the story to jar his recollection. He started to ask me to tell him stories, too. I told a lot of fibs, like the time I told him I hit fifty home runs during one game, but he'd just sit and listen.

Sometimes after one of his stories, he'd ask what the story meant. I never knew what he meant by that, and he kept telling me that there is a music to all things and events on this earth and you don't hear the music but you feel it.

He said a man has to learn to listen close with his heart and not his ears to warm to the ups and downs of life. I never understood any of that stuff about the music of good times and bad times and living and dying. But he told me to remember the stories, pay attention to things I see every day and that one day I'd make some good music of my own. He never told me stories about wars or astronauts like I asked him to a couple times. He told stories about trees and animals and storms and fishing. Especially fishing, which suited me all over because I loved to fish more than anything. He told me all of his stories were true and I believed him.

Once I'd started middle school, I didn't work for Dad as

much as I did before. I was at the ballfields or creeks more than I was in the passenger seat of his old truck. On a trip to town now and then, I'd stop in and talk to Lacy but I was too old to sit on his lap and I was in too much of a hurry anyway to listen to his stories.

I'd always noticed that Dad looked up to Lacy and seemed to ask him questions about a lot of things, so I started doing the same. I used to ask Dad about stuff but after he died, I started going to Lacy about important matters, too. It was better than talking to Momma, because she didn't want to talk at all anymore.

I had something I was dying to ask somebody that morning after the camping trip when Hollis Thrasher had shown up at midnight with a chunk of lumber in his hand and fire in his eyes. I walked up to Lacy and grabbed his suspender. He pulled his pipe away and asked if I was sick.

I shook my head. "Does Hollis Thrasher own Angel's Rest?" I asked.

"His kin have owned most of that mountain for as long as I can remember," Lacy said, leaning toward me. "Old folks still call it Thrasher's Mountain. Why you want to know?"

I stammered for a minute and proceeded to tell him what had happened the night before. He nodded his head and smoked his pipe and sat for a long time after I'd finished the story. Finally he said, "You fellers find another spot to build your fortress. There's plenty of good spots on Catawba Creek."

"Is he crazy? I heard he burned up his own family after he got out of the nut house."

Lacy toked for another long while. "Hollis got back from the war and was in the ward over in Bluff City a long time, but I don't think he's crazy. He's just one of those folks who've never found a lucky penny. He was a heck of a football player in high school and used to be a good guitar picker like his daddy."

"What about the fire?"

"They never did know what started it."

"Some still say he did it."

Lacy nodded a little. "Some folks say about anything, I reckon."

"Are you scared of him?"

"Listen, Hollis just wants to let be. He got shot up bad over there in Korea and then things went wrong for him up on the mountain."

"I heard he killed a pile of people in that war."

"Um–hmm."

"You heard that, too?"

"He's seen bad up close, child."

"Why's he live in that shack if he owns the whole mountain?"

"My figuring is it suits him or he'd live somewheres else."

"But why'd they send him off to prison after he got back from the war and out of the nut hospital?"

"He got tangled up with some rough ol' boys down South somewhere."

"In Louisiana?"

Lacy nodded.

"Why was he down there?"

"Don't know."

"Well, why'd they send him to prison?"

Lacy kept puffing but the smoke quit coming out as one of his fingers, colored like burnt molasses, rubbed back and forth across a worn groove in his corncob pipe bowl. Lacy never did talk normal back and forth like most folks do so I just kept standing there because I knew he'd eventually say something. He fired a match to whatever was left to smoke and took another toke.

"He got in a big ruckus, hit a couple of fellers and got in a bind over it," Lacy finally said.

"Why'd he beat on those fellers?"

"I reckon he thought it was the proper thing to do at the time."

"What happened to them?"

"I'm not sure exactly," Lacy said.

"Did they die?"

Lacy didn't say anything.

"I heard he killed a man in a pool hall…hit him so hard his neck broke and his head almost flew clean off."

Lacy leaned toward me again. "They tried to get his pocket-book. That's about all I know for surety."

"You don't know nothing else about it?"

"I know this. He got in a mess of trouble in a place he shouldn't have been in in the first dang place. And I think that judge did Hollis a favor throwing him in jail for a couple years so he'd quit all that dang foolishness and come back to the mountain where he belongs."

About that time, a deputy sheriff walked in with his belly

pushing on his gun belt so far that his holster banged against his knee when he walked. He took out a rag and patted a bead of sweat running down from under his straw hat and started talking to Ben Davis.

Ben had taken over Dad's business and worked up front most of the time trying to sell TVs like Dad used to do, but Dad had always told me Ben didn't have a knack for selling. Fixing. But not selling.

Dad had told me he tried to teach Ben important things like you never try to sell a customer anything until they put their hand on something, because then you know what they really want. He said it was important to figure out what folks want and their mouths won't tell you, their hands will.

Anyway, Ben ran the whole shop now that Daddy was dead and I was trying to figure out what was going on between Ben and the deputy because they were talking like someone had died. Ben came from behind the counter and called me to the back room. The deputy smiled a strange smile at me and Ben said he had some questions. I was sure the questions had to do with Dad and swallowed a big lump.

"Charlie, you seen the Wilson twins today?" the deputy asked.

I stood puzzled for a moment. "I saw them yesterday."

"Were they camping with you boys last night?"

I shook my head and backed up.

"You sure?" Ben asked.

I nodded.

The deputy got closer and put his hand on my shoulder. "This is important, Charlie. Their mom said they went up to the reservoir around dark to camp with you boys. They never came home."

I stood there unable to talk as he continued asking me the same questions over and over. I was in the middle of telling him that he should go talk to Jimmy and Alvin when I froze.

I watched as Hollis Thrasher walked into the store and stepped up to the front counter.

Ben saw me staring toward the showroom and turned around to see what had made me turn the color of warm buttermilk a week too old. He then got stern with me for the first time ever, like Dad used to do when I was in trouble. He told me to answer all of the deputy's questions, and then walked to the counter and pulled out a small transistor radio that Hollis looked over.

The deputy said a few more things to me which I didn't hear, scrubbed my head and walked to the front. Lacy got up from his straight chair and leaned toward him.

The deputy put one hand on the butt of his revolver and turned toward me, nodding his head as Lacy kept talking. Hollis was a few feet away from them and pulled a wad of money from his pocket and he started putting change on the counter. He then turned to leave with his radio. The deputy walked over and put a hand on his shoulder and then both of them turned around and looked at me. I wanted to run but instead I yelled.

"He killed them!" I screamed, pointing my finger at Hollis.

I backed up into the wall and put my finger down because it was shaking so bad.

Hollis's eyes were locked on mine and the deputy gave me a long, quizzical look before both of them walked out to his squad car. I saw Hollis saying something to the deputy and then he turned his head and those eyes locked onto me again, except this time he looked like a man who'd just found out his best coon dog had got run over by a timber truck. I ran to Lacy.

"What'd you tell the sheriff?"

"I told him what you told me. If Hollis saw you boys last night he may have seen the others. That's all, Charlie. What's got hold of you?"

"He's killed 'em and he's gonna kill me now!" I yelled.

Just then I saw the deputy sheriff nod to Hollis and get in his squad car. Hollis didn't nod back but kept looking through my Dad's store window. I remembered how Dad always told me the thing you fear most will someday end up looking you right in the eye.

After a couple hours of testing a pile of TV tubes in a tube tester machine, I got paid my wages, ran up to Jimmy's and we called an emergency meeting. He was the first one who told me they'd found the Wilson twins. They'd got scared about camping and somehow ended up with their daddy, who was rooming over in Saltville.

I felt a relief like I'd never felt before but then realized what I'd said to Hollis Thrasher and the way he'd looked at me. I ran to get the Wilson twins because we were all supposed to meet at the sinkhole behind Chapin's barn.

Miss Wilson answered the door and told me pretty directly I could play with George and Harry, but they weren't to leave the yard because they were being punished for walking four miles to Saltville in the dead of night. I told both of them what had happened and that we were going to have to build the fortress somewhere else.

"I left all those tools up there," Harry said, wearing that stupid cape.

I thought a few minutes and told him Jimmy and me would fetch the tools. George said they were only grounded until Friday so I told them to behave until then because we had lots of stuff to do over the weekend.

On the way to the sinkhole, I tried to come up with a way to get Jimmy to go up to Paradise to fetch George and Harry's tools—without me. I figured that Hollis had it in for me now and I didn't want to go anywhere near his shack up on Angel's Rest.

When I got to the sinkhole, I found Alvin sitting on a stump with his cane pole and a cupful of crickets he'd caught. He said Jimmy'd already left to find another spot for our fortress and wanted me and him to get the tools and scout book from Paradise. My legs went weak.

"What's wrong with you, Charlie?" Alvin asked. "You look like you seen Lucifer."

"Nothing. We ain't going fishing so dump them crickets and come on."

When we got up to the reservoir, I told Alvin to keep a close lookout behind us to make sure Hollis Thrasher wasn't following. As we worked our way up the ridge and down into the hollow, I stopped when I heard a noise coming from Paradise. We got on our bellies down near the stream and crawled until we could see what was making the loud racket.

"It's probably Jimmy," Alvin said.

"Shhh."

I had a sudden blast of courage and told Alvin to stay back until I yelled for him. I crawled my way through some mountain laurel and when I got behind a big beech tree, I stood up slow. I thought my knees weren't going to hold me when I saw Hollis Thrasher standing in the middle of Paradise swinging an axe. I inched my way back down the tree when I heard Jimmy running up the hollow yelling my name. I turned around, put my hand across my throat—giving him the danger signal we'd practiced—and he stopped cold. I turned back to Paradise and Hollis was staring at me, leaning on that axe.

"Come here, boys. I want to talk to you," he yelled.

For the second time in twenty-four hours, my body couldn't seem to keep up with my bare feet. Even Jimmy couldn't catch me as I made it to the gravel road. I didn't slow down until I reached my house and flew through the back door.

I went to sleep that night thinking about burning houses and axes and wolves and shacks that sit way back in the woods. Independence Day was tomorrow, so I tried my best to think of cotton candy and how many of my old friends would be at the Blue Hole.

I'd made a couple new friends but I missed doing stuff with my old buddies. No one seemed to have much to say to me after Daddy was shot, and about the time things seemed like they were going to get back to normal, a sheriff would come back up to the house asking me and Mom more questions and someone would see the police car and tongues would start wagging again all over town.

Daddy had been gone for months, but it sure didn't seem like it. It seemed like he'd never lived at all sometimes, but sometimes it seemed like he'd never left us there was so much of him left behind. Even though he was buried up on the mountain, Daddy was still everywhere but nowhere, sort of.

I wondered if me or Momma would ever get to rest in peace like the preacher told me Daddy was doing, because the whole town was sure there was a killing. And most of them said I knew what happened to Daddy and they said I was protecting a murderer.

Momma killed him, they said.

A few even whispered that I did.

Chapter Three

Fourth of July in Sunnyside was my favorite day, even more than Christmas, and it had always been me, Dad and Mom packing up for fun at the Blue Hole. I'd swim and rough-neck with my friends while Dad played in the softball tournaments between judging contests of all sorts, like he told me mayors were expected to do. Mom would sun and talk with the other ladies before helping out with the big barbequed chicken and corn-on-the-cob feed that went on there. I never remembered doing anything different, so I just figured that's where me and Mom would go that year for the fireworks show.

The Blue Hole was a wide, natural swimming hole on Catawba Creek. The town had bought the land some years before, cleared out a bunch of poison oak and scrub pine, and trucked in white sand, put in a swing-set, strung rope with floats on it across both ends, and hired the three prettiest girls in high school to be lifeguards.

I got up that next morning and ran over to Jimmy's to see if he and Alvin wanted to go to the fireworks. I'd never met Jimmy's dad and was surprised when a grown man opened the door. He looked just like Jimmy but in a bad sort of way.

"Jimmy don't stay here no more," he said.

I looked him up and down, could tell he wasn't a kind man, but I wasn't scared—even if there was something trembly about him. He stood there leaning against the door waiting for me to speak.

"Where's Jimmy and Alvin at?"

He sniffed and wiped his mouth with his collar and tried a few times to clear his throat. "They're over in Troutville staying at their grandmother's."

I tried to look behind him and saw the mess in the living room. The place stank like old clothes and whiskey.

"When's Jimmy coming back?"

"What's your name?" he asked.

"Charles W. York."

He started grinning and I saw his yellow teeth and the big wad of chewing tobacco, and pulled back.

"Charles W....I'll tell Spot when I see him that you came by." He shut the door in my face and I heard it lock.

It turned out me and Mom didn't go to the Blue Hole that year, either. She said she wasn't feeling good like she never felt good anymore and she said I couldn't walk all the way down there alone so I went up to see Harry and

George. They never went anywhere unless it was with Jimmy and me so I figured they'd be home.

I told them the big news that Jimmy and Alvin were gone and we talked about that quite a bit and just hung around the side of the mountain playing the pocketbook trick. Few cars drove by and none of them ever stopped so we ended up sitting in a ditch and tried to hit moths with the empty pocketbook and talked about the troop.

When I got home that night, Mom was outside on the screened porch hunched over a tin bucket snapping pole beans. She inched back a little in the porch swing and moved a long strand of brown hair from her face.

I climbed into the rocker across from her and rocked and rocked and didn't say anything. Her eyes never looked at me. She didn't even look at me when I'd walked in. She was barefoot and had the same dress she'd had on about all week and just kept looking at those beans, snapping each one slow into three pieces. One at a slow time. I couldn't help but notice how skinny her arms were while snapping those beans.

"Is something wrong with you, Momma?"

"No, baby," she said. "Hot night, isn't it."

I nodded to her but she was already looking back at those beans. Every now and then she'd stop and throw a bad one into a paper sack, move that strand of hair again and wipe her face or neck with a wet kitchen rag.

I kept rocking and looking at her but it seemed like she didn't even know I was there even though we'd just spoken. It was too quiet and too hot even with the electric fan blowing, so I sat for a while longer and finally decided to go in and read my Abe Lincoln book.

"You going to bed, baby?" she asked as I pulled open the screen door.

"Yeah, Ma'am."

"Sweet dreams," she said. "You're my precious angel."

I went in and got in bed and never did see the fireworks that night like I hoped. I heard them though.

A summer storm came up after I'd fallen asleep, and I woke up when the magnolia tree outside my bedroom started making noises against the window. When Dad was here I didn't get scared as much. I'd never seen him scared all my life, except in my dreams when he was on the kitchen floor bleeding and holding his stomach.

The wind kept blowing and I kept laying there and I finally started thinking about how many days I had until school started. Then I recalled one of Lacy's stories about this runt bird dog that was scared to hunt. It was my favorite story when the magnolia tree scratched on my window late at night. Sleep finally came.

It seemed like the whole troop was gone or in trouble and it was two weeks before we all decided to go back to Paradise to fetch those tools. Jimmy and Alvin had come back from their grandmother's house, and Jimmy said his dad went off to work for the railroad again. Jimmy didn't say much about his dad or why they'd left so I didn't ask.

Jimmy didn't care about the rusted tools we'd left up on Angel's Rest as much as he cared about the scout book.

"We can't kick our meetings off proper without you reading our pledges and oaths," he said.

At dark on a full moon, we all swore in the sinkhole behind Chapin's barn that we'd go to Paradise and fetch what was ours.

Jimmy had his slingshot and I had my homemade bow and arrows as we all stalked up the mountain that next morning. There was no noise this time as Jimmy snuck up to the big beech tree like I'd done before. He gave the all-clear sign and the rest of us stood up from the brush. Paradise had changed. Someone had built a small shack with half walls and a sloping roof across from where our fire had been. The chimney was torn down and all of the old timbers had been cleaned away.

We all looked in the window holes as Jimmy creaked open the door. There inside was a table and three wooden chairs. On the shelves were our scout book and tools and some military awards and old army uniforms. Alvin yelled from outside.

"Look at this, Jimmy!"

We all ran out as Alvin scrambled up wooden steps someone had nailed into a big white oak. About ten yards up there was small platform with a bell. Alvin got up there and started ringing that bell for all he was worth until we all yelled at him to stop.

I didn't know why I was so nervous and I could tell everybody was excited about using the fortress so I grabbed Jimmy.

"I don't like this place and I ain't coming up here anymore," I said.

He studied me for a long time, a real long time it seemed, then he went in and snatched the book, tools and military stuff. I felt like all of my worries were gone and didn't think I'd ever come back to Paradise as I grabbed Alvin by his collar and all of us ran down that mountain. We ran faster and faster, like the valley below was pulling us, but we slowed down all of a sudden when we got to the ridge across from Hollis Thrasher's place. Two police cars, a gray one from the state police and a brown one from the sheriff's office, were parked right next to the outhouse of his shack.

I stopped and looked over at Jimmy, who could see a lot better than me. He was standing still almost like he was a statue, except for his eyes going slow back and forth. I then looked at Alvin. He was bent over with his hands on his knees trying to get his breath. He spit and barely got his big toe out of the way of it.

"What's the law doing over there, Jimmy?" Alvin asked.

I inched closer up beside Jimmy to see what he was staring at so hard.

"I don't know," he said. "They're talking to Hollis about something. Looks like something mighty important, too."

Jimmy started to kneel down so we all got down and lay on our stomachs quiet and kept watching until we heard Hollis's voice echo over the ridge to ours. The voice was barely loud enough to hear it so far off. But we all heard it.

"This is the last time I'm gonna tell you to get the goddamned hell off my land," he said.

No mistaking it was Hollis's voice. It sounded like it had come straight out of a dungeon. We all looked at each other and then we all looked back 'cause he wasn't talking to us, he was talking to the police. I'd never heard of anyone cussing at the police to their face.

There were four lawmen total, all of them standing around Hollis. They looked like a pack of lapdogs trying to corner a black bear that wasn't about to climb no tree. Two were in gray highway patrol uniforms. The other in uniform was a county deputy I'd seen around town plenty of times, and a fourth man, a tall, lean feller who seemed to be up front and did most of the talking, wore Sunday trousers and a shirt with a gold badge pinned on it that caught the sunlight. He had a small holster attached to his belt and handcuffs dangled from the back of his pants and he wore a fancy hat. I was sure I'd never seen him before but he looked the most important of the bunch. He was the one who Hollis walked up to directly.

More commotion was going on but I couldn't figure out what was being said no matter how hard I strained. Finally all of them walked to the two police cars and got in them as Hollis opened the door of his shack and went inside.

I lay there breathing hard, my face just an inch above the leaves, and we waited until the cars backed into the woods and pulled away. We watched them creep down the rutted road and disappear into the colors of the mountain. Jimmy finally nodded his head at us, so we all inched our way over the crest of the ridge into the hollow on the other side, where Hollis couldn't see us if he was looking. Once we got through the rhododendron and pin oak and made it to the reservoir, we all stood in the middle of the dirt road but nobody said anything so we all waved at each other, split up and went our different ways, since it was getting near dinnertime and I didn't know about them, but I was starving.

On the way walking my road back to my house, I passed by Mr. Runions, who sat on his rickety porch reading the Good Book in the afternoon like he always did. I waved but he didn't wave back and it just seemed like I couldn't find my place wherever I was anymore or something. Mr. Runions always waved.

I felt like a stranger in a town I'd lived in my whole life. I did what I'd always done but nothing felt the same as it had been. I tried to tell Jimmy about it once but it was like trying to describe to somebody how your head or leg feels at night when it aches. I didn't know what changed about Sunnyside and the people in it. And I couldn't put my finger on why I was scared all the time, but it all had to do with Daddy being gone and the police who kept coming up to the house, smiling at me and asking me questions. I was sure of that.

Dad and me weren't like most other boys and their daddies. He got mad at me sometimes but not much, even when I deserved it, and he didn't get all liquored-up like some other dads in town did on weekends or when they weren't working or laid off.

He always treated me good around others. I was proud being his son because he was such a popular man in town, maybe the most popular the way people were always trying to get him to run for mayor, which he finally did. And folks said he was a shoe-in as a delegate in the Virginia General

Assembly that he was campaigning so hard for just before he died. Every service call we made that last year, Dad would shake hands after fixing the TV and say how much he'd appreciate their support when election day rolled around. They all promised they would, too.

In general, besides being a good dad, Dad was just a fine feller to look up to. My dad was my all-time hero, even more than Abe Lincoln and Jim Thorpe and Teddy Roosevelt. I wanted to be just like him when I grew up. But he was buried now and nobody could look up to him anymore. They didn't like me right off the bat for being John York's boy. They thought Mom had pulled the trigger on that shotgun and believed I saw the awful thing she'd done.

That's what the worst rumors said.

And everyone in a small town believes rumors are true when they start from the old redbrick courthouse in the town square.

I'd heard some of the talk, like how I never cried at the funeral like a normal boy should have and how Momma's story changed about what happened that night. I guess that's why when Daddy's service ended, everybody from the whole county just walked back home under their umbrellas or they got in their cars and trucks and left. It ended up just me and Momma sitting there in steel chairs listening to the rain beat off the undertaker's tarp.

Nobody came up to us and said nothing after the preacher said all he had to say, not even Granddaddy or Grandma. They all just left, except for the TV news people. One short feller had a big camera on his shoulder pointed right at us.

Standing off in the distance, they looked just like a flock of big buzzards.

Me and Momma sat there and sat there and she kept staring at Dad's coffin and the piece of green carpet beside it that covered a pile of clay. Then I looked behind me up on the hill and saw three colored men sitting under a tree with shovels in their hands. I finally grabbed Momma's hand and we walked back home.

All I knew was, the world seemed a lot different to me when Dad was still alive and I doubted I'd ever get that good feeling back.

Even though Mom didn't have to, she kept telling me that Dad was a good man. I knew that already but maybe she just needed to say it every day. She said it was a tragic accident and that it was no one's fault and he was in heaven and we'd all be together again one day.

I never did tell her that I didn't get sad when she told me Doc Lindsey said Daddy was dead at the hospital. I went back to reading a comic book, just like I finished watching a TV show after I threw up on the couch and the ambulance took him from the kitchen floor to the hospital. After I'd found out he was gone, I just couldn't really think about it for some reason.

It was too much to think about, I guess.

The best I could figure out about dying and going to heaven is that one minute you can be getting ready to eat supper, and then the next minute somebody might not be here anymore and there'd always be an empty chair at the table from then on.

Everything seemed very still and cold after Dad got buried near my schoolhouse. I could sit at my desk and stare across the two-lane highway and see his grave during that last week of school before summertime break. I tried not to, but my eyes always ended up over there.

It was too quiet at home even with Mom there, in my bedroom and everywhere else. And things looked different. Mom kept the shades drawn even when the sun wasn't bad. Every week or every other week the sheriff or someone from the state police would come up to talk some more about what happened.

The mountain always looked dark, but the older I got that year, the darker it got. I tried to listen for the music of life that Lacy said is always there if your heart's ready to hear it, but all I heard was quiet.

I started thinking that I was probably going to heaven soon, too. I just wanted to do anything that would make me feel the way I had when Dad would come home and eat supper, telling stories about what had happened that day and what he'd heard around the woodstove at the shop.

I missed how he'd come into my room every night at bedtime and say my prayers with me and tell me how he wouldn't trade me for all the gold in the China. I once asked him how much gold that was, and he told me it was more than an educated man could count.

I wanted to go away so bad sometimes it made my whole body hurt. I thought and planned on making a raft like Huck Finn did, taking off down Catawba Creek until I hit the James River and see where the current took me. Maybe to a place where there were no rumors about a killing or where eyes always glanced me or Momma's way. I built my raft in my head and got on it with Jimmy and Alvin and the Wilson twins and we had quite the adventures in my head.

But as bad as I wanted to strike off on my own, Momma was always calling me home. She didn't have any brothers or sisters and the few relatives she had lived up north—both her parents had died before I was born and all Dad's side of the family treated me and her like we had a rash that wanted to spread for the past months.

I knew she needed me. She must've told me that a hundred times a day. She even told me in my dreams. The good dreams that is.

In the bad visions, the ones that crept into my bedroom like a fog and then flashed in my mind like a lightning bolt during the darkest, most still and lonesome part of the night, Momma screamed and fell to her knees with a shotgun in her hands. She fell the same way in those awful dreams, real slow like there was something trying to hold her up at the same time, and she screamed that same terrible scream.

I never told the sheriff about those dreams.

Chapter Four

I had three more weeks of summer vacation when Lacy woke me up one early morning. It was still dark except for the red and orange colors just starting to break over the mountains outside my window. I was surprised seeing Lacy teetered over my bed and wondered for a minute if I was dreaming about one of his big tales. I'd never ever seen him in my house before. He pulled away his pipe and said he was going fishing and asked if I wanted to go. I jumped out of bed and pulled on my cut-off dungarees.

"Where we going?"

"I figured we'd try to scare up a fish down on Miss Hale's place."

By the short time it took me to do my business, Lacy already had the poles and tackle box next to the side porch door. He put my lucky cap on my head after he noticed me standing beside him and I watched him finish spreading peanut butter and damson jelly on biscuits.

I rooted in the paper sack on the counter and saw he'd already packed fried bologna sandwiches and a bunch of green apples. He finished with the jelly biscuits and put them in the sack, too, and then poked around in the refrigerator and pulled out a jar of pickled eggs and a chunk of hard cheese.

"Momma still asleep?" I asked.

"She has some things to do today," he said.

"She's not here?"

Lacy shook his head.

"Where is she?"

"Downtown," he said.

"What's she doing downtown at this time of the morning?"

"I don't rightly know. Things she need to do, I reckon."

Lacy spooned out a couple of eggs from the jar, smelled them and then wrapped them up in wax paper. Then he carved a chunk of cheese, smelled it, sliced off a skim of mold and then wrapped the chunk up in wax paper, too. A look came over his face like he knew I was curious about something.

He just kept standing there before he finally bent forward real far at the waist to get a better look at me.

"Anybody else going fishing with us?" I asked.

"Just me and you. I never did like to fish in a dang crowd. She said it's all right for just me and you to go, if you want to."

Lacy stood there all bent over wobbly until he finally rightened up straight again using the back of a chair for help.

Something about him standing in Mom's kitchen making a sack lunch and rooting around in her refrigerator and cupboards while asking me to go fishing made me a little uneasy. She wasn't home and it wasn't even daylight yet. Momma always told me stuff she was gonna be doing in town, especially after Dad died.

Mom had been sleeping in late the past few months, real late, sometimes past noon, even. So late she made me promise I'd never tell anybody. I usually needed to wake her up to make breakfast and here she was gone. I stepped down the hall to the very end and checked her bed and sure enough, it was cold and all made up. And that's when I noticed the whole house had been scrubbed clean. She hadn't cleaned like that in a long time even though she used to keep things clean all the time. She must've cleaned all night while I was asleep. I ran my fingers across her fluffed pillow and felt nervous about the whole thing.

"I ain't been fishing since Moses taught me how to catch trout by praying them into the frying pan. Just weren't sporting anymore," Lacy said real loud so I could hear it.

I walked back in the kitchen still a little shaky but couldn't help but grin because Lacy was smiling and he always came up with funny stuff about Bible people to make a person feel better about something. He once told me Jesus taught him how to walk on water and that trick had come in handy over the years when he wanted to wade to a good fishing hole but didn't want to get his feet damp.

"But if you don't want to go, I'll go by myself," he said.

I grinned all over all of a sudden.

Lacy nodded big, like we'd shook hands on the deal and he grabbed the poles and I realized that cool, dark morning with Mom gone was the first time since Dad had died that the quiet had left our house. It was the first time I'd woke up feeling good in a long time. I felt normal and realized it.

On the way out the door, Lacy put the two pickled eggs and the hunk of cheese in my creel and told me that was what he ate for breakfast when he was my age before he went fishing.

We got in the truck and just like I'd never seen Lacy in my house, I'd never seen him drive, either, and he drove Dad's paneled truck slower than I could walk backward. I wasn't even sure he could drive the way he was grinding the gears. He told me to stop asking questions until we got to the creek as we rode the rutted dirt roads down to Hale's Farm. He stared so hard out the windshield his whole body was pressed against the steering wheel. We got there though, eventually, and after I fed her pack of beagles a bologna sandwich so they wouldn't eat me up, old Miss Hale gave me the key to the gate and we parked in one of her cow pastures.

I immediately dug up some night crawlers and three spotted lizards and it wasn't long before I'd caught a couple smallmouths that were too little to keep and a bunch of bluegills.

Lacy sat on the bank leaned up against a big shaggy bark hickory tree and every now and then he'd tell me a fishing story about how he caught fish in the same spot when he was my age. I was surprised he never fell asleep sitting up like he did the one time he went along with me and Dad.

Lacy didn't sleep any but didn't fish much, either. He just sat and swatted bugs, mostly.

He finally did take a step toward the creek when I begged him to because they were starting to hit good, but I don't think he cared whether he caught anything or not.

I stood in the riffles watching my line now and then, and between that, I watched Lacy trying to get a worm on his hook. He reminded me of myself a few years before at Dollinger's pond when Granddaddy had first made me bait my own hook one evening after we'd all finished eating at the York family reunion that we went to every year, whether it was raining or not. After I'd held up my line for Granddaddy to bait my hook, he put a worm in my hand and told me real fisherman bait their own hooks.

"Ain't right to have someone else kill the worm while you just reel in the fish that eats it. Ain't right to the worm or the fish," he said.

"It ain't?" I said.

"If you can't get that worm on that hook, old as you are now, you have no business fishing, and I don't think you'll ever turn into a good hunter like your daddy, either, if you're timid of such things."

"Timid of what things?"

"Killing, son."

"But I want to fish and hunt...." I told him.

"Well, put that worm on your hook," he said.

I looked back over at Daddy, who was standing under a hay shed talking with men who were my kin even though I didn't know some of them. Daddy finally glanced at me.

For some reason he eyeballed me strange, put down his paper plate and started walking over in my direction.

"You like to eat fish?" Granddaddy asked loud.

I looked back at Granddaddy and nodded my head because I loved the big fish frys we had every summer.

"Fish taste better when you earn the right to eat them," Granddaddy said.

At that time, I'd never looked at fishing in that sort of way and I wondered how a fish would taste any different if I put the worm on the hook or someone else did. I didn't know what to say about all of that so I kept quiet. I didn't like to fish with Granddaddy anymore like I always loved to fish with Dad because we generally didn't talk about fishing when we fished.

We just fished.

"See, women aren't good at baiting hooks, don't want to hurt the worm, and they don't like to fish because you hurt the fish when you catch it, then you have to kill it and gut it and whatnot. Women just like to cook what's already dressed for the pan and eat and not have to do or think about any of that. They like to work the garden and set the table and expect the men to do the killing. It's God's design, son, for men to do the killing. You don't see no women around a hog butchering. Now bait your hook," Granddaddy said.

I remembered opening up my hand for a second and looking at that worm doing all it could to get away.

"It's time for you to start doing things like a man does. Like your daddy did when he was your age."

Dad finally walked over to me, saw my bare hook and

shoved a hand in the tin can, pulled out a worm and went to put it on my hook.

"Let the boy do it himself," Granddaddy said.

"He'll do it when he's ready," Daddy said back. He said it in a quiet but real stern way that was unusual sounding being that he was talking to Granddaddy and not me. Granddaddy and Dad never talked much about anything I'd come to realize, but when they did it was in a nicer tone, like usually around a holiday dinner one would say something good about the mashed potatoes and gravy and the other would nod. That sort of thing.

Granddaddy stood up and spit tobacco juice over one shoulder because there was a stiff breeze in his face. He didn't say nothing else and walked off.

I pulled my line out of Dad's hand, walked away a few steps and put the hook through that worm two or three times and watched it squirm something fierce each time I threaded it on. I remembered the worm blood on my hand. But when I was done, hooking that worm weren't nearly as hard to do as I always thought it would be.

That seemed like a long time ago, now. I hadn't thought twice since about putting a hook through a worm or lizard or a hellgrammite or a crawdad. Well, I guess I did feel sorry for them a little bit even though they were just bugs.

Lacy was still standing near the bank wobbling and having a hard time with his hook.

"Want me to do it?" I yelled.

He looked at me and pushed the bill of his ball cap up. "Tend your own line," he said real quiet.

I thought he was having all the trouble because he didn't want to hurt the worm, but then when he pulled the hook up next to his glasses so close it looked like he was looking at it cross-eyed, I recalled Lacy couldn't see good and figured that was the extent of the bait problem he was having.

Lacy finally got the nightcrawler on, drew back to cast and I don't know how he did it, but his line went straight up in the tree above him. I was upstream and kept looking over to see what he was going to do to get un-hung, but he just stared ahead and held the pole like his hook was in the water. The whole thing was comical to me because he looked so serious the way he held the fishing pole and kept that pipe between his teeth. I started laughing.

"What's so dern funny?" he asked.

"Your line's above your head way up in that tree, Lacy."

Lacy looked where I was pointing and pulled the rod tip close to his glasses. He finally saw the line went up into the big sycamore, gave it a tug and then studied on the whole thing while he toked on his pipe.

"That's exactly where I want it to be," he finally said, and he went back to holding his pole like he was doing before, while looking at the creek.

"Up there wrapped around a limb?"

"I guess you ain't heard of squirrel fishing."

He looked like he wasn't joking for a minute and I quit smiling and thought about it, and then he smiled and yanked his bait down using his cane and reeled in the big tree branch he'd caught.

"All this fishing's wore me out and made me hungry," he said.

I was hungry, too, so I reeled in and we ate the dinner he'd brought for us under the hickory he'd been lounging under all morning.

It was a quiet, long meal. Lacy usually didn't have much to say when he was eating and he ate about the same speed as he drove. He wiped his face with a handkerchief after every single bite. After we finished off a big jug of sweet tea, I asked him why he wanted to go fishing but didn't want to fish much.

"Fishing is one of those things that changes over the years," he said. "You get older and you don't care as much about catching fish as sitting down where you once cared about such things as catching a fish."

"So you don't like to fish now but just want to go and sit under a tree?" I asked.

"Yes, sir. When you're eighty-three years of age, Charlie, you'll understand."

Lacy reached in the side pocket of his sweater that he had buttoned all the way up the front even though it was hot out. He couldn't find his tobacco pouch, which I knew was what he was looking for. He kept rummaging around for it and then finally pulled it from one of his white socks, where he'd tucked it earlier for some reason.

He pulled the old leather pouch out, and canted his head up to look though the bottoms of his eyeglasses at what was inside, before digging his pipe in there.

"I've spent many a day on this creek and down on the

big river," he said. "Many a night, too. All the way from when I was your age to when I was a young man and came down here just after the first war with boys I went through those times with. When I got older, my old running buddies and me didn't fish as much as we acted like we were fishing when we went fishing. It was sort of a day's vacation in those days. Bunch of us wouldn't show up for work and we'd come down to the creek and fish a little, and one of the boys would always bring a banjo or mouth harp and we'd get to making homemade music and we'd drink whiskey from a bottle someone would bring and we'd pour it into tin cups and tell lies and more lies. 'Til way after dark."

"You all told lies?"

"Not real lies, just stories…things we'd done and seen in our travels. They weren't completely true. I mean a feller can't remember every detail about something so you fill in where you have to so as someone will get the point of what you're saying, you see."

I nodded.

"The stories leaned far enough in the direction of being true so they weren't really lies. Telling lies is just an old expression."

"Were they good stories?"

Lacy kept working slow but steady on getting the tobacco in his pipe just right.

"The best tales were about things we'd heard from our elders. Things the old folks had told us about how they'd found their way during their hard times and good times. Used to be a pretty rough ol' road to walk being a Negro man in this part of the country."

"It did?"

"Yes, sir. Surely did."

"Were you ever a slave?" I asked.

"No. Those bad times ended before I was born."

"Was your dad a slave?"

"He was born one but got his freedom about the time he was a boy your age thereabouts."

"Is he dead now?"

"He passed a good while back."

"How'd he die?"

Lacy pushed up his glasses and then pointed with his pipe at a green hillside way across the creek past a stand of paper birch trees.

"He got kicked in the head trying to put salve on a mule's leg just over that rise on the old Gillespie place. Pappy worked for Mr. Gillespie and his mule had got tangled up in some fence."

Lacy put the pipe back in his mouth and clapped his hands so loud all of a sudden it made me jump.

"Killed him dead just like that."

I thought about that and flicked a black ant off my leg.

"How old were you when that mule kicked him?"

"I was a little feller. Remember him, though."

"What happened to the mule?"

"Well, if I'm recollecting right, Mr. Gillespie said he shot that mule, said it was a dangerous animal, but we found out later that he sold it to a man over in Floyd County for twelve dollars."

After a last careful look at his pipe bowl, Lacy finally had the tobacco tamped down enough, but not too much. He pulled a long stick match out of his shirt pocket and got it lit on a piece of steel he kept in the same pocket.

"Do you ever come down to the creek with your old friends?"

When the smoke was all around his face he said, "They're all gone now."

"All of them?"

"Yes, sir," he said.

"You mean they all died?"

"Right."

"Did you ever bring Mrs. Coe down here?"

Lacy scratched at the back of his neck and looked at me funny out of the corner of his eye. "A time or two," he said.

"Did she like to fish?"

"She enjoyed going if it weren't too hot and the bugs weren't too bad. When you take women fishing it's more of a picnic. I mean you still bring a fishing pole but you bring other things like a blanket, and she'll bring a meal to eat, I mean real good food, not bologna sandwiches and leftover biscuits like we had. Anyhow, you just pick a pretty day to go where you can be together and spend time in nature. Alone, you see. You fish a little bit, too. She fished a little bit once or twice."

"When did Mrs. Coe go to heaven?"

Lacy didn't puff on his pipe and pull it away slow to answer a question like he usually did.

"Forty-one years ago," he said directly.

I was trying to add up in my head how long ago that

would have been, when he picked some grass from beside him and let it fly in the breeze picking up.

"You still miss her?" I asked.

"It hurt terrible for the longest time, still does now and then but it's a different sort of feeling. Warmer, I'd say."

Lacy got up on one knee and, with the hand not leaning on the cane, started picking up the wax paper from our sandwiches and stuffing them in the paper sack. He looked up at the clouds bunching up.

"If you want to wet another line, better get to it," he said.

"But you still miss that she's gone?" I asked.

"Every day, but like I said, child, it's a different sort of missing. Now I feel blessed that I ever got to spend any time with her at all. That we'd even met and she'd decided to marry a rough-around-the-ears feller like me. She deserved better."

Lacy started laughing and I always liked it when he laughed. His face looked like someone laughing but hardly any noise came out at all. He finally got up on both feet and ran a finger and thumb down the fishing line on one of my poles.

"I was lucky. Lucky to have her those twenty years."

"How'd she die?" I asked.

"Well, she got sick one winter, had a tumor in her chest. They didn't have the doctors and things they have now. She was over in this hospital in Roanoke a long time. She was kind of a fragile thing. I mean she was a fighter, don't get me wrong and she scrapped again' it, but couldn't lick it."

"So she died in the hospital?"

"It was her time to go. You come to realize things like that as you get on."

The wind suddenly picked up and blew Lacy's cap off. I ran it down before it went into the creek, knocked the dust off it and brought it back to him. A big crack of thunder hit above us. Lacy looked over his old cap more particular than seemed necessary, grabbed my fishing poles and said it was time to go.

"Do you think Daddy is in heaven with Mrs. Coe?" I asked.

On the way to the truck, Lacy patted me on the back real gentle like he'd do sometimes. "Yes, sir," he said. "I do for surety."

"Lacy, do you wish Mr. Gillespie would've killed that mule that killed your dad?"

Lacy didn't say anything else until he'd leaned our gear against the side of the truck. He looked all tuckered out from the short hike from the creek the way he was breathing so hard. He wiped his forehead and tried to clean his glasses with a handkerchief but his hands were shaking pretty bad. He gave up or cleaned them good enough before he put his bifocals back on, then he peered up at the rain starting to spit on us.

"We best get on back to town now, child," he said.

The clouds took over the sky runny and dark and they sat right down on the mountain and everything else like a heavy blanket. Big drops kicked up dust in the road and then it poured like we were under a waterfall on the way back to Sunnyside. Lacy pulled over and almost got us stuck in a ditch, saying we'd have to wait out the weather. We both sat in the paneled truck quiet after he turned off the AM radio and we listened to the rain hammering the roof between the thundering. Lacy said we were safe but he didn't look too sure about that the way he sat all hunched up and held on to the steering wheel even though we weren't moving. But he said the storm wouldn't last long and sure enough it didn't. Soon we headed back and Lacy said he had to stop by the shop for a minute, so he dropped me off at Phelps's Drug Store and gave me five dollars. I couldn't believe it. I'd seen five-dollar bills but never had had one in my pocket. I never knew Lacy ever had five dollars in his pocket, either. He told me I could get whatever I wanted and I could keep the change and I didn't argue with him.

I took a seat at the soda fountain, thought some more about him and Mrs. Coe and that mule that kicked his dad, and then I ordered a chocolate sundae with maple syrup and then ordered another one. I was about to finish the second one when Mr. Phelps asked how everyone was doing at our house and I said we were doing okay and hoped I could finish eating without him starting up a conversation about Dad. He stood there for a minute wiping his hands on a towel and I looked out the picture window and watched a big man walk up to the bench in front of the store. He wore a suit and toted a suitcase and sat down after wiping off the rain on the bench. I figured he was waiting on the bus that ran the Bluefield to Lynchburg route twice a week.

I still had four dollars and change and thought about getting some candy but then decided I'd walk to Hovack's Hardware to see if I had enough to buy real arrows for my homemade bow. I walked out of the drugstore and was double-checking my money when I looked at the man on the bench. He looked up and I turned back suddenly when I saw his eyes.

My heart pounded and I kept walking before I stopped at the corner and looked back again. The man had a short haircut and close beard but had eyes just like Hollis Thrasher. I had to know if it was him and walked back down the street. I picked up some gravels and let them sift through my fingers and slowed when I got to the bench. I stopped when he looked up at me.

"Hello, Charlie," he said.

I felt dizzy when I saw the scars on his face and heard the deep voice. All the gravel fell out of my hands. I knew it had to be him but couldn't be. "What's your name?" I finally blurted out.

"Hollis Thrasher."

I stammered a few moments and looked at him some more. Except for those eyes, he didn't look like a dangerous man.

"You don't look like Hollis Thrasher."

"You boys using the fort I built for you up on the mountain?"

I didn't know what to say.

I thought about running and looked around to see if there was anyone else on the street but he didn't look scary anymore with the short beard and crew cut and in his suit of clothes. Still big as a den tree but not scary.

"You waiting on the bus?" came out of my mouth before I could pull it back.

He nodded.

I never figured Hollis Thrasher would ever cross the county line being the strange loner that he was. "Where you going?" I asked.

"Out west."

"Where out west?"

He pulled a slick-looking piece of paper from his coat pocket and handed it to me. I looked at the picture of a white hotel with a red roof that sat next to a bright, blue ocean. I read what was under the picture and handed it back.

"Why you going to Mexico?"

"I've always wanted to go."

"What's out there that you're going for?"

Hollis took a few moments. "Good to get away from the mountain now and then."

I was trying to make sense of the man I'd been scared of my whole life all of a sudden looking cleaned up and almost normal with a suitcase heading to Mexico. Then I remembered one time Lacy told me in a story that most of God's creatures spend a good bit of their lives either running to something or running away from something, or doing both at the same time.

"When you coming back?"

Hollis grinned just barely and the expression didn't look right on him. It was the first time I'd realized he had teeth under all that hair that usually hid his face.

"You ask a lot of questions for a young feller," he said. "I'm not sure yet."

"But you're coming back?"

What grin he had disappeared. His face looked dark again. But even though it was all scarred up and burned looking, I wasn't scared looking at it anymore.

"I don't know."

Chapter Five

I wanted to ask Hollis more questions about going out west because all I thought about at night was getting on a raft and floating in some direction so I was curious about such things. But that's when I saw Toby Perkins and some of the other boys who hung around town all day walking toward me. The Perkins boys were always easy to spot in a crowd or at night because they were skinny and tall, pale-colored and all had blond hair. All of them smiled when I put my eyes on them.

I immediately knew it was best to head the other direction and did so in a hurry, but not soon enough because I soon heard the slapping of bare feet running after me.

I ran faster and jumped the fence behind the theater and was sprinting through the town parking lot when a hand locked on my shoulder and pulled me down.

Toby stood above me laughing, spit a few times and jerked

me back up when a nickel fell out of my pocket. The tallest one, a kid named Alton who never went to school and had a head the size of a cinder block, hit me in the stomach and somebody's hand went down my front pants pockets and pulled out all my money.

They were all laughing when Toby's older brother pulled a BB gun from a feedsack he had slung over one shoulder as they pushed me down again.

I knew I was in bad trouble and fought like Dad had taught me and caught a couple of them with good ones. But they stuffed me into that sack headfirst and tied off the bottom.

I was kicking and screaming trying to get out of there and they were kicking me, too. I prayed the sheriff or Lacy or Jimmy or somebody would see what was going on but they kept laughing and I got dragged across the ground in the sack, felt myself being picked up and was thrown into a culvert that ran through the middle of the lot.

I heard them run away and tried to hold my breath to tell if they'd really left, when the sack started filling up with water. I heard them pumping that BB gun.

Thwup, crack. Thwup, crack. Thwup, crack.

They kept pumping that gun and I tried to claw my way out of the culvert and I started yelling again, this time as loud as I could when they started shooting me in the sack.

"Leave that boy alone!" I heard.

Someone was coming toward me as others were running away.

I was still all balled up in the sack with my arms around

my head when the end of the sack was untied. I peeked one eye out from between my arms and saw it was Hollis Thrasher.

"Come on out of there," he said.

I inched my way out of the sack and looked around. I knew they hadn't run far.

"You hurt?"

I shook my head and wiped my face and nose with my sleeve.

"Those boys pick on you a lot?"

I tried to talk but couldn't at first and finally was able to say, "Sometimes." They never did when Dad was alive.

I looked up the alley and could see Dad's paneled truck had left. Lacy must've figured I'd gotten into something with some buddies or went home.

"Maybe you'd better go home," Hollis said.

I looked around trying to figure the best way to go home so I wouldn't run into the Perkins boys again. When I looked back at Hollis, he looked at me hard and then studied his watch.

"I'll walk a ways with you," he said.

I didn't know what to say so I just kept standing there trying to catch my breath and get myself back together. I didn't want to be walking anywhere with Hollis Thrasher, but I wasn't about to tell him that. His reputation for meanness was a lot worse than the Perkins boys was. He started heading across the lot toward Duncan Hill, and I finally felt too much by myself just standing there alone so I ran and caught up to him. I felt cold all of a sudden from being soaked in the culvert, shook off the skunk water and it hit me how Hollis knew my name when I walked up to him on that bench. But then I realized everyone in Sunnyside knew everyone else by name because there weren't a whole lot of names for a person to remember.

I kept thinking about that and he never said another word until we got to the road beside the filling station that led up to my house on Duncan Hill.

I tried to keep one eye on Hollis and the other looking behind us for Alton and the Perkins boys, even though I knew the one person they'd never mess with was Hollis, but like me they may not recognize him all cleaned up in his suit of clothes.

Hollis kept toting that big suitcase with his usual limp dragging his left leg and when we finally got to my yard, I saw Dad's paneled truck and a sheriff's car parked in front and Lacy sitting on the front porch. I thought I was going to throw up when I saw that big cherry light sitting on top of that car.

Lacy stood when he saw me. I guess I looked pretty banged up with my knees all skinned, and his eyes turned to Hollis. I think Lacy had a hard time recognizing him, too. Hollis nodded at him.

Lacy took his same always careful slow steps off the porch and looked me over. "What happened to you?"

The deputy sheriff left the porch swing and was walking toward me and I didn't know what to say and just stood there.

"Those Perkins boys were giving him a hard time behind the theater. Law in this town ought to..."

Hollis stopped what he was saying when I looked up at him and shook my head slowlike. He nodded and started to walk away.

"Where you going with your suitcase?" the deputy asked.

"None of your damned business," Hollis said without turning around.

"Might be…"

Hollis walked back until the brim of the deputy's hat was just under his chin. The deputy took two steps away from him.

"Speak your peace, Earl," Hollis said.

The deputy had one hand on his hip and the other one on the butt of his gun. Hollis put down the suitcase, which was in his huge hand close to the deputy's gun hand. Lacy pulled me to him and nobody said anything for what seemed the longest time.

"You got a shy streak when you ain't got a bunch of state troopers with you," Hollis finally said, as he picked up his suitcase and turned to leave. He stopped. "And next time you go accusing a man of something like you did, you'd better bring more law up on the mountain. I won't stand for it again. You have my word on it."

Hollis's eyes burned through the deputy before he trudged down our cracked cement walk, stepped over the ditch and walked down the street.

"Heard you're selling the mountain," the deputy said in a loud voice that sounded two hairs past shaky. "Did you sell it yet?"

Hollis turned around. "Take care of yourself, Charlie. Lacy."

And then he turned and just like that, Hollis ignored the law officer and walked back down the side of Angel's Rest, dressed for church but with that face all scarred up, going to a hotel in Mexico and dragging that bum, shot-up leg that he got in the war.

I wondered what the scuff was between him and the law as I stood there and watched him, in fact I noticed we all watched him walk away, and I thought that was the last time I'd ever see Hollis Thrasher for some odd reason.

I was dead wrong about that.

After Lacy asked me if I were okay and brushed the gravels out of my hair, he told me to sit for a few minutes on the porch. The deputy sheriff followed us, sat down beside me and started picking at green paint peeling off one of the rails. I looked at what he was doing and he stopped, chewed on his lip and started studying at his fingernails. Nobody was talking and the deputy kept looking at Lacy, who finally peered up underneath his ball cap. He'd never looked so old, I thought. Even his cap looked too big for him.

"Where's Mom?" I asked.

Lacy took off his cap, something he rarely did outdoors, and then ran a hand through the white strands of coarse hair that covered the top of his head in a few spots. He patted me on the hand.

"Your mom has to stay at the sheriff's department for a while. We'll go see her later."

I looked at him for a long time, and the edges of his mouth turned up a little but not into a smile. I'd never seen that look from him ever, and the tears started rolling out of me. I couldn't stop them. I knew then that that's why he'd taken me fishing like he did and gave me five dollars.

I tried to run away but Lacy had his hand on me. My mind was going round and round trying to figure out if I'd said something I wasn't supposed to. Mom had told me over and over how we had to tell the same story about how Dad died or she'd get into trouble with the police and go to jail. My belly hurt so bad bent over on that porch, I thought I was going to die right there.

"She's in the jailhouse?" I finally asked to make sure. I looked up at Lacy and he slowly nodded his head and kept patting my hand.

"It's gonna be okay, child. We'll go down there this evening. You can visit with her."

I stopped crying and looked across the road at the neighbors peeping out their windows and the ones out sweeping their porches that didn't need sweeping. They kept glancing over and I hated all of them. The same glances I'd seen from everyone in that town for months. No words. They saved what they had to say to whoever they were with when they thought me or Mom were out of earshot. Just glances. Suddenly I felt like I couldn't take in another breath.

The deputy stood and rubbed my hair but I yanked my head away. He looked at me and said, "Lacy's supposed to stay and take care of you for a while. It's what your mom wants. If that ain't okay, let me know now. You got kin who can look after you, Charlie. You don't have to stay here with Lacy. Would you like to stay with somebody else…like your grandfolks?"

I looked at Lacy, who was studying his pipe. I'd just been thinking about Mom being in jail and what a terrible thing that was, not who'd be looking after me. But when I thought about that, about me not having a mom or dad when I woke up or went to bed, it felt like I didn't even have a place to be, anymore.

I couldn't figure why Mom would want me to stay here with Lacy when I did have relatives on Dad's side who lived all over the side of that mountain who I could stay with. But they weren't sitting here now, Lacy was.

There weren't any coloreds who stayed up on Duncan Hill; they all lived in Town Heights. You never even saw a black person near Duncan Hill unless they were tilling up some old lady's garden or something. And you never saw them up there at night. Never. The way I understood it, that's the way everybody wanted it to be, too. They had their place and we had ours and that's the way the Good Lord wanted it, Granddaddy had told me one time.

I was so shook up sitting on the porch with Lacy and that sheriff that I could hardly think about staying here with Lacy watching over me or staying there at all without Momma around. But I figured it'd probably work out all right for a day so I finally peered up past the belly of the sheriff, tried to find his eyeballs and said, "I'll stay here with Lacy."

The deputy looked like I'd just told him terrible news and it got real quiet on that porch. Sitting there it really hit me how if Lacy weren't around, nobody would want to take care of me or they'd be here now instead of him. I'd probably have to be like Huck Finn or Oliver Twist because none of my blood relatives acted like they were my kin anymore. I wanted to run off that porch and never look back but I could never run away with Momma in trouble.

I figured the only reason Lacy was here was that he was the only person in the whole world Mom thought we could lean on now. Even though I liked Lacy and was glad at least he was there, that weren't a good feeling that he was all we had, especially being that he was so old and colored. It wasn't a good feeling at all. I looked at him and he was looking far away at the mountain ridges. He put the pipe between his teeth slow and careful and I wondered why he still liked me and Mom and wanted to help when so many didn't. Maybe Mom was paying him a wage, or he'd get free meals or something like he did at the shop.

The deputy hiked up his pants before heading to his car.

"If the boy wants to see his mom, visiting hours are six to seven, Slim. Don't be late," he said in his usual too-loud voice that wasn't shaking anymore like it was when he talked to Hollis. I noticed he talked to Lacy in the same way someone would tell a dog to sit.

I looked across the road and saw the neighbors straining while standing in their bean patches or on their front porches to make out what the deputy had said. The operator running the phone lines in Sunnyside would be busy tonight, I figured.

Lacy waved to the deputy and I ran into my room, slamming the door. I dove on my bed and lay still until it quit creaking and bouncing up and down. I turned my head to look out my window at the magnolia tree and that's when

Lacy knocked on my door and pushed it open a crack before he decided to walk in. He had an envelope in the hand not holding his cane.

"Your Momma asked me to give this to you."

Lacy had the same look on his face that he'd just had while sitting on the porch. It made me even more scared of whatever was in that envelope. I turned over away from him and soon heard his footsteps and cane leaving my room. After he shut the door, I saw where he'd placed the envelope next to my pillow. I didn't touch it but studied the outside. It had my name on it in Momma's handwriting. I wanted to read what was inside but didn't want to at the same time, so I just smelled it. It just smelled like paper. I closed my eyes, felt cold and started thinking about everything I'd ever told the police about how Daddy had died that night.

When I woke up, I was covered up by a quilt Mom always kept on the back of the sofa in the living room. I stood with the unopened envelope still in my hand and could smell collard greens cooking. I hoped they'd let Mom go and ran into the kitchen. Lacy was standing over the stove cutting a tin of corn bread. I never knew a man to cook before.

"We'll go see your mom in a minute," he said, while he kept messing with a hot skillet on the stove.

"When did Momma give you that envelope?"

"Yesterday, before suppertime. She came out to my house for a visit."

"So you knew she was gonna be put in jail?"

Lacy turned around to look at me. "No, sir. She told me

she had some business downtown with the sheriff's office and asked if I'd look after you until she got back. I told her I would and she asked me to give you that letter this evening if she was late getting home."

"You should have told me this morning before we went fishing, Lacy. You should have told me."

"I didn't know enough to tell you anything so I just did what your mom asked of me. I was hoping your mom would be coming home today and she'd be doing the explaining of things. Now I figure we best get cleaned up and eat a bite of supper before we go. She's waiting to see you, child."

He nodded and nodded at me and I didn't know what else to say about it so I went back to my room, changed into my dungarees and pulled my church shoes out of the closet and saw the bright clay mud still stuck to the bottoms. I put them on for the first time since Daddy's funeral and rocked back and forth until they felt right then sat with the letter and smelled it again. I held it up to the light and felt how thin it was. I opened it up, tearing it across the top and tore off half the letter at the same time. I held the pieces in my hands, one of them was blank and I carefully placed it on the bed. I made sure Lacy was still in the kitchen and unfolded the rest and began to read.

My Charlie,
Remember our talks. Say your prayers and listen to Lacy.
You are strong. Don't ever forget that. I will always be your
Mommy even when I'm away. I love you, Charlie. Your

*Daddy loved you. Don't ever forget either of those things.
Coldest time of the day is always right before dawn. Remember how we talked about these things. Dawn is coming to reveal the most beautiful day. Bundle up for now
but don't forget the sunshine is coming. Remember our
talks. Listen to Lacy. Don't fret for a moment.
I love you,
Mommy*

I reread the letter a couple of times, tried to put it back
together with the torn piece, gave up and placed it all back
into the envelope best I could. I stuffed it under my mat-
tress and walked back into the kitchen. Lacy was at the table
pouring molasses over my corn bread.

I sat down and looked at the sliced tomatoes, cucumbers,
bread and collards. After putting a few slabs of fried side-
meat next to my corn bread, he took off his cap, grabbed
my hand and his head dropped. I dropped my head, too, and
closed my eyes but when I didn't hear any blessing, I peeped
over and saw his lips were moving but no words came out.
I wondered if the things he was saying to himself was a
Negro prayer and I wished he'd of said those things out
loud, too, so I could've heard it.

I guess he finally finished whatever he was saying to himself and then he said out loud the normal sort of things
white folks thank God for before having the evening meal.

As long as I'd known Lacy and he'd been good to me,
and now that we'd even fished together and everything, it
still felt funny the two of us sitting at a table for a meal all

quiet like it was except for the both of us chewing. I'd never seen a black person eating in our kitchen. But we ate everything but the plates and silverware sitting on that shiny wood table that Dad had bought Mom just the year before for Christmas. I remembered how she loved that table and how much he loved that she loved it when he stomped the snow off his feet and wrestled it through the front door.

After we wiped our faces, Lacy washed up and I went into the bedroom. I reread my letter and afterward he made me comb my hair and button the top button of my shirt, and we got in the paneled truck and drove down to the jail.

It took a while with Lacy driving and as we went down all of those narrow dirt streets, I looked at the faces peeping out their windows at us. I was determined to try and keep looking people in the eye like Daddy had taught me to do. He always told me it would be hard to do sometimes, and that's when you really need to do it.

I'd never been inside a jail but had seen them on television and read about them. Cold, mean, dark places. I knew most of the town drunks and the oldest Perkins boys got locked up about every month for something and stayed there. I couldn't imagine my mom in such a terrible place. I just couldn't imagine it.

There wasn't time for me to say anything it came up so quick. I just opened up the truck door and lost my supper right there on Main Street. Lacy pulled over until I was finished, then drove me back to the house and tried to pour me a spoonful of paregoric. His fingers shook so bad I ended up holding the spoon as he poured from the bottle. It tasted terrible but made me feel better.

I think Lacy felt puny, too, because I'd never noticed his hands shaking so bad before. After I went back outside, I watched through the window as he found the mason jar that Dad used to keep behind the dry goods in the top cupboard. Lacy searched quite a while to find it.

He unscrewed the lid, pulled the top piece off with a thumbnail, smelled it, and then took a pretty good swig right from the jar, shook his head for a minute, and then took another one. I didn't know if Daddy would like Lacy swilling right from the jar like that being colored and all, but I didn't say anything 'cause I guess it didn't even matter, Daddy being dead like he was.

A few minutes later, me and Lacy got back in the paneled truck and this time, made it all the way to the jail to visit Momma.

Chapter Six

We walked past the rusted iron fence with the pointy tops to the red front door of the jailhouse. Lacy had never grabbed my hand before walking anywhere but I was glad he did it that time. I don't know if he did it cause he was shaky or he thought I was. Maybe he knew holding on like that would help the both of us.

Lacy knocked, tamped his pipe out on the brick and after the door swung open, the old jailkeeper talked to him for a minute with their heads close together as the jailer started saying how it was all such a tragedy.

"Tragedy," he kept saying. "Such a tragedy."

Lacy just kept nodding, but not at me or the jailer. He just kept looking down moving his head a little.

The jailer kept glancing at me through smudged eyeglasses that had to be thicker than the bottom of a pop bottle. I wondered if he could even see me at all and that's why he kept looking at me so many times.

He finally quit talking and Lacy quit nodding and then Lacy patted me on the head and went back to wait in the truck like he told me he'd do.

The jailer told me he had to search me so I raised up my arms fast like they do on TV. I was shaking I was so nervous while he patted my clothes. He made me pull out my wallet from my back pocket and my pocketknife in my front pocket that Dad had given me for my birthday when I'd turned ten the year before. The jailer told me I could keep the wallet and said he'd give my Uncle Henry back when I left. Then he made me take off my church shoes and he looked in them and then at the bottoms of my feet before handing my shoes back to me.

As I put the stiff things back on, a jail matron who I also recognized as the typist at the county farm office smiled at me. She was a big woman, much bigger than most women I'd ever seen and she smiled like an upside-down frown for a minute, but I just stood there until I finally asked if I could see my mom.

"Of course you can, sweetie pie," she said.

She led me down a dark, brick hallway that smelled like a stink they'd been trying to scrub out of there for a hundred years.

We passed one dark cell that didn't have a window but I heard a rustling in there. A haggard-looking wiry feller, who all the town knew used to be a divine preacher of the gospel at the "Mount Olives Highness Church of the Disciples of the Arisen Savior" before he submitted to the booze and flesh demons, leaped up from his bunk and walked up to the bars in a hurry. I jumped when he leaped out of the dark and then I walked around and got on the other side of the matron, who stopped.

"I can't eat this, Claudine," he said.

He held an apple up and it looked like he'd been gnawing on it to no use.

"Slide your tray out and I'll get the trustee to mash it up for you," the matron said.

"I need some teeth," the preacher said.

"County's buying you teeth next week."

The big matron turned to walk again.

"You John York's boy?" the old man asked.

"Doesn't concern you, Preacher Spangler," the matron said as we kept walking.

"Hey, boy!" he yelled. His voice echoed like he'd shouted it from a pulpit.

I turned around but the matron grabbed my hand and we kept walking.

"Your daddy would've never shot himself. Never!" He kept looking at me and I kept looking at him getting farther away as he pressed his face to the bars. "Guilt is eating your soul. I can feel it! Cleanse yourself to the police and repent to the Almighty...or your father's ghost will surely haunt you from this day forward into the fiery hereafter. A place for the evil you don't want to go. Your mother will be waiting on you there, boy. I've seen it! I've been there. You hear me, boy! You hear me!"

The matron let go of my hand, pulled a big stick from the ring in her belt and she marched back to the man's cell and banged that stick against it. I thought my head was going to split open from the noise.

"I've warned you to watch your sermons in here when I'm on duty, Preacher Spangler."

I couldn't see the preacher anymore and he didn't say anything else. The matron put the big stick back in the metal ring on her belt and as she walked toward me, she smiled. I don't think I smiled back. We took a few more steps, went around a corner, then through a door with bars on it and both of us ended up standing beside a thick wooden door she knocked on. She turned a big gold key and it swung open.

I saw Mom sitting at a table and flew across the room to her. She stood up and I almost knocked her and the chair over. I held her for a long time and she held me back. Finally I opened my eyes and looked at the strange green dress that looked like something you'd wear in the hospital.

"You sick, Momma?"

She was crying and shook her head and smiled, really smiled. It was a smile I hadn't seen in a long time.

She must have good news so I asked her, "When you coming home?" as she gently pushed me away.

She started to say something when I saw out of the corner of my eye someone rising from another chair at the table. I hadn't even noticed anyone else in the room up until then and it scared me for a minute.

I turned around and there stood Malcolm J. Boone.

Now I'd always heard that Malcolm J. Boone was a distant relation of Daniel Boone but he sure didn't look like it. Standing there in that fancy suit that looked too small for him I couldn't picture him blazing a trail through the Cumberland Gap or fighting Indians, but everyone in Southwest Virginia knew he was a fighter of the oddest sort.

Malcolm probably only went about five feet tall with shoes on. He leaned like a bent-over sapling and had a giant head with thick gray hair that stuck straight up and made him look bigger from a distance than he was.

Malcolm served as a senator in West Virginia before I was born, but as I'd learned listening to stuff I wasn't supposed to be understanding, he got in some trouble up there in the Capitol. It was something about a newspaper article about him living with another feller and a big stink broke out. He denied it but it got started that Malcolm was funny. He ended up in a whole bunch of other scandals involving betting and all sorts of things and none of that went over well in West Virginia. He was run out of Washington and West Virginia, and he moved back to the homeplace of his great-great-great grandfather who'd built Sunnyside and named it after the nickname "Sunnyside" of his youngest daughter just after the Revolution.

"Charlie, you know Malcolm Boone. He's going to be helping me," Mom said.

Malcolm nodded and began collecting papers he had on the table and putting them in a shiny black briefcase. I couldn't help but notice all the rings he had on his fingers. Never seen a man with so many rings on his fingers.

"Your mom's a good woman, Charlie," he said, not looking at me. "She's told me the greatest things about you." Malcolm closed his case, winked at me and looked at Mom and said kind of quiet, like I wasn't even standing right there, "I'll let you all talk. Be back tomorrow morning, Love."

Malcolm patted my shoulder and I'd never heard Mom called "Love," but knew Malcolm called about everyone that name. He banged on the door, the female guard opened it and he was gone like a breeze.

Folks always said that before he was going bust, Malcolm owned about as much of Sunnyside and the surrounding county as he wanted. At one time all of the business people in town hoped he might do for Sunnyside what Vanderbilt did for Asheville. There were all kinds of rumors you heard all the time what deals Malcolm was into, but the fact was, he was going broke quicker than a gambler with bad luck, which I think described Malcolm pretty well since everyone said he gambled a lot and had poor luck at it.

At one time he owned whatever property he wanted, the apartment buildings that housed the storefronts downtown, both gas stations, and he'd started a big project turning a farm into a golf course but there were still cow piles on number one green. No one played golf in Sunnyside but I guess Malcolm wanted to. He did still own some property and had most of the town government in his pocket. They'd never extend a finger to touch him and that's what Malcolm Boone liked best about Sunnyside, Virginia, Dad always said.

Every time I did see Malcolm, I always wondered why

someone like him who could live about anywhere even if he was funny and disgraced, would live in such a small place as Sunnyside.

But even going broke he was still land rich and was probably the most educated person who'd ever stepped foot in our county. His farm was the farm of all farms in that part of the state. The house he built looked almost exactly like Thomas Jefferson's house in Charlottesville, except Malcolm's was bigger, some folks said.

Most people got a chuckle thinking how Malcolm probably always figured himself cut from similar cloth as President Jefferson with the reddish hair that had turned a shade of gray and the noble nature and building the same house, but no one ever chuckled in Malcolm's presence.

No one would ever do that.

He was one of only two lawyers in town but that wasn't the biggest reason folks smiled too big when he passed, for Malcolm gave out hunting and fishing permits every year to the chosen few.

As bad as people were in Sunnyside at times about treating someone not like them pretty standoffish with their rumors and glances, they always treated Malcolm Boone like the king of the county.

"He could decide to sleep in the middle of Main Street and the law would block traffic so as not to wake him," Dad had told Mom one time.

Malcolm was the one man to be reckoned with in Sunnyside it seemed, and it shocked me in the best way I could imagine when I saw that he was sitting at the same table as

Mom and he was on her side. Her side. I felt like I could breathe again and my stomach felt better already.

I believed that if anyone in the whole world could get Momma out of that stinky, dark jail, Malcolm J. Boone could.

"What happened to you?"

Mom's eyes told me she'd noticed the red marks on my face and her fingers found the big knot on my head.

"Did you get in a fight?"

"No, ma'am."

She looked me over some more and as hard as I tried, I could tell she didn't believe me. I figured she had enough to worry about besides me getting beat up again by the Perkins boys.

"Who did this to you?"

"We was playing football," I said.

"Hmmm…"

She scooted the chair Malcolm had been sitting in across the cracked cement floor until it was next to her. It looked like the same exact chair I'd sat in at Daddy's funeral. I had so much on my mind that I could hardly sit.

I looked at her long, dark hair and noticed it wasn't put up into a ball on top of her head like it usually was, and I don't know why, but she just looked younger to me than she'd ever looked before. And she looked pretty in a way I don't think I'd noticed before. Sitting in that jail was the first time I'd really noticed just how pretty my mom was. In fact, I think it was the first time I ever thought she was pretty at all even though I guess she always had been.

She grabbed my hand and eased me down and I tried to look at her blue eyes all watery until I couldn't look at them anymore so I ended up looking at our hands in the lap of her hospital dress. She started pushing the small diamond sitting on top of one ring back and forth with a thumb.

"Where's your clothes?" I asked.

Mom sniffed and took a deep breath and smiled. "This is what they want me to wear in here. Did you get any supper?"

"It's cold in here, Momma. Aren't you cold?"

She grabbed me and hugged me tight and talked real quiet just over my head as she ran her fingers through my hair at the same time, stopping occasionally to feel the knot again.

"I'm fine. I'm going to be fine so I don't want you worrying about me."

She pulled my head down for a closer inspection.

"I'll be very upset if you worry, Charlie."

I nodded and when she was finished poking on my head it stayed quiet, and then I heard a tractor-trailer rumbling down Main Street just outside the window. I wondered if she had to listen to that racket all day.

"When they going to let you come back home?" I asked.

"Well, I go to court in a couple days and we'll find out."

"You're not coming home for a couple days?"

"Mr. Boone is a good lawyer. The best in the state they say. He's going to do everything he can so I can come home soon."

Mom paused and I had so many things I wanted to ask her but my mind was swimming so I just sat and let her keep holding me. I didn't know it would be a couple of days until she came home.

"What have you and your friends been doing today?" she asked. "Besides football."

I couldn't think about the fact that it seemed like I didn't have hardly any friends left to do nothing with even if I wanted to.

"Didn't Lacy take you fishing?" she asked.

I nodded.

"Is it okay, Lacy staying with you until I come home?"

"How long is it gonna be 'til you come home?"

"I don't know yet."

"It ain't gonna be a week, is it?"

"Baby, we'll just have to wait a couple of days to find out."

"So I'm just gonna stay up there with Lacy 'til you come home?"

"He's a good, decent man."

"He's colored," I said.

"Yes, he's black."

"Folks on the hill won't like it."

"I don't care anymore what folks on the hill think about anything. We're lucky we have Lacy to help out."

"But why ain't nobody else helping, Momma?"

"They will. After all of this gets sorted out…things will get back to…people will treat us like they used to before the accident." Momma finished but kept nodding at me.

"So why's Lacy helping?"

"Your dad was good to Lacy, and I think in Lacy's way he's returning the favor. He was fond of your dad and he's always been very fond of you."

"I like Lacy, Momma, but I don't know if Dad would want him in our house."

"Your dad wouldn't mind. Your dad looked up to Lacy."

"He never took him to our house before."

"Well, he's there now."

I wondered what Mom would think about Lacy getting into Dad's corn liquor an hour ago but didn't say anything. It got awfully quiet.

"Talk to me, baby," Mom said.

"Why they have you in here? You need to come back home."

Mom looked over at the closed door real quick and went to spinning that diamond ring on her finger again.

"You're going to hear this soon enough so I'll go ahead and tell you. They've brought in a policeman from Richmond who says your father couldn't have accidentally shot himself. The police think I didn't tell them the truth when I told them what happened."

I started trembling all over and the more I shook the harder she held me. I pulled my head away so I could look at her eyes. I just had to ask with all the talk around town and now this. I had to.

"But it was an accident like you said it was, wasn't it?"

She grabbed me all of a sudden by both shoulders and held me in front of her.

"You're telling the truth, aren't you, Momma?"

She didn't do or say anything for a long time and then she pulled me toward her again. I could feel her breathing on my neck.

"We're telling the police what your dad told us to tell them…that it was an accident. A horrible accident. Because that's what it was."

"When'd he tell you to say that?"

"Before the rescue squad got to the house…."

She turned to look at me and she looked so upset. But all I could remember was Dad's white face and his eyes and mouth open like a dead deer I'd seen roped to the hood of a pickup truck as they took him out of our house on a stretcher. The blanket they'd thrown over him was a dark red in the middle. I remembered that. I didn't remember Daddy saying anything to anybody. He didn't look like he could say anything because he just looked dead to me. He looked so dead on that stretcher that he didn't even look like my dad anymore. He didn't even look real. It was the worst thing I'd ever seen and I wish I'd never seen it.

Mom took a big gulp of air and wiped her eyes with the top of that ugly green jail dress.

"This was coming, Charlie. They want to blame someone. I want you to listen…if any police officers try to talk to you about this, you tell them to speak to Malcolm Boone, your mom's lawyer. Don't say anything else. They can't make you say anything and I want you to tell me if any police try to talk to you. Understand?"

I nodded.

"Just like we've always said, we don't know how your dad died. We were in the living room while he was cleaning his gun in the kitchen, heard the shot and that's all we know. That's all. It was some sort of horrible accident."

I pulled away quick and stood in front of her, trying my best to swallow. Mom didn't look pretty anymore with her eyes all a mess, but I couldn't help what I had to say.

"I don't remember you in the living room before it happened. You were out in the yard putting clothes on the line and I heard you talking to somebody and then you came in the kitchen. You were in there—"

"Don't say that again."

That frog in my throat grew bigger and bigger and I started crying all of a sudden. "You didn't kill Daddy, did you, Momma?"

I was surprised how easy that question I'd been wondering about like a horrible secret that should never be told finally jumped out. It jumped out of me so fast I couldn't take it back even if I'd tried.

Mom jumped up in a whirlwind and slapped the eternal damnation out of me. But I didn't have time to feel the sting of it before she had both arms around me. I guess I yelled or made some kind of noise because the matron pushed open the door and looked in on us for a minute before closing it again.

"Listen to me...listen to me!"

I was looking down. She pulled my chin up and looked right into my eyes.

"We didn't see anything. We don't know what happened. It's what your dad wanted us to say and that's the way it is. It was a terrible accident. And if anyone asks you anything, you say nothing except for what?"

I yanked my face out of her hand and buried my head in that dress and she kept asking me what I'd say over and over.

Her voice was shaky, and I could tell she was worried to death about all of it. I was, too, but in a real bad way now, so I finally muffled out the answer I knew she needed to hear in that small, smelly brick room in the Sunnyside jailhouse. Besides her needing to hear it, I just didn't know what else to say so I finally said, "I'll tell them to go talk to Malcolm J. Boone."

She was still crying but smiled and rocked me and told me how much she loved me and told me how much Dad loved me. For the first time in the most terrible, lonesome place in my stomach, I really wondered if Momma was telling the truth. Did she know more than she was letting on…just like people in town had been saying for months, especially the police and all of our kin on Dad's side who seemed to hate the sight of both of us.

Granddaddy York didn't act the same. He didn't give me his pocket change anymore or hardly say anything to me when I'd be with Momma and we'd see him in town or up on the mountain somewhere. He'd never say a word to Momma but just stare at her. It'd been months since Grandma had made me a sack of sugar cookies to dunk in coffee. We hadn't been up to their house once since Daddy died and neither of them had stepped foot in our house, either, after the funeral, like they used to all the time without invitation.

After all those years when it seemed like that whole town was ready to do anything for us day or night, all of a sudden I just had Mom and Lacy, and Lacy was already into Daddy's liquor and Mom was in jail and it looked like she'd done fell apart.

I wondered when they buried Daddy, if me and Mom

would've been better off getting buried right there beside him on that wet, cold day.

I looked Mom over best I could, her in that faded ugly dress that was thin as an old sheet. Just like me, she could never get away with telling a big lie, just the little ones like everybody does. She looked and acted like she was telling one big lie, but I tried to believe her as hard as I could. I wanted to run out of there all of a sudden, but I realized I was locked in that room with her. I felt like she'd covered me up in some kind of terrible lie, too, just like Preacher Spangler had said.

I wondered if she'd covered me up in it from the beginning with her talks about what she said Dad wanted us to tell the police.

Thinking about Mom lying and doing what everybody said she'd done made me cold all over, like someone had poured water from a deep, dark well straight down my backbone. I couldn't imagine my mom ever hurting nobody, especially my dad, but she was in the kitchen before it happened. I remembered that.

And she always got so nervous whenever I tried to talk about that terrible day. I think Momma knew the awful things I was thinking about her, too, because I could feel her heart pounding right through that dress.

The matron finally opened the door and after looking us both over, she got that big upside-down smile on her face again and said I needed to go.

I didn't kiss Mom or anything when I got up. I didn't even look at her because I couldn't, even though I wanted to. I didn't know what to do. She asked me to come back twice and I felt her hand grab the back of my shirt, but I just walked out of there and never turned back.

Chapter Seven

"You got to call Doc Lindsey. Call him now!"

"What do you want me to tell him?"

"I can't breathe, Lacy, like I'm trying to tell you and it feels like somebody's got me around the throat."

"You look to be getting air in. Might just be you—"

I jumped out of bed and ran in the kitchen crying. Lacy was trying to catch up to me wearing his robe and telling me to becalm myself. I went to grab the phone off the cradle and he put a hand on it.

"You go on back to bed now and I'll call the doctor."

I looked at him and could tell he was all nervous over me but still sleepy in the head. I ran back to my room and got under the covers but as hard as I tried, I still couldn't get a full breath of air in. I'd been trying for a half hour. And it wasn't just that, my heart was going so fast and I was so light-headed I didn't know what to do. I knew something was bad wrong with me, and it all started as soon as me and Lacy got home from seeing Momma at the jail.

I was sure I was dying.

I looked at my alarm clock and it was just before midnight as I rolled over panting and was sure I'd go unconscious listening to Lacy try to reach Doctor Lindsey and then explain why he was calling about me. Finally I just jumped out of bed, ran in the kitchen, grabbed the phone from Lacy and he took a step away from me and patted me on the back as the doctor asked me a bunch of questions.

I was leaning against the wall, sweating through my bed-clothes and trying my best to get the doctor to hurry up with all the phone talking so he'd come up and take a look at me. But he ended up saying the same thing Lacy had said—I was breathing fine because I wasn't having any trouble talking about not being able to breathe and you have to be able to breathe good to be able to talk so much.

Doctor Lindsey said he wanted to talk some more to Lacy, so that's when I handed Lacy the phone and ran back into my bedroom for the second time that night.

I heard Lacy say a bunch of "yes sirs" over and over until he hung the phone up all careful, like he tended to do.

Lacy walked in looking like he had real bad news and told me just for surety, that Doc Lindsey had told him to take me over to the emergency room at the hospital in Winslow.

He couldn't make a house call because he was attending to another matter. I knew what he was attending to when

I was talking to him because he kept yawning while I was talking to him.

Lacy looked so worried about driving in the dark the 30 miles over to Winslow that I told him I was feeling better even though I wasn't. But then I realized I was a little bit. I'd forgot about all the breathing problems while getting so aggravated that Lacy was so slow doing anything about it.

Lacy told me that sometimes when a feller gets real upset about something, a feller can get all stoved-up and excitable in the middle of the night but it weren't nothing serious. He said it was nature's way to let a feller know he's having a rough time is all. But all I knew was, I laid there listening to him and still couldn't get a full gulp of air no matter how hard I tried. Lacy told me to stop trying and I would before I knew it.

He went into the kitchen and fixed me a big remedy of shine with sugar, lemon and ice and said sipping on it was good for night heart palpitations. I did what he said and finished the whole glass like he told me to even though it tasted terrible. I eventually did fall off to sleep so we didn't have to make the trip to the hospital, and that next morning I woke up breathing good again like I always had before that long night, but now my head was splitting in two. Lacy was snoring all slumped over in the chair next to my bed when the sun came through the curtains.

Those first few days without Momma around were lonesome and the nights were even more lonesome. It took some getting used to in that small house, but even with everything going on, me and Lacy ended up getting along pretty good after that first week of bumping into each other all the time. I got used to him being so slow, and I guess he got used to me being in a hurry.

I said a cross word a time or two about different things he'd tell me to do or not do, but Lacy never said a cross word to me. And he promised that he wouldn't say nothing to Momma about me having a hard time getting my wind that one night.

I started liking Lacy even more than I ever did before, but the neighbors didn't like him. I wasn't sure if it was more because he was colored or if it was because they didn't like anybody who stayed in that house anymore, but I noticed folks didn't wave or speak to him even when he waved or spoke. It didn't seem to bother Lacy at all, though, like it bothered me.

After a while, I started hoping Mom would let Lacy stay with us if they ever let her go and she came back home. Just like Dad had always let Lacy loaf at the shop because he said he just liked having him around, it got to where I just liked that Lacy was around the house, too.

Lacy tried his best to raise me proper and that wore on him the way he seemed to get more tired day after day and week after week. He and Momma tried to keep me away from the cameras and rude people around the courthouse, but I'd still sneak down there and try to find out everything I could about how Daddy died and whatever I could about Momma's trial coming up.

After that first jail visit, I didn't want to visit with Momma anymore but Lacy made me go see her twice a week. Each visit was harder than the last one but other than that they were pretty much the same.

I hated that Mom wasn't home and hated that she was in there, and I started hating her for being in there, too. I hated that Daddy was gone and hated her even more for that. I just started to hate her for all kinds of reasons, and that made me hate her even more for feeling and thinking such things.

But I didn't hate her all of the time. It was mostly late at night or in the still hours of morning when you're feeling all by yourself.

During the day I kept telling myself that Momma was innocent no matter what kind of talking I was around because I think the biggest part of me still believed her. There just wasn't a reason I could think of why she would do what they said she did. And I kept hoping that she was gonna come home all smiling any day with the news of how they finally proved she'd been telling the truth all along. It would never bring Daddy back, but it would at least bring her back.

But with each jail visit those daytime hopes got pushed away little by little. Momma just looked weaker each time, and worse than that she looked like she was trying her best to hold on to a lie even though nobody believed her anymore. It looked like she didn't even believe it sometimes. I didn't know what to think anymore but just kept trying to believe in her like Lacy told me to do. Still it was harder each time I walked down those brick hallways and got let into that little room.

So I was glad the day came when Lacy told me that Mom didn't want me to visit more than once a week until the trial came because so much was going on and she wanted me to stay clear of all of it.

I was glad, and sometimes I came up with a good excuse to even get out of those weekly visits. But every day I still kept hoping she'd show up home. I hoped for that more than anything.

During that same time it was hard for Lacy to keep all of the nosy people with notebooks and cameras away from the house. Finally he went out on the porch one evening and started throwing rocks at bats that flew under the one street-light above their heads. His aim wasn't too good I noticed, and they noticed, too, after he almost pelted a couple of them by mistake.

They left us alone after that, at least during twilight hours.

Lacy told me over supper one evening that it'd been over twenty years since Sunnyside had so many newspaper people hanging around as that fall and winter of 1967. The biggest news story around our parts was usually something like twins being born to an old childless woman, or a farmer who'd grown a six-pound tomato that looked like Jesus if you looked at it the right way on Sunday, or somebody's daughter had graduated from the college in Charlottesville and was going off to work in New York or Paris or some big place like that for someone important who none of us had ever heard of but it all sounded like big things shaking to us.

Things like that.

Lacy recollected the last time so many cared about the go-ings on in our rural county was to cover the grand funeral of a 102-year-old Civil War soldier who'd become a crusader against the KKK in his later years. Lacy had known him and said he'd matured late about some things but had turned out to be a fine feller when he finally did. That old soldier had been one of the officers under General Lee's command at Appomattox and had written a book about the great general in his worst but finest hour, Lacy said.

But I knew the cameras and reporters didn't come this time to record some big event like a funeral of an old rebel hero who'd lived through so much, they came from as far-away as Richmond and even Washington because they smelled a dark secret in our small town. It was a story that would sell newspapers, Lacy told me, and that's why they were there. I thought about it and supposed that it weren't too often when the law believes a mayor's wife killed her husband with a shotgun. Particularly in a small town like Sunnyside where nobody locked their doors at night because nobody ever killed nobody else on purpose.

All I knew was, I just wanted them all to pack up and go back to where they came from. I wanted to wake up to see Daddy reading the paper at the kitchen table and find that all of had been a terrible dream. A dream so bad you wouldn't even ever tell anybody about it because it was so bad.

But that didn't happen. Lacy kept waking me up every morning except when I had to wake him up. He'd always fix a big breakfast of eggs and bacon or homemade sausage and fried apples because he always said a growing young 'un needs a big, hot breakfast and then he'd send me off to school.

I remember wearing several shiners from Halloween to Thanksgiving during that time, and even lost one of my bottom teeth to Lucas Chambliss's right fist. Before Daddy died, Lucas was a good friend of mine but he stopped liking me about the same time everybody else did. Anyway, Lucas had to go get his hand stitched and I had to spend time in the dentist's chair. Lacy went down to talk to the principal. I pleaded with him not to and he knew why, but he said Mom made him.

Things got worse every day after that, especially after the principal called in Lucas and a bunch of other boys and told them to leave me alone and quit calling me names like mamma's boy and nigger lover and other stuff. That talk the principal had with them made me all the more fair game to make fun of or beat the tar out of when they could get away with it. They tended to get away with it pretty frequently.

I finally started cutting class and then cutting school all together because I was flunking everything anyway. I was just basically scared all the time and would rather be by myself.

Even though it was way too big and sometimes too warm to wear, I always grabbed Daddy's big blue wool coat and the lunch sack Lacy fixed for me each morning. I'd wave to Lacy as he stood rigid on that front porch sniffing the air to see if it would rain.

"Keep your chin up," he'd say.

I once asked Lacy why it was important to keep my chin up and he said he weren't sure but at least I'd see what I was about to run into before I'd run into it.

So I'd nod, put my chin up a little, veer off the school

route near Long Curve Road and walk the railroad tracks through Burton's farm down to Catawba Creek.

I'd sit on the creek bank all day and skip rocks and whittle and lay in the sun if it were out, and I even snuck a fishing pole down there, but didn't fish much it was so cold. I'd wonder about a lot of things and stare at the sky moving above me, and when it started getting gray in the late afternoon, I'd creep back to a cut cornfield across from the schoolyard. When all the kids were let out I'd make my way home.

I'd always make a new story up about school that I could tell Lacy when I got home if he weren't asleep, which he was most of the time so that worked out good.

After a few weeks, Jimmy started cutting because he found out after his own share of bloody noses that he couldn't help me fight all those who wanted to take a poke at me. He started going with me to the creek and then Alvin started tagging along, too, sometimes like we both knew he would once he found out what we were doing or he'd snitch out the both of us.

Jimmy said his mom would probably never find out they were skipping school because the teachers probably wouldn't notice him or Alvin missing in their chairs, and even if they did, his dad wouldn't care one way or the other if word got back to his house so he and Alvin seemed happy about the whole arrangement.

Both of them hated books anyway.

No one had seen George or Harry Wilson in some time so they weren't with us. Jimmy said that their dad, who was a traveling insurance salesman who made a right good living he'd heard, had arranged it so they could go to some school for the gifted or the slow-witted, no one was sure which, somewhere in upstate New York, wherever that was. We missed those two boys, odd as they were. The troop had gotten thin with just the three of us.

On a cold Tuesday morning, me, Jimmy and Alvin started building the raft of my dreams out of a downfall of timber and a sail made out of an old piece of canvas that we found. We made plans to head off to our destinies by Friday once we had enough provisions, but once we finished tying all the logs, the raft was so heavy and we'd built it so far from the water, we'd need a mule or a miracle to get it to the creek bank.

Well, we got the miracle and it came in time but it came at the wrong time because none of us were on it at the time.

A huge, cold November rain came one night, and I reckon that raft eventually did what we'd built it for, because when the weather cleared and me and Jimmy went to check on it, we found the side of the hill had washed away and it was gone. We walked the creek searching for it until we got to the mouth where Catawba Creek dumped into the James River.

I wondered where in the world that raft ended up as we watched all the logs and odd things spin around and float down the brown current. Maybe it made it all the way the Chesapeake Bay and then the Atlantic Ocean. I hoped it got that far. I wondered and wondered about that raft for a long time.

Walking back up the creek bank to go home because it was already turning dark, Jimmy grabbed me by the arm of my coat and turned me around.

"What really happened…how your dad died…?"

I stumbled for a minute because me and Jimmy never asked each other questions about hard things, but just generally let one or the other talk about whatever we wanted to.

He finally shrugged his shoulders and said, "That's all right."

He started walking away, dodging the briars and quicksand holes. I caught up and grabbed the back of his brown corduroy coat that looked like he'd outgrown it a couple years before, the way his arms poked out the sleeves too far.

"I don't know what happened," I said. "It was an accident. It was a terrible accident, Mom said."

Jimmy took a couple of steps backward and sat down on a big river rock. He looked down and pulled off a piece of moss and then looked at me.

"You never said nothing about it so I just thought I'd ask with all the dang talking going on," Jimmy said. He stood from the rock and put one hand on my shoulder. "Let's go."

"That day's fuzzy, like a dream or something."

Jimmy nodded. "You don't have to say nothing."

"I remember Momma screaming and all the police and ambulance people in the house, all of them getting real close in my face as they were asking me stuff. I remember Miss Dobbins from the infirmary in her rescue uniform looking me over from top to bottom and wiping blood off of me."

"You had blood on you?"

"It was on my hands and my shirt and was on my face, too, because I remember her wiping my face with a cloth, and when she pulled it away it was red."

"Was it your blood?" Jimmy asked.

"I don't think so. They didn't take me to the hospital or nothing."

"Was it your dad's blood?"

"I guess it was. Momma told me I was hugging him in the floor before the hospital people got there."

"But you never…you don't know what happened?"

I shook my head. I looked at Jimmy and knew he believed me. I just knew it because me and Jimmy were that way from the very beginning.

"You didn't see him die, did you?" he asked.

"I saw them taking him out of the house but I'm not sure if he was dead then yet. He looked like it, though. It was a terrible thing to see, Jimmy."

Jimmy pulled his coat sleeves down as far as they'd go.

"Were you in the house when the gun went off?" he asked.

"I think I was but I don't remember hearing it. I just remember Momma screaming."

"I don't see how you couldn't hear a dang gun going off in a house," Jimmy said.

"I don't know. I don't remember hearing no gun."

We stared at each other for the longest time and then he looked away real quick and he couldn't say anything I guess so I started going back up the creek. I felt better in some way for finally talking about it with someone who weren't a police officer but it still made me want to throw up, which I stopped and did.

Jimmy caught up and patted me on the back.

"I wish I knew what happened, Jimmy. I'd give anything to know."

I got myself together and washed my face in the creek and we walked almost a half mile tramping along, not saying anything before he said, "I didn't know whether to tell you this or not but figure I'll go ahead and do it."

I turned around. Jimmy pushed me forward to keep walking ahead of him and I did.

"Me and Alvin were downtown looking for change and we got to the Tastee-Freez. We were searching around cars, and I heard Deputy Reed talking with a man from the state about Hollis Thrasher. Reed said they got some kind of paper on him and they're looking for him. Got people even looking for him in Mexico. Said they need to ask him questions about your dad dying."

I stopped. Jimmy pushed me forward again but I didn't move.

"I'm just telling you what I heard with my own ears because I thought you'd want to know. I think that's why the law was up at his place that time…remember when we seen them up there?"

"Do they think he may have done it?"

"I don't know but it sorta sounded like it. Or he knows who did."

Jimmy shrugged and I took a shiver that I couldn't shake off. I started digging a hole in the creek bank with the heel of my boot. I felt like I was gonna throw up again and just couldn't figure that Hollis Thrasher would kill my dad. My dad was always good to Hollis, giving him rides, and I saw him buy him a cold bottle of pop a time or two. After talking to him on that bench, Hollis didn't seem to me anymore

like someone who'd hurt anybody just to hurt them like
Lacy had told me once, he just looked like he would, though
he had spent time in prison for hurting people and some
folks in town still thought he'd killed his wife and daughter years ago after he'd got out of the mental hospital when
he got back from the war. And they say he killed piles of
people in that war and had the medals to prove it.

"Did you hear anything else about it?"

"They said somebody saw him up at your house about
the time people heard the gun go off. That was all me and
Alvin could hear because the man from the state turned
around and saw us snooping and they went inside."

My mind and stomach were racing a hundred miles an
hour as we started walking, and when the trail finally split
where Jimmy would go to his house and I'd go to mine, we
never said anything more, just stood there until finally he
waved and headed off and I walked up Duncan Hill. I felt
so tired and lost I didn't think I could take another step. I
knew one thing walking in the dark, even though Hollis was
in Mexico, I was scared of him again even more than I ever
had been before.

When I was almost at the top, I saw a streetlight glowing
off two heads of blond, wiry hair. Two of the Perkins boys
were pushing an old tire down the street, and I looked
around real quick to see if Alton was with them. When I
looked back around I could tell those boys spotted me because they pushed the tire in a ditch and took off running
down the street as hard as they could in my direction.

I stood there for a minute. I don't know what welled up

inside of me, but I took off charging at them as hard as I could, yelling my head off with both arms straight up in the air. They stopped about a half block from me for what reason I don't know, but I kept running at them as hard as I could.

But I was running so fast, that when I was finally on top of them, I just ran right over the both of them swinging both fists. All three of us hit the ground, and I was somehow on top. I was still yelling and swinging when one got away from me even though I pulled his boot off. He took off down the hill back toward town with just the one boot and stopped and watched me whip the snot out of his older brother.

I finally let him up when he yelled for me to a couple of times and then I threw the boot at the younger brother, told him to come back and get what he'd asked for and called him a big sissy.

I stood still on guard, ready to go again with the other one, and like usual expected I'd caught a couple good blows and would start feeling it. But the only thing that hurt was my lungs burning for air and my knuckles.

Ricky Perkins got up, half fell down and then walked away and then started to run trying to get his coat from overtop his head where I'd pulled it before he fell again. He eventually got his brains together and his coat fixed and both of them took off like the sheriff was after them.

I stayed in the middle of that road like I was the king of that mountain until they were both out of sight, and I had the biggest feeling in the world when I turned to go home that that was the last time the Perkins boys would ever pick on Charles W. York, unless they had Alton with them, maybe. But maybe I could even take him, too.

I looked myself over real good, tried to get the dirt off my coat, and as I walked the rest of the way up the side of the mountain to my house, I saw Malcolm's big red Cadillac shining in the dark beside my front yard. That car almost took up the whole dirt street and for some reason just seeing it there made me feel all hollowed out again.

I guessed he had some bad news to tell me or a note to pass on from Mom. I used to hope when I saw his car that he was bringing Momma home. Maybe he'd convinced the judge to let her go or maybe they'd decided she didn't do it like we'd always said, but as the days and weeks passed and she kept staying in jail, it seemed less likely to me that she'd ever come back home and that was so empty to think about I tried not to. I just hoped Malcolm had good news of some sort because I sure could use some.

Before I stepped up onto the porch, I took one last look around. I wasn't looking for the Perkins boys. I looked up on the mountain ridge where I could usually see the faint yellow speck of lantern light that came from Hollis Thrasher's shack. But the whole mountain was still misty and dark like it had been since he'd took the bus for Mexico.

Chapter Eight

They both stared at me when I walked in but it didn't look like I'd interrupted any big conversation. Malcolm was sitting at one end of the kitchen table with Lacy at the other. The first thought I had seeing the two of them was you couldn't find two more different looking and acting people in one room. Malcolm with his pale color and his fancy manners and loud ways, and Lacy with his face and hands the shade of the rainy side of a tree and his slow Southern way of always going around the barn like small town folks do when talking to people instead of being direct like city people and Yankees do in general.

Lacy didn't say anything, stood and pulled out my plate warming in the stove. He put it on the table, took off the foil and put down my silverware one piece at a time like it mattered a lot exactly where the fork or knife was placed, and then told me to wash up.

I half smiled at Malcolm because he smiled at me before he took a sip of the hot tea with lemon Lacy always made for him on his visits.

I went to the bathroom mirror to make sure my nose wasn't busted because I couldn't get much air through it and saw the tear marks streaked through the dirt on my face. I guess I got them when I talked to Jimmy about Dad dying or when I was beating up the Perkins boys. Maybe both. I was embarrassed wondering if Lacy and Malcolm had noticed and I gave my face a good scrubbing until I was red from ear to ear.

Walking back in the kitchen and getting used to Lacy's dinner rules, I stood with my legs still all aquiver from the battle and from thinking about Hollis Thrasher as Lacy tucked a kitchen rag into the collar of my shirt before I could sit. I then bowed my head for a minute like he expected me to do. I never prayed anything because nothing came to mind but I figured they thought I did. I did say, "Amen."

Supper that night was a usual supper people ate in Sunnyside about four days a week. A big bowl of pinto beans with fatback and chow-chow, canned tomatoes, turnip greens and corn bread.

I was so tired and so sick I wasn't hungry, but when I sat it was quiet, way too quiet especially with Malcolm in the house. So I went ahead and put some chow-chow and butter on the beans and tore into them and hoped he wouldn't note my hands trembling like they were.

Lacy poured me buttermilk into a glass he'd kept cold in the refrigerator, and then he walked out and I heard the TV come on in the living room. I looked over at Malcolm and he was staring at me smiling. I never ever saw anyone who smiled so much as Malcolm Boone. It was tiresome to be around someone who smiled so much, especially on a day like today when the raft you've been building goes down the river without you and it felt like you'd been in battle after battle, I thought.

"How's school, Charles?" he asked.

I hadn't been for some time but said, "Pretty good, Mr. Boone," and kept eating.

"I know it's a really hard time for you right now. We're trying to push the trial date up to get this over with so your mother can come back home."

I listened to him go on and on between his sips of tea, but it seemed like forever before Mom's trial got going in a proper fashion. And even though Malcolm made it seem like it was the judge or the commonwealth attorney who was slowing things up, it seemed by the newspapers and TV that Malcolm was giving them all a fit and that's why the trial was being put off.

The other thing I'd noticed was he sure seemed to enjoy answering the evening questions hurled at him in front of the cameras on the courthouse green from the times I snuck down there to find out what was going on. Then I'd come home and, if Lacy were asleep in Dad's old chair, I'd watch Malcolm on the news with the volume way down as he talked loud and fast, getting all worked up with his eyes looking like they'd shoot right out of his head and break a window if they didn't kill somebody first.

Lacy wouldn't let me watch the news except for when Walter Cronkite talked about the war in Vietnam, or when the blacks and whites were fighting somewhere or when it was time for the local weather and baseball scores because he said the rest generally wasn't fit for any ears, old or young. He said the news was pretty much just a show to tell you things put in a slanted way so you'd be more apt to watch it and wealthy folks could sell laundry powders or biscuit mix and whatnot on the commercials and get even more wealthy. It was all a moneymaking venture, Lacy said. But I watched it anyway if Lacy was snoring. I figured some of it were true and tried to figure out which parts.

There were all kinds of different court hearings that fall. They showed Momma in that green dress walking with chains on her legs once. Her head was down and she tried to cover her face with her hands. It was the worst thing I ever saw on TV.

I'd hoped Malcolm had good news tonight, but he didn't or he'd of said so already. Even though that made me even less hungry, I kept eating anyway because it beat just sitting there with Malcolm smiling at me and listening to Lacy snore.

By the time I finished supper and spooned out the last of the corn bread dunked in buttermilk, Lacy's snoring got even louder in the living room. Malcolm was not his usual fire-and-brimstone self that evening, either, and said very little by his standards. His thick hair was sticking up in all kinds of directions like he'd been fighting bad winds all day. He finally got up to leave and that's when I had to ask him a couple things I'd been dying to know but had never had the courage to ask.

"Why do they think Mom killed Dad?"

Malcolm sat down slow and adjusted a small gold chain around one wrist.

"A firearms expert has stated that the wound your father received had to have come from the barrel of a shotgun from a distance of at least two feet from his body, and in a horizontal line. Basically, it would be impossible for him to accidentally shoot himself in the stomach. He would have had to hold it out from himself, by the end of the barrel, and somehow pull the trigger. You understand what I'm saying?"

"Maybe he dropped it and it went off," I said.

Malcolm shook his head. "Again, and only by their interpretation of the evidence, your dad would have had to be perpendicular to the shotgun, like a 'T', even if he dropped it and it…well, basically they believe the evidence doesn't suggest that he dropped the gun and it somehow fired."

I started to pick at my face and moved around my silverware. Malcolm acted like he was waiting for me to say something, but I couldn't say it right then with him eyeballing me so hard so I just looked down.

After a long time of silence, I finally glanced at him and Malcolm had quit smiling and his bloodshot eyes were still drilling into mine. He had a serious look about him sometimes, between all that smiling that would scare a spook.

"But why do they think Momma would do something like that?" I finally asked.

"A deputy sheriff and rescue squad members have said that your mother had red marks on her face, her cheeks, and her hair looked like it had been torn out from her bun. That along with a neighbor saying she heard yelling from your house before she heard the gunshot makes it seem like there was some sort of altercation in the house before your father was shot. An altercation between your father and mother."

"What's an altercation?"

"It's…a heated disagreement. Someone can become angry and—"

"It means people fighting?"

"Yes. Two witnesses have said your mother screamed before the gunshot was heard."

I couldn't slow down my breathing as hard as I tried.

"Are you okay, Charles?"

A vision came on me and I wasn't okay at all. A big drop of sweat rolled down the middle of my back.

"Maybe we shouldn't talk about this now," Malcolm said.

"And you don't think she did it?" I asked.

Malcolm pulled his hand down his long face, stretching it even more.

"Charles, I truly believe your mother didn't murder your father."

"If it weren't an accident, could somebody else have done it besides Momma?"

"I'm confident it was an accident."

"Does that mean you're sure it was?"

"I believe that, yes."

"And you think she'll get out of jail?"

Malcolm's smile returned. "I wouldn't be here if I thought otherwise. Your mother doesn't want you to worry about the trial. She just wants you to be a young boy and think good thoughts and go to school and do your homework and all of those things. This will be over very soon and like I told you, I've gotten the commonwealth attorney to agree that unless there is some dire need on their part, which I'll fight, you probably won't have to testify per your mom's wishes. They're going to introduce the statements you've made to the police. That's—"

The kitchen door slammed back against the wall so hard the whole house shook.

"This county has had enough of your lies, Mr. Boone."

I was suddenly standing from the loud bang and recognized the strained voice of my Granddaddy York even though I couldn't see him clear. He was standing on the side porch in a shadow next to the kindling box. He took a step inside and I'd never seen the strange look on his face before. That look was pointed right at Malcolm.

"What are you trying to do to my grandson?" he said.

Granddaddy took off a red hunting cap and stuffed it into a back pocket of the tan work overalls that he wore all the time except on Sundays.

I looked over at Malcolm and noticed he was standing, too. All got still and I walked and then ran to Granddaddy because he got down on one knee and held his arms out for me. He grabbed hold of me and I grabbed hold of him tight. I was so glad it seemed like he liked me again, but even on his knee holding me, he was still staring at Malcolm with a wild look I'd seen on faces at the playground a few times from someone who wasn't about to fight, but was already in the middle of one.

He finally pushed me away a step before he stood, then he walked up to Malcolm and the two of them stood nose to nose. Malcolm was as thin as my granddaddy was thick, like a willow sapling poking up in front of a fifty-five-gallon drum.

Malcolm stuck out a hand and flashed that TV smile of his for a moment. His expression changed and got crooked on one side when Granddaddy looked at Malcolm's hand, but didn't take it.

Granddaddy raised a thick finger with scars and calluses all over it from framing half of the houses in Sunnyside for forty years. That finger sat stone-still in the middle of the room right in Malcolm's face.

"You're not gonna ruin that boy."

Granddaddy kept his finger in that one spot and Malcolm pulled back his hand that obviously wasn't gonna get shook.

"I was speaking with—"

Granddaddy slammed his hand on the table and my fork and knife flew into the floor.

"Enough!" he yelled.

I backed up next to the refrigerator and Granddaddy wiped his mouth and looked at me for a flash like he was ashamed of what I'd just seen. I'd seen him serious lots of times, like the time he wanted me to bait my own hook, but I'd never seen him worked up like he was. I'd never seen him mad. He turned with his gray eyes all squinted up to Malcolm.

Malcolm's crooked smile disappeared altogether and a stern look came over his face, like he'd get with the newspaper reporters, and then it looked like he grew a couple inches taller all of a sudden. As thin and weak as he looked sometimes, it now looked like it would take ten men to move him if he didn't want to be moved.

"Don't do this, Ethan," he said.

"You address me as Mr. York."

Malcolm didn't budge in any way except his look just got harder by the second, like it was setting in concrete.

"I'll address you how I please," he said.

The sudden loud way Granddaddy had came in the house had gave me a startle, but now I was scared because like I said, I'd never seen him mad at anything or anybody and I'd never heard him say much at all my whole life except good things now and then or things I needed to do to become a strong man like Daddy.

I knew Malcolm was always aggravating people over this or that with his strange ways but I wondered what Malcolm had done to make Granddaddy so mad. Most people Malcolm aggravated kept it to themselves and said stuff about him behind his back, not direct like Granddaddy was doing.

I kept backing up and peeped through the door that led into the living room when I heard Lacy get up from Dad's lounging chair.

Lacy walked in and adjusted his horned-rimmed glasses, which had fallen down on his nose. He looked like he didn't know where in the world he was at for a minute as we all stood there and stared at him. He finally stopped and leaned on his cane but wobbled and grabbed the wall, too. He looked at all of us one at a time and when his eyes found Granddaddy, he backed up a step.

"I'm taking Charlie home to me and Mother like I told you yesterday, Slim. He's gonna live with us for a while. Boy needs his family now."

Granddaddy looked at me and I guess the thought of getting out of my house that seemed so empty and visiting with them and eating Grandma's cooking and sleeping in a big feather bed and doing all the things I liked to do up there took hold of me because I walked toward him ready to go. It made me feel a lot less lonesome and feel stronger all of a sudden or something.

"His mom wants him to stay here," Lacy said.

I stopped at the coatrack when Lacy said that. I looked at him and my Granddaddy stare at each other across the small space in that kitchen until Lacy looked down. I put my coat on and Malcolm grabbed his teacup, put it in both hands and took a sip. Then he shook his head slow at me.

Granddaddy looked at Malcolm like he'd like to swat him like a fly, then he moved to me and put a hand on my shoulder and pulled me to him. He patted me on the shoulder and then his face changed and he looked at me like he used to. I was just happy he was acting like he liked me again and I felt good. Real good.

"Me and your grandma want to take care of you…'til things get worked out with your mom and everything," he said, his voice now back to normal.

Lacy dug in his sweater pocket and pulled out his pipe. I

could hear him pulling air through the stem and he finally took it away and pointed it at me.

"Now I've talked to his momma like I told you I'd do and she wants him to stay here. She was firm about it."

"I wanna go up there, Lacy," I said.

"We have to tend to her wishes."

"But she wouldn't mind me staying with Granddaddy," I said.

"We'll both go down and you can talk to her about it in the morning."

"You do all the talking to whoever you need to do to-morrow, Lacy. We're going, and you're going, too. I'm taking you back over to Town Heights. Get your things together."

"No, sir, Mr. York. And he's to stay here," Lacy said.

"I ain't staying here," I said.

"But you got to, child," Lacy said.

"He ain't got to do nothing you say," Granddaddy said. "And I'm not gonna have words with you over it in front of the boy because that's the way it's gonna be. Now get your things together."

Lacy took careful steps across the floor and pulled a chair and sat in it all tuckered out like he'd just finished digging postholes all day. "Charlie, go in your room for a minute, please, sir," he said.

"Charlie's fine where he's at. And I'm not gonna tell you again—get your belongings together!"

I wanted to go but didn't like Granddaddy talking to Lacy like that. I didn't like it at all. I'd never heard him talk to anybody that loud. Lacy reached over and patted my hand. "Go on now, let us talk."

I looked up at Granddaddy and saw his face changing again and I felt some of the weight of his hand lift from my shoulder. I buttoned up my coat and walked out of the kitchen and down the hall but didn't go in my room. I stood where I could hear what was going on from just inside the bathroom.

"You and Miss Ruth know you can come down here and visit anytime you want. You know that. But this is still his home, you see."

"You think you're gonna sit there and tell me what I can and can't do with my own grandson!"

"I'm just telling you what his momma—"

"You should've paid more mind to the talk we had yesterday...."

"Why you doing this now...you ain't had a thing to say to that boy in—"

"Slim, get your things together. I ain't telling you again."

I started hearing hushed talking and then heard Malcolm's voice.

"You try to take Charlie out of this house without his mother's permission, and I'll call the sheriff."

"Call him," Granddaddy said.

"If you have custody issues, you need to discuss—"

"I talked to the sheriff and I talked to the judge and I talked to a lawyer. I heard what you been saying everywhere and telling that boy and I'm through talking. Between your lies and his mom's lies he doesn't know right from wrong anymore. And I don't know what you're doing up here to begin with, Slim. This ain't your place to be and I know you damned sure know it."

Malcolm picked the phone off the cradle and I heard the numbers spinning.

"Mr. Boone, put the phone down, please sir," Lacy said.

I stood trying to breathe as quiet as I could and inched closer when everybody got quiet for the longest time.

"Come on out, Charlie!" Granddaddy yelled.

I took a couple steps and heard him say to Lacy real low, "I offered you a ride, but you can get your own ride back. But if I were you, I wouldn't stay up here one minute once we leave."

I kept standing there in the hall and didn't know what to do. I felt sorry for Lacy. He'd been too good to me and Momma for Granddaddy to talk to him like that.

"Your grandma has made you a big supper! Come on, son."

I walked in and looked at Lacy. As much as I wanted to go up there a minute ago, I didn't want to leave now if Mom and Lacy didn't want me to. I weren't sure about Mom anymore, but Lacy had never steered me wrong about nothing and was about the only friend I had left except for Jimmy. If he was saying I shouldn't go up there for some reason, I started thinking maybe I shouldn't until I talked to Momma about it. I knew Momma and Granddaddy never got along real good and were cold around each other for what reason I didn't know, but she'd never told me I couldn't go up there before now.

I sat back down at the table between Lacy and Granddaddy.

Granddaddy grabbed my hand and pulled me up slow. Then we started walking toward the porch, but I pulled back and looked at Lacy just before we went out the door.

"Come on now. Let's go," he said.

Lacy looked me in the eyes and limped over to the kitchen door as quick as I'd ever seen him walk. He put his cane across it.

"Now I mean what I say," Lacy said, but he sure didn't say what he'd just said like he meant it.

His voice was trembling and I could tell he was scared a lot more than I was. Granddaddy let go of my hand and took a step directly in front of the cane. It looked like he was gonna rip it right out of Lacy's hand if Lacy didn't drop it out of fright first.

"I'm staying here, Granddaddy. Why don't you and Grandma come down here and stay with us?" I asked.

He turned around and looked at me and then at Malcolm, who had the phone in one hand while holding down the cradle with the other.

"This isn't the way to do this, Mr. York," Malcolm said.

Granddaddy looked at everybody on all sides of him and then focused on Lacy, who finally lowered his cane.

"You don't know what you're doing to that boy," Granddaddy said quiet, leaning right up to Lacy's ear.

Lacy didn't say anything and just stood there breathing heavy and looking frailer by the second. Granddaddy leaned in even closer and Lacy pulled back his head from him.

"It ain't right and nigger, you're gonna wish you'd of taken that ride I offered tonight."

"Did you just threaten him?" Malcolm asked, walking toward the two of them.

"No, sir, he didn't," Lacy said.

"Charlie, go to your room," Malcolm said.

I took a step but stopped.

"Now, Charlie," he said.

Malcolm looked at me hard but I didn't move another inch because all this talking was about me and I wanted to find out what the fuss was. Malcolm finally decided I wasn't gonna do as he said. He looked at Granddaddy. "What did you just say to Lacy?"

"That's between him and me," Granddaddy said.

"You'd better be careful before you cross a very serious line here, Mr. York."

Granddaddy nodded his head. "Lacy is the one who done crossed a line...and you'd best be careful of yourself up on this mountain, Mr. Boone."

"Keep talking...." Malcolm said.

Granddaddy put his cap back on all of a sudden, bent down and I flinched. But he picked me up and kissed me on the cheek before he held me for a long time and lowered me back down.

"I got the whole county on my side, Mr. Boone. We'll be taking this back up soon."

Granddaddy put his hand on my head and nodded, and then Lacy got out of his way quick or he'd of gotten run right over as Granddaddy stormed out the kitchen door into the night.

Chapter Nine

I looked at Malcolm and he definitely wasn't smiling now.

Lacy looked like he barely made it back to the table to sit back down as we all listened to Granddaddy's pickup truck tear down the mountain. Malcolm sat, too, and finished his tea after he gave the last sip a swirl. He then stood, put on his big leather coat and tucked his scarf in.

"It's a tough time for everyone who was close to your father, especially your grandparents. But Lacy's going to continue to take very good care of you just as he has been, okay?"

"For how long?" I asked.

"Until your mother's trial is over."

"And then what happens?"

Malcolm smiled and winked. "Good things happen. Have faith, young man."

He went to leave and I wanted to ask him about what I'd

heard from Jimmy about Hollis Thrasher, but I couldn't find the words to say anything more. Malcolm shook hands with Lacy and said quiet, "Come see me tomorrow, around noon."

Lacy took a big shaky breath and nodded barely, and then Malcolm stepped out the door with a smile and another wink as a cold gust blew into the kitchen that went right through me.

I felt that sharp chill and thought as smart as everyone said he was, I never did think Malcolm thought I was too bright the way he said everything to me with a smile and wink at the end. That worried me because there was nothing to smile about, no matter how much he polished it all up. I just hoped Malcolm didn't think all of this was like one of his high-stakes poker games that I'd always heard he liked to play so much, and lost at.

But somehow I was glad at least he was smiling, even if I knew it was fake because his eyes had stopped smiling weeks ago.

I'd usually put on a fake smile, too, almost like I was trained to do now no matter what terrible things were going on. So that's what I did when he left.

I smiled.

But it dropped from my face before the door closed and winter air filled that small kitchen where Daddy had laid dying on the yellow linoleum floor just months before. I remember seeing Mom crying and trying to scrub it all up after she came back from the hospital with the news that Daddy was dead.

Lacy stood and started picking up my dirty dishes and I

got the silverware off the floor. It was quiet for a long time as he started running the dishwater. Lacy had his back to me and leaned over that sink like if he let go of it he'd fall into pieces like a box puzzle.

"He shouldn't have called you that name, Lacy."

Lacy turned around and looked at me for a minute. "It's all right, child," he said.

"Why's Granddaddy so mad?"

Lacy turned off the spigot and looked out the kitchen window where the curtains didn't meet all the way.

"What he thinks is best for you and what your momma thinks is best is two different varmints."

"He don't want me staying here with you."

"No, sir, it surely don't sound like it."

"'Cause you're colored?"

"Well, I got it figured that we got to do what your mom says on account of she's your mom and moms always know about these sorts of particulars."

"He says you crossed a line...."

Lacy kept standing with his back to me. He ran a finger down one of Momma's lace curtains and I kept waiting for him to say something but he never did.

"Why are the police looking for Hollis Thrasher?" I asked.

Lacy turned around quick for him. "Who told you that?"

"I just heard it from somebody who heard a sheriff saying that down at the Tastee-Freez to somebody else."

"They have a few questions for him, I reckon. Normal sorts of things they've asked about everybody who lives up on the mountain."

"You don't think Hollis Thrasher had anything to do with Daddy dying, do you?"

"I believe what your momma says happened."

"The sheriff don't. Nobody else does, either."

Lacy turned back toward the sink and stacked all the dishes in one at a time. He started scrubbing on them.

"I don't want you to give two cares to whatever the dang law in this town thinks."

"Do you trust Malcolm?"

Lacy turned off the water, and after he'd finished the dishes and dried them and put them in the cupboard, he walked to the table, took a seat and wiped his forehead with his handkerchief. It was a good two minutes before he answered my question but Lacy was like that.

"He's one smart feller. Your mom's getting out of that jail. Don't you ever think anything different, not for a minute."

He looked at me stern like I'd never seen him look at me before.

"Not for a minute, you hear?" he said.

I nodded.

"You think Granddaddy is gonna come back mad again like he was?"

"I don't rightly know."

"You ever seen him mad like that?"

Lacy pulled out a pocketknife and started whittling away the tar from the inside of his pipe bowl.

"Do you think he'll come back tonight and take me up to his house?"

"You're to stay here, if it's okay."

"I don't mind staying here with you," I said.

Lacy nodded and got up all of a sudden to peer out the window again when a car drove up. Headlights flashed across the curtains, but whoever it was kept driving. He stood there a long time looking all around with his fingers on the window.

"Are you scared of Granddaddy?"

Lacy folded his penknife and put it back in his pocket. He turned and wiped his mouth with a handkerchief.

"Times like these it's hard for folks to figure what's the right thing to do. Your granddad's used to getting his way about things in this county, but your mom is to get her way when it comes to her own young 'un, you see. She knows what's best for you."

I thought about Granddaddy. He'd taught me how to play checkers and read a watch and tell whether a turkey you're tracking is a tom or a hen just by looking at its poop and how to tell where a deer has slept and how to eat a wild apple so you don't eat the wormy parts and lots of other things. I loved him and always looked up to him like I looked up to Lacy. Seemed to me he'd always been good to me and Dad and Mom in his serious sort of way about things. That's why it hurt so bad when it seemed like he didn't have nothing to say to us since Dad died until tonight.

"Things will shake out proper in due time," Lacy said. "Always do."

I wanted to ask Lacy some more things but I was so worn out, and he wasn't looking good, either, the way he kept looking out the curtains every time a car was going up the mountain. I realized he never said whether he was scared of my granddaddy or not. But he looked scared of him when they were face-to-face a few minutes ago and he looked more scared of something out there in the dark since Granddaddy had left. In some way I felt scared of Granddaddy now, too. I wasn't sure why but I was and that was an empty and troublesome feeling.

Lacy walked over and patted me on the hand and nodded, and then went into the bathroom humming an old Mother Maybelle Carter tune with his pipe between his teeth. I thought again how he told me that Mom was getting out of jail.

Lacy had never lied to me.

Ever.

I don't know why with so many things going on, but for some strange reason that empty, troublesome feeling left and I ended up feeling pretty good at the very end of that long day, almost normal, and at first I went to sleep like I hadn't slept since the smells and sounds of my Dad were in the house every night.

I know I didn't say my prayers before I fell asleep, because I'd quit doing that after Dad was gone because he always said them with me. It just didn't seem the same saying them by myself to an empty room.

And I don't remember dreaming anything like I usually did as soon as I'd start falling asleep, but I do remember thinking that I was glad I didn't take off on that raft after all. I was still on fire from teaching those Perkins boys a lesson about messing with Charles W. York. Dad would have been proud of me.

I did keep wondering where that raft ended up, though. I hoped the way it left without me in a rainstorm was some kind of sign that I was supposed to stay. Then I wondered if it was a bad sign because I never understood signs like some people could. But I didn't worry about that for long, I don't think. I was just glad that besides Malcolm Boone, Lacy still believed Mom was telling the truth. Both of them said she'd come home soon and things would get straightened out and that was good enough for me after that long day.

But that good feeling of just feeling normal didn't last but a few hours. Me and Lacy were about to get another visitor that night.

I lay under the quilts hearing the knock, still heavy in my arms and legs and wondered if I was in the beginnings of a terrible vision. Another knock, this one louder. I woke sudden and then all I could hear was my breathing. Hardly nobody ever came to the front door and I never heard a knock there in the middle of the night.

"Sheriff's office, open up."

I sat up and looked out the corner window where I could see the street in front of the house. A sheriff's car sat, engine still running with the headlights off. A cloud of blue smoke puffed from the tailpipe.

I went to get Lacy and there was a bang even louder at the door, so loud this time it made me jump and I thought the door was gonna come off the hinges. I recognized the voice that followed the banging. It was the deputy sheriff who'd been up to the house what seemed like a lifetime ago to break the news that Momma was in jail. There were only three deputies in our county so it weren't hard telling who was who.

I ran to the living room and looked at the clock and it said it was a little before four in the morning. I thought about opening the door but then ran to Lacy's room when the knock turned into the law now kicking on the door.

"Open up, Lacy!"

I shook Lacy and he didn't move and I kept shaking on him until he sat up. I told him Earl Potts was outside.

Lacy looked around in the room, which used to be Mom and Dad's room. He propped himself all the way up on both arms and there was another kick. This time it came from the kitchen door.

"Earl Potts?"

I nodded.

"What's he want?" Lacy asked.

"I don't know. He's been beating to get in for a couple minutes."

"Let 'em in, child. I'll be in directly."

I ran to the kitchen in my long underwear and saw the deputy's face plastered against the glass like something you'd see in a scary movie.

He saw me at the same time, and he pointed for me to open the door.

I did.

The deputy walked in and looked to be in a hurry because he didn't wipe his feet or take off his hat or anything. He shook the chill off for a second, nodded and asked where Lacy was.

"He said he'd be in directly," I said.

The deputy looked around the kitchen, and I guess his nose led him to a pot of cooked brown beans on the stove that Lacy was letting set to fry up for breakfast. He didn't open the lid but stared at the pot. I was still standing there beside him for what seemed to be forever. But he never said nothing else to me and that's when I noticed that my feet were freezing on that linoleum floor because I didn't have any socks on.

Lacy walked in with his raggedy green robe wrapped around him and he looked around in the dark for us. He searched for a light pull-string in the wrong places so I reached above the kitchen table and pulled the string and it got bright as the blazes in that kitchen. Me and Lacy both squinted up.

The deputy went right past me and put a hand on Lacy's shoulder turning him around. He grabbed him so hard Lacy almost turned in a whole circle before the deputy got hold of him good and got him going in the direction he wanted. They both walked into the living room and the deputy looked back at me and held up a finger for me not to follow them but I did.

Lacy turned on the light next to Momma's china display and I started to walk in and Lacy shook his head for me not to. I took a step down the hall and stopped because I knew this was something serious and I was sure it had to do with Momma. It just had to. A pang of something bad shot up from my stomach into my throat. I tried to hear what was going on but couldn't. But that's when I heard the sounds of sirens far off.

All of a sudden Lacy came around the corner with his cane popping against the wood floor, and he almost fell when one of my legs got tangled up with his cane. He didn't say nothing as I tried to get out of his way and I watched him go to his bedroom.

I ran in my bedroom and pulled on socks and my overalls and a new pair of hunting boots Lacy had picked up for me. I heard radio static coming from the kitchen. I crept near the doorway with a sweatshirt in my hand and saw the deputy trying to get a whole piece of Lacy's leftover corn bread in his mouth while talking into a walkie-talkie.

He said something about a fire.

Chapter Ten

Flames shot out the windows and doors like arms trying to grab hold of us. One big flame went through the roof near the cement block chimney. Even sitting in the back seat of a patrol car with the windows rolled up, I could smell the smoke and feel the heat from it and I watched as the firemen tried to put it out with two hoses hooked to the Sunnyside volunteer fire truck.

I looked over at Lacy sitting beside me in the back seat, but he just kept staring at the fire. I saw most of his neighbors in Town Heights were out in their yards and standing in their driveways watching Lacy's house burn to the ground. One man stood with a wooden bucket in one hand and had a little girl in the other.

A fireman wearing a heavy coat and black helmet ran over to us and fell when his feet went out from under him on the wet grass. He got up and yelled something and waved us back.

Deputy Potts backed up the sheriff's car about fifty feet from where we'd been sitting, and after we stopped, Lacy leaned forward and said a few words to him I couldn't hear. The deputy got out, walked around and opened Lacy's door. Lacy got out and I wanted to get out, too, but he shook his head.

Lacy stood beside the car and leaned on his cane, and I saw him look up to the sky a couple of times and back at his house. I decided to go ahead and get out since it looked like the whole town was standing outside but when I tried to, I noticed there weren't any door handles. Then I noticed there weren't any way to roll down the windows.

I sat there by myself a minute and looked through the steel wire that kept the front seat divided from the back seat. I pounded on the window but, with all the commotion and the sirens going, Lacy and the deputy couldn't hear me. They started to walk a few steps closer to the house and that's when a big gust of smoke flew over the car and I couldn't see anything. I yelled. Nobody heard me so I yelled louder. The deputy finally turned around and walked back. When he opened the door, I didn't ask if I could get out, I just jumped out and ran and stood by Lacy. Lacy didn't notice me beside him for a few minutes as the roof started to give and then the whole house fell in on one side and loud noises and flames shot out everywhere.

Lacy had both hands leaning on that cane, and I saw the tears in his eyes even though they were all squinted up.

When I coughed a couple of times 'cause the wind shifted and blew the smoke our way again, he finally noticed me standing there. He patted me on the back and we both went back to the car.

We got in and the deputy soon got in, and after that the house started burning all over and the firemen had to back away farther from where they'd been standing. They started watering down the other houses and mobile homes next to Lacy's house. Lacy looked at me, but said to the deputy, "Take us back up on the mountain, please, sir."

The deputy turned around and chewed on the side of his mouth like he did all the time. Then he said, "Why don't you stay with one of your relatives over here, tonight. I know you got a pile of nieces and nephews who live over here."

Lacy didn't say anything and took a big shaky breath.

"Don't you still have a brother who lives here, Slim?" the deputy asked.

Lacy let out the air he'd just took in slow and then sat still like an old, weathered rock. "No, sir."

"Well, I'll take Charlie to the sheriff's office and we'll work it out with his mom for somebody to stay with him. Probably be best for you to stay tonight with your people…so as you can take care of your own things here in the morning."

"Take us back up Duncan Hill, please, sir," Lacy said again.

"I don't think that's a good idea."

"Do as I ask, now," Lacy said.

"Listen, we're gonna have to ask you some questions and whatnot. Gonna take a while."

"I'm wore out and need to go up and get back to bed for a couple hours."

"Ain't you worried about your house?"

"Ain't nothing left to worry about."

"You have insurance on it?"

"No, sir."

"Well, like I was saying, we're gonna have to talk to you about how the fire could've got started, that sort of thing."

"We'll do all that after the sun comes up," Lacy said.

"You know how it could've got started?"

"I figure it was meant to burn down is about all I know."

"What do you mean by that?"

"I mean it started on its own or somebody started it. Either way, it's gone."

The deputy pushed up on his hat and turned on the interior light. He started backing up the car and then when we pulled away he looked in the rearview mirror and said, "We're gonna go on down to the sheriff's office."

"No, sir."

"Now I got a right to take you down to ask you questions about how it might have gotten started."

"I think you got a good idea already, Earl. And you know I didn't burn down my own dern house. Now take us back up on the mountain like I'm asking you to do."

"So you thinking somebody burned it down?"

Lacy didn't say anything for a long time. He had both hands resting on his legs and looked out the side window.

"I'll come down to the sheriff's office around dinner time and we'll speak on it," Lacy said.

The deputy's eyes looked at me quick in the mirror and then back at Lacy.

"I was just thinking if you had any ideas about how the fire started and who could have started it, it would be good for the law to know now."

"You know dern well who it would be," Lacy said.

The deputy kept glancing back and forth at Lacy in the mirror.

"I guess I wouldn't know," the deputy said.

"It's the same folks who've been doing this sort of foolishness since I was a young 'un," Lacy said. "I'm too old and have seen too many things for you to be playing stupid with me. Now take us back up on Duncan Hill," Lacy said.

The more talking that deputy was doing with Lacy, the shakier and louder Lacy's voice was getting. I'd never seen him so worked up mad.

The deputy shook his head and got a look on his face like this boy I'd seen one time who was mistreating his momma's cat and was enjoying doing it too much.

We drove the few miles in quiet. The deputy turned off the interior light but I could see he would still turn his eyes to Lacy now and then. When we got to Main Street and started going up Duncan Hill, Lacy patted my hand and told me it would be all right.

"I'm real sorry about your house, Lacy," I said.

He looked at me and nodded and then my throat got all tight and I started crying because his eyes were still all watery.

"Shhh now," he said. "Weren't much in there no-ways."

"But you don't have a house no more."

"Surely don't look like it."

"What're you gonna do?"

Lacy blew his nose and refolded his handkerchief before he started kneading it in one hand. "Well, I still own the piece of dirt it sat on. Still be there in the morning, I suspect," he finally said.

As we got out and the deputy pulled away without saying another word to either of us, me and Lacy walked up the steps to my house and stopped on the porch.

We looked north way across town, past the courthouse and all the small houses and church steeples shining up white through the nighttime. Out past that, it was all darkness, except for the bluff called Town Heights that overlooked the big bend in the river.

I could see the red lights from the fire truck going around and around and Lacy's house still burning. It was still so bright I could see the shacks and trailers and the tin roofs shining with old tires piled on them. The wind then shifted and the smoke looked like a coiled-up snake and it started rolling back toward the mountain. It spread out slow and looked like a dark cloud was about to cover Sunnyside.

Lacy put his nose up in the air and sniffed several times. I thought he was smelling the smoke.

"Bad weather coming in," he said.

After me and Lacy ate the beans he fried and the peaches he heated up with brown sugar that we poured over biscuits, we both went back to bed for a few hours. I didn't think I'd be able to sleep getting in bed at daylight, and I didn't think he would, either, the way I kept hearing those floorboards in his bedroom creak and creak. I knew he was in there walking the floor because his cane made a noise that wasn't like no other sound.

But I did sleep and I slept a long time, and when I woke it was far into the day and the house was cold. I opened a curtain sort of bewildered like a person does when they sleep too late and couldn't believe my eyes. Snow was coming down in big heavy flakes and the ground was white. And it weren't even Thanksgiving yet. I grinned and prayed it'd keep snowing and they'd cancel school so I wouldn't have to skip anymore.

I ran to get Lacy up and pushed open the door in his bedroom, but it was empty and his bed was sort of made up. I checked in the bathroom and he weren't in there, either, then I looked through the whole house and called out his name but he never hollered back.

I figured he was outside somewhere and after I put on my clothes, I was almost out the door of my bedroom when I saw the note he'd left on my bureau. Lacy couldn't spell good but in big pencil letters he wrote that he had to go downtown and would be back before suppertime. His last line told me to stay put because the weather was gonna worsen and he needed to talk with me about a few things. So that's what I did, I stayed put because Lacy was never wrong about the weather and whatever he needed to tell me, I figured I needed to know. I fed the stove when it needed it and ate cold cereal all day and watched the snow and the TV.

But Lacy never did get home at suppertime.

After dark set in, I started getting worried about him not being there. Lacy was so old and I knew he was half-blind in the dark and he was a poor driver and here it had been snowing all day. I gave the whole thing a lot of thought and ended up trying to get hold of Malcolm Boone. An old woman who answered the phone saying, "Malcolm Boone's residence," said Malcolm was away on business and would be back tomorrow. I couldn't figure who else to call about Lacy being gone so I called the jail and asked to speak to Momma. They'd let me speak to her once when I called just to see if they'd let me talk to her, if I ever just needed to.

The jailer asked me what I needed and I didn't want to say, but he wouldn't let me talk to her unless I did. So I told him Lacy was late for supper and it was well past dark.

The jailer still wouldn't let me talk to Momma but said he'd pass the note on to her and said Lacy would probably be home soon.

I waited up past midnight watching the clock every few minutes. The two TV stations we picked up from Roanoke and Beckley finally went off the air playing "America the Beautiful" while waving a flag.

I called back down to the jail and the phone rang about twenty times before the same man answered it who'd answered it hours before. He didn't seem happy I was calling back.

About the third time I was telling him who I was, I heard a knock on the front door. It scared me and I froze until I heard Lacy's voice. I said "never mind" into the phone, hung up, ran and threw open the door.

Lacy wobbled like a town drunk and looked almost froze to death. He didn't have his ball hat or coat on and looked so strange, and then I noticed he didn't have his glasses on, either.

I couldn't say anything and kept waiting for him to come inside and say something. He finally took a step and was shaking all over. I noticed he didn't have his cane when he dropped a big stick he'd been leaning on. He grabbed on to me and the walls, and then I noticed he didn't have any shoes or socks on, either, but had rags tied around his feet.

He patted me light on the shoulder between his steps, and then grabbed me with a hard grip when he put a foot down. He tottered his way all the way inside and then pointed at a hard chair that sat in the corner of the living room.

"Pull it next to the stove," he said in a voice so high and raspy I could hardly hear it.

He let go of me and I did as he said. He sat slow, like none of his bones would move the right way. But he finally got situated and tried to say something else but I couldn't figure what he was saying.

"Get me a blanket," he finally got out.

I went to do what he said but that's when I smelled something. I stopped and looked back at him. Lacy peered up at me and saw what I was wondering because he said, "Had an accident in my britches, child."

I didn't say anything back, ran to my bedroom and pulled off two quilts and knocked the snow off his shoulders before I wrapped the blankets around him. Lacy pointed at his feet with a long finger that was shaking like he had no control over it. I took one of the quilts and went to wrap it around his feet. I noticed the rags were wet so I pulled them off first and then wrapped the quilt around his lower legs and when I touched one foot, it was ice cold.

Lacy nodded like he was pleased but kept shivering.

I ran to the kitchen, loaded up the coffee basket all the way, poured the percolator full of water and plugged it in. Then I dumped a canning jar of Momma's vegetable soup in a pot and set it on the woodstove.

"Come here," I heard.

I walked back in slow, hearing the weak way he'd said that, pulled on another light and was scared of what I'd see. Lacy looked worse. His skin looked like one of those mummies I'd seen in schoolbooks and his eyes looked hazy. He was so woozy he still looked drunk but I knew he wasn't.

"What happened?" I asked.

Lacy didn't say anything. He leaned toward the stove and rubbed his hands against each other between trying to clench and unclench them.

"Want me to call the doctor?" I asked.

Lacy shook his head.

"You don't look too good, Lacy."

About that time it hit me that I never saw headlights or heard Daddy's paneled truck pull in before Lacy knocked, and I'd been looking and listening for hours. I ran to the window, looked out through the snow still coming down and the paneled truck wasn't parked out front. I ran back to the kitchen, looked out the side window and didn't see it out back, either.

"Where's Daddy's truck?" I asked, still looking out the window.

He didn't answer. I went back next to him and he was trying to hold a foot up next to the stove. I fetched him a stool for him to set it on.

"Did you get in a wreck?" I asked.

He shook his head.

"Where's Daddy's truck?"

"Call Malcolm," he said.

"I already did and he's not home."

Lacy's body jerked all of a sudden in one terrible motion and then he nodded his head.

"What happened?" I asked again.

He didn't say anything and just sat there still for one moment and then started shaking life a leaf the next.

"You want me to get your pipe?"

"Hmmm-ummm."

"What happened to your clothes?" I asked.

Lacy's eyes squinted tight and then it looked like he was about to start crying or had a terrible pain or something.

"Some men took me for a ride. They took them from me."

"What'd they take your clothes for?"

"For meanness."

"Where'd you ride to?"

"Don't know."

"You don't?"

Lacy shook his head, still trembling all over.

"You don't want me to call a doctor?"

With the tips of his fingers he patted my hand that was

hanging down one side of me all tensed up. He tried to take in a deep breath and told me to call Malcolm again and to tell them that Lacy Coe had to speak to him and it couldn't wait.

"But he ain't there."

"They'll reach him," he said.

"Call right now?"

"Right now, child," he said.

"Lacy, what happened on that ride?"

"We'll speak on it," he said.

"Want me to call the sheriff?"

Lacy turned toward me quick and but his eyes still looked hazy. He shook his head and turned back to the fire.

Chapter Eleven

✦

Malcolm's Cadillac woke me up the next morning as it swerved up Duncan Hill with tires screaming trying to find something to hold on to. I peeked out my bedroom window and saw two men in the car. The driver looked like Mr. Brewster, who worked up front at Malcolm's law office. The car slid back twice, once going completely sideways, but Mr. Brewster kept gunning it and gunning it getting a little farther each try until he got in front of the house. It looked like there was over a foot of snow piled on Malcolm's hood, and it was still snowing.

I threw my clothes on, opened the front door and a blast of cold hit me. I was so happy to see so much snow that I didn't know what to do. I'd been praying for more bad weather and had never seen that much of it as I looked at the drift taking over Momma's porch. And then I saw a gray truck that I'd never seen before sitting just at the corner of our lot. It sat up high and had a bar across the cab with red and blue lights fixed to it, and the seal of Virginia showing a lady wearing a sheet stomping on somebody was painted on the door. A man I'd never seen before sat inside.

Malcolm jumped out of the passenger side of his car wearing a fur hat. He waved to me but never came toward the house. He walked over to the gray truck and talked to the man, who rolled his window down and poked his head out. Malcolm pointed all over the place talking a hundred miles an hour and looked to be really carrying on to whoever was in that truck. Then he finished, waved again at me and got back in his car. I waved back, shut the door all the way almost to keep the cold out of the house, but watched as him and Mr. Brewster slid down the hill going right through a couple of front yards until they found the road again, but not for long as they almost went off Mr. Tate's rock wall into Mr. Tate's orchard, but they finally got turned all the way around and went out of sight. I'd never seen such a piece of driving and I kept hearing whooping and hollering from that car and as curious as it was, it sounded like Malcolm doing all of it.

I heard Lacy's footsteps behind me about the time I shut the door and that's when I smelled coffee and knew he'd already been up. I was worried of what I'd see come around the corner, but at first sight Lacy looked like he'd finally warmed up and he actually looked cheerful for some reason, but he still looked weak by the way he was teetering around.

"You feeling all right, Lacy?" I asked.

He stood still all of a sudden. "How do I look?"

"You look all right sort of."

"Must be, then," he said.

I nodded and opened the window curtain. "Who's that man in the truck out there?"

Lacy didn't look where I wanted him to because he was already pacing slow to the kitchen woodstove. I followed him and he stood a minute with his backside to it.

"Don't recall a storm like this in November," he said.

He turned around using a black cane with a silver handle that I'd never seen. He tucked it under one arm and warmed his hands.

"Do you know who that feller outside is?" I asked.

"Have a seat, child," Lacy said. He said it like he was finally gonna talk about all that had gone on the past days, not like he was fixing to make us something to eat, which was good because I still had a terrible sick stomach from the long night that had just passed.

I sat down at the table and after he chunked a couple of logs I'd split into the stove, he sat beside me wearing his old robe. I saw the glasses on his face. They looked crooked.

"You found your glasses."

"I keep a few pair from the drugstore," he said.

I nodded and gave him a pretty good look over. He looked almost like he usually did and a lot better than he did when he'd come home so late hours ago, but his whole body was still quaking now and then.

"Want me to open the drafts?" I asked.

Charles Davis

Lacy leaned and took a careful look at the stove drafts and then peered back at me. "I'll warm up directly."

We both just sat there across from each other but then Lacy acted like he didn't have anything to say. He just kept sitting. Didn't smoke his pipe or nothing.

"We gonna talk about something?" I finally asked.

He took a deep breath. "Yes, sir. Malcolm talked to a judge and they decided to give us some company up here for a few days, until your mom's trial is over."

"What kind of company?"

"They're gonna have a policeman stay outside."

I walked to the window over the sink and looked outside and didn't recognize the man in the car as a policeman I'd ever seen.

"He's with the state," Lacy finished saying.

"A trooper?" I asked.

Lacy nodded.

"What's he outside our house for?"

"From my understanding, when there's a big trial in a small place like Sunnyside, they do that just to make sure there ain't no foolishness. Kind of a standard thing Malcolm said they do during a trial to make sure everything happens proper. Nothing worrisome about it, he said."

The last thing Lacy had called foolishness was the fire at his house.

"What kind of foolishness?" I asked.

"I'm not rightly sure."

"Did you find out yesterday if somebody burned your house down?"

152

Lacy shook his head.

"Do you think you will?"

"I don't reckon."

"But you think somebody done it on purpose...."

"Don't know."

"Does that trooper sitting outside have to do with those men who took your clothes last night?"

Lacy pointed at me like he was gonna say something, then didn't and walked back to the stove. He eyed the drafts a little more and used his cane to open them up another crack.

"It's just what they do to make sure the trial goes off proper like I'm telling you. Malcolm arranged it through federal people. He said it was usual procedure."

"Somebody's not gonna burn Daddy's house up, are they?"

Lacy turned around. "Now nobody's gonna bother your house."

He took a step toward me to make sure I believed him before he quit looking at me, then he got out a dark brown pipe I'd never seen before and wiped the stem down with a handkerchief. He looked at it close up to his glasses, where he studied on it with his fingers.

"I think it's just a way for the police to make overtime money before Christmastime. About all it is."

I knew there was more to it than Lacy was letting on. Just like he'd done hours ago when he told me some fellers had put him in a car and taken him for a ride through the countryside and dropped him off at the bottom of Duncan Hill without some of his clothes. He said they did it just for meanness but I knew it had to do with him being up here looking after me.

"Are you gonna leave?" I asked.

Lacy put the empty pipe in his mouth. He popped that new cane against the floor and dragged his feet several steps to the window and looked out.

"Snow's awful pretty when it comes early like this," he said.

"Lacy, people don't want you staying with me."

He came back over careful but took a hurried seat because his legs were unsteady beneath him.

"Seems like you're in some trouble or something being up here," I said.

"You're in no harm with me being here or I wouldn't be here. I talked to folks who know about such things. Now this is your home and you're as safe and sound in it as you always have been. Don't go to thinking nothing different."

"But I ain't scared for me, Lacy."

"Well, I'm in a mind to stay, if it's okay with you."

"It's okay with me," I said.

"Everything's all right, Charlie. And I'm safe, too, so don't worry about such things. All this will be over soon. Want some breakfast?"

"So you don't think nothing else is gonna happen to you?" I asked.

"No, sir."

"Why not?"

"Just won't."

"But why?"

"Well, I reckon 'cause anybody who'd want to do something to me has done run out of things to do. You just can't take much away from an old feller who ain't got nothing left. The folks who do all the mistreating and hating against black folks who ain't done a dang thing to them…their times is ending, you see. Some of them just don't know it yet."

"Who are those folks?"

"You never know for surety."

I started thinking that Lacy was brave, a lot braver than me.

"You should go back to Town Heights where people treat you good, Lacy."

Lacy went to the cabinet, where he found a saucer and cup, then he poured himself coffee from the percolator, which he always said he learned to take black from his days soldiering in the U.S. Army.

I saw he was having a hard time with the coffee missing his cup, but I didn't offer to help, just like Daddy never did when Lacy was having a hard time doing something. Lacy mopped up the coffee from the saucer with a rag and made his way back to the table, easing the saucer and cup onto the table.

"Most of the folks in Town Heights fell out with me some years ago. It were my fault, I reckon."

I sat back. I'd never, ever heard that and couldn't imagine anybody falling out with Lacy about anything but then I remembered how the coloreds never said much to Lacy at Dad's shop. Dad had told me that when he was growing up, Lacy was the one black man who would come to town meetings, and he'd speak up for the people in Town Heights. He'd raise a ruckus about this and that just like a lawyer would, pointing all around with his pipe and talking loud and looking people in the eye, Dad told me. He was kind of the mayor of Town Heights even though they didn't have a mayor. So they must've used to like him if they had him speak up for them.

"Would you eat some hen fruit and country ham if I warmed up a skillet?" he asked.

I couldn't even think about breakfast. I couldn't believe he could think about breakfast.

"They don't like you over there?"

"It ain't so much they don't like me, it's I didn't live up to their expectations. I backed away from some things I shouldn't have a good while back and it hurt them."

"What'd you back away from?"

"I quit standing up again' things, child."

"What things?"

"So the black folks would have a fairer shake around here."

"Why'd you quit standing up for black folks?"

Lacy looked colder and he took a lot longer than the usual couple of minutes it'd take him to get his pipe loaded and lit up proper. But once he did, he just sat it in the palm of one hand and looked at the tobacco smolder.

"I stood tall when I was a younger man a time or two, but never really had the stomach for it. See, when it comes down to it, I ain't a brave sort of person. Being brave is a rough path to walk, you see, 'cause you find yourself walking all by yourself. Much easier to just sit on a porch around other folks."

"Or just sit in the shop?"

Lacy looked at me for a long spell before he nodded at me, just barely.

"I've turned away from ugliness for some time. One of those fellers that some of the white folks could shoo away or could do harm to without much of a peep. You see what I'm telling you?"

I shook my head.

"I'm looked at by folks around here as a coward, Charlie."

I couldn't believe Lacy had just said that. And he said it looking me right in he eyes like he believed it, too, as he put the pipe in his mouth and took a few slow tokes.

"So the reason you're up here is you're trying to prove to everybody you're not a coward 'cause some people don't want you up here?"

Lacy went to pat one of my hands but I pulled it back. "No, child," he said. "See, I know your dad would want me here being the way things are…I dang know he would if I know anything, and I owe him that. Besides, me and you were always friends and it's good for a boy to have an older person around, same as it's good for the old to have a young 'un around. Ain't no more to it than that."

"Why do you owe Daddy?"

Lacy took to toking again, but this time he pulled the pipe away quick and pointed it at me and I just sat there looking at it shake in front of me.

"Because he was a good man and he got me out of a peck of trouble one time. Ummm. And he gave me a place to be, when I couldn't find no place to be. Your dad called me Mr. Coe around white folks, too, even when treating a

Negro man like that around here might get a feller in bad regard with some of the people who run things in this town. He had a fairness in him. Always good to the folks in Town Heights. Your dad stood up for things, child. You will too. You're standing up for your momma now when it ain't an easy thing to do."

I felt sick when Lacy said that because most of the time I wasn't standing up for Momma. I was too busy trying to stand up for myself and find people to stand up for me, to stand up for anybody. It was quiet for a long time in the kitchen and then I wondered if Lacy wanted me to call him Mr. Coe like Dad did so I asked him.

"I want you to call me Lacy. That's what I told you to call me when you weren't knee-high and asked what my name was. It's just I've been called a lot of names by white folks, but never was called Mr. Coe like a white man is addressed by a younger white man. Things like that mean something to an old black feller. It may be silliness but it's the truth as I'm sitting here. It matters is what I'm saying."

I looked at Lacy sitting with both feet on the floor like he always did. He still looked like an old ship captain to me sitting in his chair, not a coward. He just looked like he was a wore-out old ship captain. "You always seemed brave to me, Lacy," I said.

"No, sir. Wished I was. But it don't take no bravery on my part to be here anyway so it don't matter none. I just told your mom I'd help out a little bit, and as long as she wants me up here and you don't mind my company, I mean to do it."

"Even though people don't want you up here?"

"I reckon I just ain't in a mind no more to let a bunch of dang knot-heads run me off this hill. Plum wears a feller out turning his back on things and running away from things he knows he shouldn't, you see. Now let's have us something to eat. Does red-eye gravy and pone bread hit you anywhere good?"

I shook my head because my stomach was so uneasy. I couldn't even ask any more questions because it just seemed like the more I found out about stuff the worse everything got and the more confused I got. But then I wondered why so many white people hated black people like he'd said before so I asked him.

"It'd take a educated feller to figure that out but I know hating folks is learned young. It's hard to get it out of a man if he grows up in it."

"Why's that?"

"Easiest thing in the world to do is to hate. Don't take no effort at all, you see."

"It don't?"

"No, sir, 'cause you don't have to work to not care about nothing. Hating's a lazy feeling. Dark feeling. A person never has to look far into their own heart and own failings when they hate, you see. It's a dangerous feeling, too. We all give harbor to it but ain't much good in it."

"Is hating always bad?"

"I'd have to give a good think on that."

"But it usually is?"

"Well, what we're speaking on is the sort of general hate

where some people just hate or mistreat a bunch of other folks, folks they don't even know enough about to figure if they should hate them or not. That kind of hate don't do nobody no good. Just breeds more hating."

"Do black people hate white people?"

"Some do."

"All white people?"

"I suspect. See, hate's a fire that won't never go out in some white folks and black folks. Get a little wind or gasoline on it and you got trouble."

"Do some black people have a good reason to hate all white people?"

"No, sir," Lacy said. "Same as the white folks who hate all black folks. I reckon the worst thing for some folks around here is they never get out of these hollers and hills to see how other folks live and what they're like. Some of the folks on this here hill won't even take a nice meal if invited to another man's house in a neighborhood by the river a mile from here. It's too far for them to travel from where they live inside, you see. This mountain and their place on it is the whole world to them, when the town ain't nothing more than a dang speck on a map. Like the folks around here are all faithful praying Christians, and now there ain't a thing wrong with that. No, sir. I pray quite a bit myself, not gonna say who I pray to 'cause that's my own business, but I do my fair share of knee thanking and asking.

"But so many of them will tell you theirs is the only one true way of knowing our Maker. If you don't believe what they believe in and do what they do, then they're apt to get agin you quick, when the truth is, the only reason they believe what they do in the first place is because that's what they were raised on. They don't hear or think of nothing different 'til they get some age on them, and then they don't want to listen to none of that because they've been told if a man believes other than what they already believe, then that man is wrong. They think it's the dang devil talking to them, you see, but it ain't, child. It's their heart and head a-talking. And some of them will go so far as to say that other man is a real bad man for believing in something different. A sinner, and not the kind going off to heaven someday like them, of course.

"Now the truth is if those same folks were born somewheres else, they'd be taught some other religion and they'd be shaking their fists the same way they do now but then they'd be saying that other religion is the one true religion and if you don't believe in it you're wrong. You see what I'm saying?"

I shook my head.

"I'm just trying to show you how these folks I'm speaking about stay thinking the same old things about lots of things like they were taught to think as young 'uns just like their parents were taught as young 'uns. It makes them feel safe in it, you see. Makes them sleep good nights like they did as children. The world makes some sense to them when they wake, and it keeps a little money in their pockets and the peace the way they like it. But when you got too many folks in charge of one small place all thinking alike, it ain't a good thing. They're so apt to go against somebody who don't think and live and look like they do. I mean to ask you something now but you don't have to say nothing if you don't want to."

I sat up straight when he said that 'cause he'd said it so serious.

"Do you think a God up there in the heavens would judge a feller by what color his skin is, child?"

I thought he might, but I didn't say nothing.

Lacy gave me a minute and then patted my hand. Then he got going again.

"Most black *and* white folks around here are poor, too, and are fighting for the same nickel. Now you have more a problem 'cause there ain't enough nickels to go around like there never is and there never will be no matter how many dang nickels there are because people can't never get enough nickels, so if one group is taking most all the nickels from the other group, it makes the group in charge sleep better if they don't like and look down on the people they're taking from. They know way down deep somewhere that they're taking and hurting and hate calms the guilt, you see. Hate's a powerful thing, child. Will make a person feel like they deserve the jingle in their pockets when they pretty much done stole from people with no pockets. Makes them think they're better when they ain't 'cause we're really all the same. But they start feeling good and patting themselves on the back for their hard work and lot in life. They leave the less fortunate their crumbs so as they'll feel charitable, too. Got to be charitable, you see. Now I ain't talking about everybody, I'm just talking about the dang folks who like to keep their foot down on other folks so it makes them stand taller. You following what I'm trying to say to you?"

Lacy had lost me ten minutes ago when he said folks thought he was a coward. I wished he'd of never said that and had just sat down and told me a story like he used to about a man caught out on a lake in a thunderstorm, or a story about an old mother oak tree or something like he used to instead of saying all this stuff because at least I was starting to understood some of his old stories.

"You asked me about hating, child. It just seems to me that ignorance and fear is the things that causes the most hating, which ends up causing the pain. Things dressed up pretty on the outside but ugly on the inside like greed come from fear, too. Lot comes from fear. Good stuff comes from it, too. I reckon being afraid is the weakest sort of feeling a person can have and the easy road out of it leads to hate. A lot of wars start with hate. Lot of them. Keeps them going, too. You mix fearfulness with ignorance, throw in some guns and folks who don't think they're being treated right on one side or the other, and you got a bad time a-coming."

Lacy went to going on with more but then took a deep breath like even he was trying to figure out what he was talking about. Either that or he'd talked himself tired. But then he pushed himself upright in his chair and instead of looking at the table like he'd been doing, he looked at me.

"It's just a shame how so many folks learn as young 'uns to either love or hate. That's where ugliness starts 'cause there's no middle where the understanding of things lays where people can learn to tolerate one another. Respect one another. Terrible thing when there's no middle ground, child, and there ain't with too many folks. Nothing in the gray, so then there can't be no justice for nobody because that's where justice is. See, nobody or no group of people is just all good or all bad. We're all a mix of it, just like life ain't all good or all bad."

Lacy nodded and had taken on a pale color for him. I was still sitting and waiting in case he got going again with something else but he never did. He looked down at his pipe and it had went cold with all his talking and it looked to surprise him. I didn't understand hardly anything he'd said, but sitting there while he worked his pipe, I still thought he was tough and brave even though he said he wasn't. I think he was just feeling low, talking like he was doing, and even wondered if he had a fever with all the talking so much crazy like he was doing.

Lacy had never talked like that to me. I'd never even heard such talk, even in church. And I don't know what he was thinking when he said people who hated black folks couldn't do nothing else bad to him, because I'd seen pictures in a library book of Negro men hanged from trees.

I got up when I had that terrible vision and went to the window where Lacy had just peered out before he'd got all wound up about the blacks and whites. Even though I still wasn't sure why he was out there, I was glad that trooper was parked outside in his big truck even if he did look asleep with his head leaning forward against a book.

When I looked back at Lacy, he was all hunched over and it looked like he didn't care anymore how much coffee he spilled from his cup as he took another drink. Momma needed me and I needed Lacy, but now it seemed like Lacy needed somebody, too. He wasn't acting right and I'd never seen his hands so bad. He caught me looking at him.

"Let's have some breakfast," he said.

"I just ain't real hungry, Lacy."

"How 'bout a stack of buckwheat cakes?"

I shook my head.

"Cream of wheat?"

I looked at him for a while and he looked at me back, then he said, "I reckon I ain't too hungry, either. We'll just hold off and cook dinner in a while, then."

Lacy stood and walked over and patted me on the shoulder. I could feel him looking at me and then he took his cane and pushed the drafts back on the stove. "Don't you be worrying about things, now."

I nodded.

"I'm gonna get on back to bed for a spell, child, if you don't need nothing," Lacy said.

"I don't need nothing."

"I was just rattling on. Old folks do that now and again. Don't pay no mind to it."

"We gonna be all right here, Lacy?"

"Yes, sir. Yes, sir, we will for surety."

Lacy patted me again before he walked back down the hall. He didn't sing or hum anything like he usually did walking toward the bathroom.

Even though he was trying to act normal, I could tell he wasn't. He was either bad sick or shook up about something.

Shook up in a down deep sort of way and it made him tremble all over and talk way too much. He couldn't be cold, either, because I was roasting in that hot kitchen.

I looked outside again at the snow coming down and then heard Lacy singing real raspy and quiet in the bathroom. It was a lonesome tune I'd never heard him sing before.

Chapter Twelve

It turned out the snow that started the same day Lacy's house burned down was one of the biggest snows Lacy could ever recall and it kept snowing and snowing.

The whole town soon closed down and it made everything brighter and cleaner looking, especially Angel's Rest and the front yard of our house which had gone downhill since Daddy had died, and especially since Mom got put in jail.

I never said anything to Lacy about the state of Mom's flowerbeds and window boxes. I knew she'd have thrown a fit seeing all those dried up weeds poking out all over the yard and under the windows. The snow covered all of it like a great big white quilt.

Me and Lacy kept the square woodstove in the kitchen fired up day and night, along with the potbellied one in the living room, except when we had to clean the ashes out of them every couple of days, and then we'd stoke them up again and get more put-up goods from the root cellar to keep handy if we needed them.

After Thanksgiving the power flickered off and on through December. Much of the time for days and days. It got more lonely than usual at first without the TV or radio, but every evening Lacy kept me busy busting kindling and teaching me how to cook on the woodstove by oil lamps and candlelight. Lacy said a woodstove was all he'd ever cooked on so he knew all about it because he'd bachelored all those years after his wife passed.

Jimmy banged on the back door one evening all in a rush not long after the big snow. I went to the door and unlocked it and Jimmy came in out of breath, saying he had something to tell me. I noticed he'd got a new, old coat that fit him better. Lacy had just fixed me a big plate of corned beef hash so he put another plate out for Jimmy before walking into the living room.

Jimmy waited until Lacy was settled, then leaned over one side of the table toward me so I leaned toward him over the other side.

"Your mom got some kind of court paper where your granddad ain't supposed to come near you without her permission. That's why he's been steering clear of here, sounds like. Your granddad's been trying to take you away from your mom, and they've been fighting over you ever since your dad got buried."

I put my fork down. Jimmy had my attention and my heart started racing up, but sometimes Jimmy would unintentionally tell a person all sorts of things that turned out not to be true because he'd heard it from people like his brother, Alvin, who'd completely make up stuff just to do it so I asked, "Where'd you hear this?"

"People talking quiet about it everywhere 'cause it got in the newspaper."

"Did you read it?"

Jimmy shook his head. I knew he couldn't read good but he could read a little. "I been listening to people who did," he said. "Heard something else, too. The FBI's been talking to people all over town, and they've been up at your grand-daddy's house several times in the evenings. All of it's about Lacy's house burning and the ride men took him on."

Jimmy's voice then got so quiet I could barely hear it. I leaned forward as close as I could and he stretched his neck as far as it would go to see if Lacy was still in the living room. Then he looked dead at me.

"The men who took Lacy on that ride hanged him out of an old barn loft by his neck, but they quit hoisting him up just before his feet were all the way off the ground. Word is that it was a final warning to leave Duncan Hill and if he ever said a word about that ride to anyone, they were gonna kill him. And if he didn't leave Duncan Hill that night, they'd hoist him up until his feet were off the ground next time. And the next time would be soon. They did all that to him before they took him back to town and dumped him out."

Jimmy quit talking, his eyes full of everything he'd just told me and I pushed back from the table. I heard Lacy snoring already in the living room and couldn't get my breath. I wanted to ask Jimmy a bunch of questions, but I told him he had to leave because I felt like it was an emergency. I had to talk to Lacy. I had to talk to him now. Jimmy looked at the plate of hash so I told him to hurry up with it and he did. His plate was cleaned by the time I got back from peering in at Lacy.

Jimmy put his new coat back on, and he made me swear I wouldn't tell Lacy what he told me. I swore I wouldn't before I realized what I was swearing to, and he took off out the back door as fast as he'd come in. I locked it behind him like me and Lacy did all the time now.

After he left, I walked in the living room quiet for some reason, but then prodded Lacy hard in the shoulder until he woke up in the chair all confused. I waited until he leaned forward and then I told him about what I'd heard. That's when it hit me that I'd broke my swear already, but I vowed to myself that I wouldn't tell Lacy where I heard it from. I was shaking standing there and couldn't hardly finish, and he just kept sitting and staring at me the whole time.

"Sit down, child," he said.

"No."

"Please, sir."

I shook my head, so he finally waved me back a little with his fingers. I stepped back a step to give him some breathing room.

"You just told me some men took your clothes. You should've told me the rest of it, Lacy."

Lacy went to stand for a second but it looked like his legs

decided not to. He grabbed his pipe out of his sweater and pointed it up at me.

"You listen to me now. The worse thing you could do is listen to all the jabbering that's floating around. Now I told you some men tried to scare me and that's all I'm gonna say about it right now."

"But Lacy, what if they—"

"That's all I'm saying about it, and we're not speaking no more on it!"

Lacy let his pipe down and I realized that was the first time he'd ever raised his voice to me. I'm sure he realized it, too, by the way he was looking at me. But we were gonna speak on it no matter what he said.

"Why are FBI men talking to Granddaddy?"

Lacy stood and finally got balanced before he walked toward the bathroom. On the way past me he said, "That's business between your granddad and the federal people."

"You've been lying, Lacy!" I said.

He stopped in the hall and was still as he could be except he shook his head with his back to me.

I got madder so sudden and yelled loud, "Why won't you tell me what's going on?"

Lacy came back and put a hand on my shoulder. It seemed like he was trying to find something to say but it wouldn't come out. I asked him again about Granddaddy but he wouldn't say nothing bad about him as much as I poked for him to say something. But he didn't say nothing good about him, either. I finally got calmed down a little and my eyes were drying.

"Why won't you tell me what really happened on the ride?"

"It wouldn't be right for me to speculate about muddy waters where I'm not sure of the bottom. When I am, we'll have a talk on it."

"Was Granddaddy one of the men who did that to you?"

"They wear hoods, child."

"Lacy, is Granddaddy a bad man?"

"It just ain't my place to be talking things to you about your family. Just ain't my place."

"But you're sorta family now, too, Lacy."

He patted me and nodded. He kept patting me and then he walked off into the bathroom without saying another word. I stood there and it seemed like there were so many dark secrets swirling around me and everybody who was close to me. I felt like I was drowning in those muddy waters he was talking about.

My heart started beating even faster like it did the first night they put Momma in jail and I was having so much trouble getting a good breath of air that I went in the kitchen and fixed one of Lacy's night heart palpitation remedies.

After Lacy came out he saw what I'd done, I don't think he knew what to say to me about it. So he just took a good look at my remedy through the bottom of his eyeglasses, then smelled the jar of shine and decided to make himself a remedy, too.

Over the next few days I didn't find out anymore about anything. Jimmy hadn't heard nothing more and Lacy would either ignore my questions or talk about something like what I wanted for supper. He said as soon as the police finished their investigating, he'd tell me everything he knew, but he couldn't say nothing more about it until then because he wasn't supposed to say nothing. I thought he was just saying that for an excuse and told him so. But Lacy just kept asking me to trust him and stand by Momma and keep believing in the music of things because things were gonna change for the better soon. I don't know what Lacy was thinking when he said that, 'cause things were about to get worse.

As the trial creeped near, it got to where I couldn't stand being inside because I found out that in the winter, Lacy liked a house so hot it would make everybody else want to go outside in the cold. But he told me too hot was always better than freezing to death and we should be thankful we had a good fire, good health and plenty of provisions to make it through the winter.

School was cancelled for over two weeks and I'd hear my old friends yelling and hollering heading down Duncan Hill on inner tubes and pasteboard boxes.

I even heard Mary Elouise Jennings's voice one time. It hit me that her mother finally decided to let her stay out later than usual and have fun for once.

Mary Elouise lived behind us and our yards were separated by an old wooden fence and her dog, Chucky, which was the meanest dog in Sunnyside in my opinion. Until just around the time Daddy died, I'd never really liked Mary Elouise or especially her big furry dog, because she always went inside too early and didn't like to do the things me and the other boys on the mountain did. I didn't like her dog because he bit me one time after chasing me up a maple tree that I fell out of.

But something started happening around fifth grade for no good reason I could put my finger on, and I found myself thinking about her a lot and I think the same thing was going on with my old buddies. All of us seemed to spend more time trying to show Mary Elouise how fast we could run or how far we could throw a rock than actually doing things we all used to do.

I heard my old gang sled riding down the hill, and I know it was Mary Elouise's voice I heard. Lacy asked me if that was that Jennings girl doing all that hollering, and I told him I thought so.

I wanted to go sledding, too. But knew I wouldn't be welcomed there.

Lacy tried to get me to go and play with them but I told him I didn't want to. He said he'd walk down there with me but both of us knew it would take him a month to walk through all that snow as slow as he walked in good weather, and besides that, one of the troopers always followed us when we went somewhere together. They'd even drive us to the post office and grocery store once a week. I'd noticed they followed Lacy around when we were apart, not me.

So anyway, with the silence between us most of time, me and Lacy pretty much both just sat in the house with the curtains open and the law outside. We watched the snow come down most of the time and it seemed to pass the hours for both of us.

I don't know if he thought I was bored or he was just

particularly blabby again, but for the first time, he started really telling me things about himself. I was just glad he didn't get all wound up preaching again.

He told me how he'd done some roaming as a young man and even lived in New York City for a spell before he signed up for the army. He was in the first big war, and told stories about all his colored buddies and the times they had and how nice the French folks were to them. He said some of the soldiers had to live in this trench for months and it was so cold and wet and there were rats and people dying little by little day by day and he lost four good friends. He never told me about how they died, just that they did and then he'd get all wound up and tell me about some big time they had over there in Europe. He said looking back they were much more farm boys or poor city kids than soldiers.

"Scared but adventuresome," he said.

I didn't know coloreds fought in wars back then. Lacy said they all grew up too fast those two years and especially the ones who had to live and die in those trenches. Then he got quiet for a spell after he said that.

But he'd get started again and tell me how he'd worked all these jobs after the war trying to find his place and make a couple nickels to rub together, how he'd shined shoes and barbered, ushered in a Negro theater in Richmond, hauled ice and rode in a meat truck for a couple years, worked for a timber company cutting brush and draining swamps and then got on a construction gang as a carpenter's helper before he got on a gang stringing power lines through the coal camps of West Virginia. Seemed like Lacy had done about everything there was a person could do, black or white.

"See the hard times and the good times tend to go together as a set, and sometimes it takes some looking back on to tell which is which," he said.

It seemed to me listening to him while watching that oil lamp burn beside the window with the snow and the state men on the other side that his whole life was mostly one hard time, what with his dad getting kicked in the head by a mule, then his wife dying so young and his only child passing on before he even got to be my age just from getting sick with the influenza. Lacy told me his son's name was Lacy Albert Coe Junior and they called him Albert.

It sounded like it was all hard to me, every bit of it, with only a good time thrown in now and then. But I don't think Lacy looked at it like that by the way he told his stories.

"Yes, sir, the good and bad just happen for their own wandering reasons, not ours," he'd said.

It did seem like he had some of his fondest memories about the toughest times.

I wondered the way he was talking if I'd ever have fond memories of this time. I couldn't imagine that I ever would.

But I'd listen to him ramble on about old times until he'd pretty much talk himself to sleep. Then I'd blow out all of the lamps except for the one I'd take to my bedroom, and he'd take his and proceed to check all the windows and doors two or three times. I'd crawl into my cold bed in all my clothes until I got warm, pull off my duds and let the heavy quilts settle on me just right until I got too hot and had to stick a foot out.

It would get quiet real late after the sledders went home, except for the sounds of Lacy's snoring, the wood crackling in the stoves and the strange sound snow makes when it falls just outside a window on a windless night. I always liked that sound. It was the only thing I liked about nighttime in the winter.

I'd lay there still as I could be and try not to worry about what may happen in my head when I closed my eyes. I'd think about some particular thing Lacy had said, then think about Dad and then Mom in the jailhouse, and I thought about Mary Elouise a lot. She'd always liked me in some way I hoped, and I wondered if she still did when everyone else didn't anymore. I believe that thought helped to keep the bad visions out of my dreams sometimes, and that always made me feel better when I woke to bad on a new day, like when I looked outside one morning and saw somebody had written "Die Nigger" in red spray-paint across the snowdrift in our front yard.

I heard the trooper who'd been watching the house got in a lot of trouble over that, especially since he sat right in front of where it happened. He was in a good hurry to cover it over with clean snow but before he found our shovel, a man from the newspaper took a picture of it and it made the TV news, too.

After that we got two troopers outside our house, one out front and one out back. Lacy told me Malcolm arranged it through the federal people over in Roanoke again. I figured it did make the odds better that with two troopers out there, one might be awake at any one time. Never saw grown men who needed so much sleep as those troopers.

I just wished they'd wake up because I had a terrible feeling we might need them some dark night soon because with everything else, we'd been getting bad phone calls. Lacy wouldn't let me answer the phone anymore, and it got to where he wouldn't answer it, either. We'd just sit and let it ring a good bit of the time. But that wasn't the worst of what was going on. A coon hunter said he'd spotted Hollis Thrasher late one night up near his shack on the mountain.

The police were all over the county looking for him.

Chapter Thirteen

It was on a Friday evening when the snow had finally stopped falling that Lacy and me got the first company in a long time that wasn't Malcolm Boone.

I was sitting on the big colored rag rug in the living room drawing a scuba diver with a shark after him on a pad that Lacy had picked up for me, and I heard a soft knock on the front door. I opened it and prayed one of the troopers wasn't gonna want to use the bathroom again and sniff around the kitchen after he'd done his business.

The best surprise of my life was standing there about three or four feet tall with a grin on her face.

Mary Elouise Jennings was all bundled up on the porch with a great big cap and mittens on and she had board games in her hand and asked if I wanted to play Monopoly. Her nose was red as a sundae cherry.

I'd never played Monopoly but nodded, and about that time Lacy came to the door to see who it was and invited her in because I was standing right there in her way and letting the hot out of the house.

"Does your Momma and Daddy know you're down here," Lacy asked.

Mary Elouise nodded and stood inside the doorway still bundled up.

Lacy took her coat and I just stood there because I felt like a possum who'd climbed its first tree and now had to get down.

Lacy finally said I'd be in in a minute and he pulled me by one overall strap into my bedroom.

I started getting a little miffed at Lacy because it looked like he was trying to keep from chuckling. I didn't think it was funny at all that I was so nervous my knees were shaking and I couldn't say anything.

"Just go in there and talk to her, Charlie," he finally said. "She's just a girl…you've known her all your life. Just sit down and talk to her. I'll get you all a couple bottles of pop."

I went back in because I knew I couldn't stay in my room and she was still standing in her light blue dress with her knit hat on. I sat down on the couch and wished like crazy the TV would start working again just for the noise and fuzzy pictures of the two channels we got, but it didn't.

Lacy finally walked in with two bottles of Coke he'd wrapped napkins around the bottoms of for some reason and handed her one bottle, then me the other.

"I have some work to do in the kitchen," he said real loud on his way out.

I looked over my shoulder at Lacy until he was gone and then turned slow and kept sitting there and she kept standing there and finally I said, "I don't know how to play Monopoly."

Evidently those were the right words to Mary Elouise because she took off her cap and sat down on the floor and got everything out on the coffee table while talking a hundred miles an hour about how to play Monopoly. It looked like I wouldn't have to say anything the rest of the evening as we played, and she won the first game and talked and talked and talked.

I never knew a person would have so much to say about a dang board game.

It was during the second game when I was doing better but still losing that she drew a "get out of jail free" card and looked at me.

"I'm sorry your mom's in jail and what happened to your dad. I always liked your dad. I heard my daddy tell my mom that any woman who shoots her husband just because he came home and gave her 'what for' for straying should stay in jail 'til she dies. He said everybody knows your dad would've never accidentally shot himself cleaning his gun being the good hunter he was and everything. Dad said most folks clean guns on the porch, too, not where you sit for dinner."

Mary Elouise moved her silver shoe piece, which she'd said earlier brought her good luck, across the board and as she kept talking, she nodded at me to roll the dice and take my turn.

"My dad said a good man like John York should've never died like that, young and everything, being a mayor and having a good business he'd built with his own two hands and the whole world going for him and leaving a boy without a daddy. Dad said in a few years your dad would've probably become a congressman or a senator he had such a way with people and fixing their problems. And he said that even Malcolm Boone will never find a jury in this county that will keep your mom from going to prison for the terrible thing she did."

Mary Elouise finally ran out of air at some point, I guess, and stuck her get out of jail free card next to one of her knees and looked at me, but I was so hot and dizzy and just felt like she'd been whacking me in the stomach with a baseball bat.

"I have to go down there to court and testify," she said.

"You have to go down there?"

She nodded her head.

I felt like she'd just hit me again.

"I heard your dad yelling real loud that day, and I was in my backyard so I climbed on top of Chucky's doghouse to see what was going on. And then I heard your Mom yelling. That's when I saw the door open and he had you by the arm and threw you down the steps out into the yard. You turned around and looked right at me for a second, remember?"

I shook my head.

"You don't remember? You got up and ran around the

side of the house and that's the last thing I saw, and then I heard your daddy and mom screaming more and the gun go off so I ran into my house and my mom called the police."

I couldn't say a word and just kept looking at the Monopoly board feeling worse by the second. Even though she told me it was my go, I just couldn't play anymore and wished I hadn't drunk all that pop.

"So anyway, I have to go down there and tell the judge what I saw. I also heard Mom tell Dad that she never really trusted your mom, never since they were in high school. She said your mom always had a wandering eye and thought she was better than everyone else in Sunnyside because her family had come from Charlottesville when she was little, and like all those people from Charlottesville, nothing ever satisfied them and nothing ever will, men included. She said she always knew it would get her in the end and that's why nobody liked her much around here to begin with."

I felt like I couldn't breathe at all. I stood up.

"And Mom saw Hollis Thrasher at your back door before it all happened looking to be trying to sell a sack of wood like he does, and then she saw him heading up through the woods to his shack after the shot. She told the police she thinks your daddy caught him there because she said everybody in town knew Hollis spent time with your mom down at the library past closing time now and then, but nobody ever thought nothing of it 'til the murder because your mom was married to John York. And Hollis is so off in the head and always needs a shave and a bath. Nobody figured it was more than Hollis being a nuisance to people being mean and crazy like he does."

The knock on the door almost sent me through the cracked plaster ceiling above my head.

Lacy walked in from the kitchen, peeked outside and then opened the door and I saw it was Mr. Jennings. He ran the bank downtown and as affable as he usually acted, he didn't look happy standing on our porch.

"Come in, Mr. Jennings," Lacy said.

Mr. Jennings stomped off the snow on his boots and stayed outside the door. He looked around Lacy and saw Mary Elouise and his face got madder looking.

"Time for supper, Mary Elouise."

As she got up and walked to him, he helped her put her coat and mittens on and said, "We've talked about this, now haven't we."

Lacy peered over at me out of the corner of his eye, pulled his pipe away from his mouth and pointed it at me.

"Help her get the game together, Charlie," he said. "Hurry up, now."

There was fake money everywhere where we'd hidden our stashes, but I put everything back in the box best I could and handed it to Mr. Jennings before backing away.

He half smiled at me and didn't look at Lacy at all before he grabbed Mary Elouise's hand and helped her down the steps. Lacy nodded with his head for me to come back to the door, which I did as they left. Mary Elouise looked over her shoulder at me once and waved with her free hand and I waved back. She had a smile on her face.

When she walked out of the house I turned to Lacy and he asked if we had fun. I felt my face turning even hotter and then he asked me if I was coming down with something 'cause I didn't look so good.

I couldn't answer him and just wished Mary Elouise had never told me the terrible things Mrs. Jennings thought about my mom. I wished I'd never heard her say the word murder, either.

I was glad Mary Elouise had come over and we'd played Monopoly but was awfully troubled by her news. Maybe it wasn't troubled and I was just sad about it, I'm not sure. I did start wondering if I was going crazy because I didn't remember anything she'd said about that day, but pieces of what she'd said had showed up in my dreams before.

Thinking about Hollis and what she'd said gave me a shiver all the way down and then I thought about Mom and wondered how many other neighbors were going to be testifying against her in her trial. Maybe all of them. I wondered if the whole danged town knew more than I did and they were going to line up at the courthouse to say what a bad person Mom was and that she should go to prison for the rest of her life.

I didn't know how in the world Mom would ever get out of jail and back in good graces with the church, the library, her neighbors and Dad's kin. And my stomach still didn't even know if she was innocent like she kept telling me over and over and that was the worst of it. It made me hurt so bad I laid down on the couch and closed my eyes.

I sat up like I was thrown from the couch when the gunshot went off in my head.

I couldn't figure out where I was until I saw the orange

peeking out around the woodstove doors and realized I'd fallen asleep. My throat ached. I didn't know if I'd screamed out loud or just dreamed I did. I moved my feet from under the afghan Mom had knitted onto the living room floor. I guess Lacy had thrown it over me. I took a few steps to the kitchen door and felt like I'd just been standing in that same spot…I was almost afraid of what I'd see but all I saw was the streetlight coming in through the window above the sink.

My nightmare was fading like they always did when I woke, but I could still see and hear some of it.

Momma was talking to somebody outside, a vehicle pulled up, a car door slammed and then the screen door threw open and there were footsteps in the kitchen.

Something was going on, it sounded like, so I went to turn down the TV sound dial and that's when Momma screamed.

A chair fell over and something heavy hit the floor.

I kneeled up from in front of the TV. She kept screaming.

I started to run toward the kitchen when I heard a man's voice…like somebody grunting as he was talking, breathing heavy. I didn't know who it was.

I looked outside and saw Dad's truck and then ran in the kitchen. It was Daddy standing in front of Momma and she was on her knees. He had her hair in one fist and smacked her on the side of her face with an open hand, then he looked at me.

"Get out of here!" he yelled in a terrible voice.

Daddy had never yelled at me so I just stood there for a second unsure of what to do.

He came toward me in wide steps with his hands out in front. Daddy grabbed me and lifted me off the floor by my collar.

"Let go of him!" Momma yelled as she ran toward the bedroom. "Daddy!"

That was all I could remember, except for the sound of the gunshot. I got a glass of water and then walked down the hall and creaked Lacy's door open. He was laying there on his back in his nightshirt, and except for his lips blowing in and out, he looked dead to me and it scared me even more for a minute. He looked so small and old without his collar buttoned up high like he always kept it, and without his teeth in and without his glasses and hat on and pipe stuck in his mouth. It was then that I saw a wide, puffy scar that went long around both sides of his neck. I wondered at first if he got it when those men had hoisted him up, but it was a real old scar that looked smooth compared to the rest of his wrinkly skin.

I stared at it for a minute before pushing on him a few times. He finally roused awake and sat up quick.

"Is the house on fire?" he asked.

That threw me even worse. "No," I said.

He looked around for a bit and then asked me again like he had earlier if I was sick.

"I'm not sick," I said.

Lacy looked at his clock. "Well, what in the dang blazes are you doing poking on me and waking me up at two in the morning?"

"Lacy, it didn't happen like Momma said. I'm sure of it. She killed him. She killed him Lacy because he was mad and I think he was beating on her about something. I think he may have beat on me, too."

"What're you talking about?"

"Daddy. Momma killed him."

Lacy's head dropped and he took a big breath of air and without looking at me, motioned me to move back from the bed.

"What're we gonna do? She killed him, Lacy. She killed him."

Lacy motioned me back some more, threw both legs over real shaky and took a big chill. He told me to go to my bedroom and that he'd be in directly.

I did what he said while I heard him rattling around the bathroom putting his teeth in and then he checked the stove in the kitchen. He finally walked in wearing his big slippers and robe that dragged the ground and I think he had a hard time seeing me but I could see him fine standing there in the dark, and, after he found the edge of the bed, he took a slow seat on it.

"Your momma told me about it the very day it happened. She came over to my house a mess like I'd never seen anybody in my life and told me everything. It was a terrible, terrible thing to happen to your dad, to your mom, and to you, especially with you being so young. They did have a fuss that evening, but she didn't shoot him like they're saying. It was an accident. I dern know it was. I know you'd do anything to bring your daddy back. But we can't. But we can have faith knowing your mom is getting out of that jail. You need your momma and she needs you. You understand what I'm telling you?"

"But it don't make sense. It just—"

"It will one day. Don't think bad things about your momma, 'cause if you do you're wrong and you're wronging her."

"Everyone in the whole county thinks she did it."

"They sense a justice in pointing a finger at somebody. They need to, see, 'cause they loved your dad so much. There's more to it than you can understand right now, but you will one day."

"Why won't they let her come home, now? Malcolm kept saying he'd get her out before the trial but they won't let her go."

"Well, the judge set the bail at a high mark—more than she can pay. See, all your mom's money and the shop and everything is tied up right now. The insurance your dad had. Everything. It's tied up until they rule how your dad died. She's having enough problems just paying Malcolm to be her lawyer and I don't know how she's doing that. I'd help her, but a poor feller like me doesn't have that kind of purse."

"Do you know why Dad and Mom were fussing like the neighbors say?"

Lacy ran a hand across his whiskers, patted me on the leg and stood and wobbled for a minute until he got his balance.

"That's between your mom and dad, child."

"If she did it, she should go to prison for what she done, Lacy, shouldn't she?"

"Now get that bad vision out of your head right now."

"So you think Malcolm's going to be able to make them know she's innocent?"

"Something like that. Now I want you to keep believing in her. Be brave, and get all those worries off your heart 'cause they don't belong there."

Lacy walked to the hall door and held on to the wall for a minute before he turned around.

"Trial's gonna be here before you know it, and you'll need to be strong like we talk about. But you can do it. You're a fine little feller, just like your daddy was. Strong, too. Never forget that. No, sir, never forget that."

"I don't feel strong, Lacy."

"Your dad would want you to be on your mom's side. I don't know much but I know that. Put your faith in the music of things like we've talked about. I'll pray on it with you if you want to."

"I don't feel like praying."

"Well, I'll say one for you then. I've lived long enough where I'm on pretty good terms with the Maker."

"He let your house burn down."

Lacy tamped his cane up and down a few time. "Yes, sir, he surely did."

"Why'd he do that?"

"I don't know. Most of his works ain't for my understanding. I do know I still got a nice place to lay my head. He gave that to me about the same time I lost my house."

"He took Daddy for good."

Lacy nodded. "I lost my daddy as a young 'un, too, so I know some of the hurting you're feeling."

"I just don't think I'm on good terms with our Maker like you are."

"You are, you just don't know it. When you're older, some things will start—"

"I don't want to grow up, Lacy. Sometimes I wish I'd never wake up in the morning because it's the same old terrible thing getting worse. Something awful is gonna happen soon, I can feel it."

"Well, I've felt like that a time or two myself," he said. "But you're gonna grow up. Life ain't gonna always be so hard as it is right now. A feller never knows what kind of music will be playing when he wakes, you see. Let's rest on it tonight. Let it rest, child. And if you don't want to pray on things, at least say a little something for your momma."

"Why?" I said.

"Because she's praying in that jailhouse for you."

"I'd rather pray for Daddy."

"But he don't need your prayers no more, unless you just want to speak with him on things. Your momma needs your praying now."

Lacy kept nodding in his slow way. I finally told him I'd pray something for Mom even though I figured I probably wouldn't unless something snuck in. Lacy walked a step or two toward his bedroom.

"How'd you get that scar on your neck?" I asked.

Lacy raised a finger to just under his jaw-line and picked at his skin. "Dang old razor, need to get it stropped."

"No. That old long one around the bottom of your neck."

He pulled the collar of his robe up and walked down the hall. As his door started to squeak shut he said, "It's a birth-mark of sorts, I reckon. Good night, Charlie."

* * *

The clock on the kitchen wall seemed to tick slower as the days of December passed one by one. I walked over to it so I could watch the hands move up close and that's the first time I noticed tiny drops of Daddy's blood stuck on the glass that Momma had missed in her cleaning. I studied on it a while and then walked to the window. The sky had stopped snowing but it was still cold and the worst part was, Jimmy and Alvin had gone again to their grandmother's in Troutville for over a week. I wished every day that their drunk daddy would go back working on the railroad again so they'd come back to Sunnyside but this time it looked like they were gone for good. I missed Jimmy.

Missing the only best friend I still had besides Lacy made me keep hoping that Mary Elouise would come over to play board games again, but she never did. I suspect she got in trouble for coming down here that one time, and I never did quite muster up the courage to go up there to see if she wanted to play checkers or cards.

There was a lot going on during that month with Momma's trial and Malcolm was at the house several days a week. I'd started noticing that he still smiled but didn't wink as much. And Mom had put a stop to all my jailhouse visits because of all the folks hanging around, pointing at me and asking me the same things.

I was glad when I found out I didn't have to go no more. Momma'd ask me the same old questions about nothing and she'd hug me but each time there was more and more quiet and I'd always feel lower leaving than when I went in there.

I suspect she did, too. We both just kept dying a little more each visit, it seemed.

She didn't look pretty anymore, either.

Her eyes were always watery and her face was the same ashy color all of the other prisoners' faces looked like. I tried to keep from hating her for being in there and have faith in her like Lacy said but it grew harder every day.

Lacy was smart but even a smart man don't know all. He'd told me that one time and I was starting to wonder the same about him. Me and Mom passed notes through Lacy and Malcolm and through that big jail matron who seemed to like Mom, even though she was the one keeping her behind bars. Mom told me she was a kind woman. I guess she was always nice to me.

The judge finally set the trial date for December 12th, and the biggest event of Sunnyside in twenty years was scheduled to go for two days, Malcolm told me.

Waiting the final days for Mom's trial to get going and get over with was like watching water drip out of the kitchen faucet, which I actually did once. Malcolm had arranged through school that my lessons be dropped off twice a week. Lacy was pretty hard on me about doing all the homework. He said after the trial I'd go back to school and everything would work out. I didn't know about all of that so I tried not to think much about it. What I did think about all the time between doing homework and listening to dripping water and a ticking bloody clock was why Daddy died and who done it. I couldn't wait for that trial. And even worse I couldn't wait for it to be over.

But it did finally come just like Lacy said it always would. And every time I tried to sneak down to the courthouse, Lacy would have me busy doing something else like going up on the mountain with him and a trooper to chop down a Christmas tree, or putting up the decorations Mom wanted us to put out.

Lacy didn't sleep during the day like he had been doing, especially since I got wind that he'd been getting bad things in the mail. They never did catch who was sending the bad letters or the person who spray-painted our yard.

I said little to him about the letters and the spray-painting because every time I tried, Lacy would change the subject or just ignore my questions altogether. He acted like he couldn't hear me more and more, when I was pretty sure he could.

I woke up one morning and found two presents in brown paper with my name on them that Lacy had wrapped, even though they said on them that they were from Santa Claus. Looked like Lacy's writing on the paper and they smelled like pipe tobacco, and I'd known for some time that Santa Claus wasn't real. I didn't see any presents from Momma but figured she gave Lacy the money to buy them, if she had any money left.

It sure didn't feel like Christmastime to me no matter what we did, so I wasn't excited about all of that like usual. But doing chores did help pass the hours, especially because the trial went five days longer than the judge thought it would when one of the jurors took pneumonia.

Malcolm was tearing into everyone the prosecutor would put on the stand using his loud voice and theatrical ways, Lacy said. He told me he'd heard from a man at the colored barbershop that Malcolm chewed up policemen like they were rough lumber and spit them out like sawdust when he was done with them.

The days did creep by and one night Lacy sat me down at the kitchen table after he'd tucked a rag into the collar of my sweater I'd gotten the year before for Christmas. The smell of what he was cooking made me sick to my stomach.

He'd made me a big meal of country-style steak in mushroom gravy, potato cakes, apple butter biscuits, green beans and fatback cooked down, and had bought a big chocolate pie from Miss Beulah's bakery. It was one of my favorite meals, but I told him I wasn't hungry so he just picked up his plate and my plate and put both back in the oven to warm.

He came back and sat and looked so wobbly I thought he was gonna fall right out of the chair as he took off his blue cap and hung it on the cane he'd propped up beside the table.

Lacy looked like he was getting older by the second. His skin looked so thin that I thought I could almost see right through him even with him being so dark.

"They found your Mom guilty at the courthouse this evening," he finally said in a high but real loud voice for him.

Lacy patted my hand slow like he did when giving bad news. I think he was expecting some kind of terrible reaction from me, but I knew all of that already because instead of going up to Jimmy's like I promised him I would—who was still gone but Lacy didn't know that—I was down at the courthouse hiding behind a big snowdrift when all of the reporters rushed out toward the phone booth.

I stayed a long time hiding behind that big drift with my ear in the wind watching the clouds roll past the mountain. It seemed like I laid there forever.

I knew Momma was just on the other side of that thick, brick wall, and I stayed until I got so cold and felt so empty I had to leave or freeze to death. The thing that kept running through my mind was that she did kill Daddy. The judge declared she did. I couldn't believe after all those terrible months of hoping, my very worst nightmare came true.

I didn't let on about any of that as Lacy finally said that even though the court said she was guilty, we knew better, and like he'd told me before, she was getting out of that dern jail.

I looked up from the table. For some reason it was almost like I didn't care anymore what happened to Momma and especially what happened to me. Didn't even matter anymore or something because whatever happened wouldn't change anything except the whole thing would just get worse. But I thought again about what Lacy had just said, mostly because of the strong way he'd said it.

"She's getting out?" I asked.

Lacy nodded.

"When?"

Lacy stood and went into his bedroom and walked out with a handful of pillowcases. I sat up.

"That jury is wrong, Charlie. You got to be trusting me on this now. Pack all your clothes that still fit out of your dresser and closet into these. Your coat. Warm clothes. Your shoes, too."

"They gonna send me off somewhere, Lacy?"

"Do what I say, child. Then we'll have a nice supper. You're gonna need it tomorrow."

"Where am I going?"

"I told you a long time ago that one way or another, your mom was gonna get out of that jail. Now I meant what I said. Pack your things."

I'd never seen him act so serious and his voice was deeper and didn't have any quiver in it, so I didn't ask any more questions right then. I walked into my room with the sacks and packed for what or for how long I had no idea.

I turned around and started to say something because I saw him standing there watching me.

"Do what I'm telling you."

All of a sudden I cared again what happened to me and Momma, at first it was just a little bit, but after a couple of minutes I was stuffing those sacks as fast as I could.

Chapter Fourteen

I thought it was Lacy banging around in the dark without his teeth in or glasses on, passing water like he had to do a dozen times a night. I looked at the alarm clock wide-awake because there was no way I'd sleep that night anyway.

It was after midnight and I heard more noises in the kitchen and couldn't figure what in the world he'd be doing in there so late after that big meal we'd had earlier, so I got up and wrapped a blanket around me to take a look.

There weren't any lights on when I walked in, but I stopped when I saw the back of a big man hunched over the table. He had on a military long coat with the collar pulled up over short, dark hair. I thought at first it was one of the state policemen who'd come inside to get out of the weather. I don't know how long I stood right there looking at him, but it may have been a minute or more.

I started getting scared because he didn't look like any of the troopers I'd seen before, so I inched my way to the corner and tried to make it to Lacy's room to tell him some man was in the house.

I was halfway across the floor when the man turned.

Even in the dark, I could see his face from the moonlight coming through the kitchen window. It was Hollis Thrasher. He was drinking coffee and carefully put down the cup.

"Sorry to scare you, Charlie," he said.

He went to stand and I took a quick step to yank the string on the hall light.

"Don't. We don't want to wake anybody."

I wondered for a minute if I was dreaming and then looked in those black eyes and knew I wasn't. I jerked on the light string, dropped my blanket and shot down the hall to wake up Lacy. I knew something was bad wrong. Bad wrong. Before I got to the end of the hall Hollis had turned off the light and it was pitch-dark.

"Lacy's in the bathroom. He'll be out in a minute," he said.

I could hear sink water running and threw open the bathroom door.

"Hollis Thrasher's sitting in the kitchen," I said as fast as it could come out.

Lacy was in the dark with his pipe in his mouth wearing his long johns and scrubbing on his dentures with soda.

"I know. I was just going to wake you up," he said. "Be out in a minute."

"It's Hollis Thrasher!"

"I know. I let him in."

"You let him in?"

"I'll be out directly. Get dressed."

"But Lacy…"

"Do what I say, now."

"I'm gonna get one of the troopers."

Lacy turned around sudden. "No. Now do what I'm telling you."

I looked around back down the dark hall toward the kitchen. "I ain't going back in there. He's—"

Lacy bent down. "It's all right. Trust me, child."

"What's wrong with you?"

"Trust me. Trust me, now, child."

My head was spinning but I finally did as told and ran to my room, locked the door and pulled on my overalls and sweater. A few minutes later after Lacy fetched me, we all sat in the dark kitchen as Lacy fixed me an apple butter biscuit left over from supper.

One of my legs was going a hundred miles an hour up and down waiting for someone to tell me what in the world was going on as I stared at that biscuit. Hollis sat still as a stump and by his face, he looked to me like a man who'd done a lot of bad in his life and I couldn't believe he was sitting in my house. I wondered if Lacy was in his right mind letting him in with the police looking for him to ask more questions about Daddy getting killed. It felt like the whole house was about to explode or at least I felt like I was. I knew for sure looking at Lacy that I wasn't the only one feeling nervous at that table.

Lacy leaned forward and in a voice like a whisper said, "You're gonna go down and get your mom out of jail tonight with Hollis."

What he said took a minute to set. My leg quit shaking. "They're letting her go right now?" I asked.

Lacy shook his head. "Child, in the morning they'll be taking her to the woman's prison over in Andersonville. We're not going to stand by and watch her go to prison for the rest of her life. It just ain't right. We're going to get her out of that jail."

The quiet that suddenly came over that house was the scariest thing I've ever listened to. All I could hear was Lacy's raspy breathing and the wind whipping around outside banging the inside kitchen screen door back and forth a little.

Lacy finally patted my hand. "It's the only thing left to do. You'll understand one day I surely believe."

Lacy stood and went back to Mom and Dad's bedroom. I started to get up because it was just me and Hollis at the table, and I still had no idea why he was in our house at midnight and somehow part of a big plan to bust Momma out of jail. I kept wondering why he wasn't still in Mexico like I'd heard or holed up in his shack up on Angel's Rest.

"Sit for a minute, Charlie," he said. "I know this is a shock and it's gonna be tough on you because you're just a boy, but your mom needs you tonight."

"What're you doing here?" I asked.

Hollis reached up and grabbed for nothing on his face, I guess out of an old habit of scratching his big beard that wasn't there anymore. I stared at a thin, pink scar that went down the side of his forehead to the top of one eye. It sliced right through one black eyebrow. Seemed like everybody in that house was all scarred up but me.

"I'm here to help your mom," he said. "We've known each other since we were kids."

"She always told me to stay away from you."

Hollis looked down for a minute and then raised his head. Those eyes of his lit up in a direct way. "Your mom and I went to school together. I know all of this is hard to understand, but you have to believe me, and she'll tell you so in just a few minutes."

I was still scared of him and I don't know why it bothered me so much that he was in my dad's house, where he was sitting and drinking coffee, but it did. It bothered me so bad it went right through me.

"You're sitting in Dad's chair," I said.

Hollis nodded and pushed his cup and saucer in front of another chair and stood to move but about the same time, Lacy walked in with a crumpled old piece of luggage.

"Bring your clothes in here, then go in your room and whatever else you'd like to take with you, put it in here. Your ball glove, picture books, tackle box...whatever you want to take."

"Where am I going?" I asked.

"Just do as I say, now," Lacy said.

"How long we gonna be gone?"

"For a good while."

I wanted to disobey Lacy over a big thing for the first time ever that he'd catch me doing it and tell those troopers Hollis Thrasher was in the house, but Lacy looked so serious and so old and just plain tuckered out, and I was so stunned by that point with everything, that if he'd of told me I needed to walk off a cliff while singing "Dixie" I'd have probably done it.

I didn't ask any more questions, took the bag and walked in my room. The first thing I saw was Dad's picture and my fishing poles propped up in the corner. Lacy must've seen me looking at them.

"Take them with you."

When he said that a terrible feeling went through me because it would be months before it would be time to fish again.

I pulled open my drawers and put some comic books, my Abe Lincoln and Jim Thorpe books and my arrowhead collection in the bag, and then started putting the pictures on my dresser in, too.

It was then, when I grabbed the picture of Dad that Mom had framed for me on the day of his funeral, that I knew I'd never ever be coming back to this house after tonight. I just knew it. And it was then that I fell on my bed with his picture and cried until I couldn't cry anymore.

When I was finished, I wrapped the picture of Dad in an old T-shirt, put it in the bag along with my fishing plugs and extra reel and a few other things, and the strangest feeling in the world came over me.

I was glad I would never come back to Sunnyside or this house. Both were just too hard to live in anymore. I'd never been gladder of anything in my whole life that I was going and I wondered if I was going nutty for thinking such a terrible thing.

I walked in the kitchen with the bags of clothes and the other heavy bag of stuff and Lacy and Hollis both stood.

"You ready, Charlie?" Hollis asked.

I didn't say anything and Lacy then asked the same thing. I nodded and Hollis patted my back kind of gingerly that gave me a shiver and he took my fishing poles and bags and we all moved quiet to the cellar door like mice would in the middle of the night. I saw Hollis had Mom's suitcase with the sewn daisies on it under one arm.

Lacy prodded me to walk in front of him down the rickety pine steps to the dirt floor of the basement.

"Where's your bags?" I asked Lacy.

We kept walking and Hollis was all stooped over to keep from bumping his head. He shook hands with Lacy really formal-like, then after he looked around out the bulkhead door, he went up the steps and I saw him trying to run with his limp through the deep snow where Mom's vegetable garden used to be. Lacy then looked down at me and put both old hands on my shoulders.

"I'm not going. You're just going with Hollis. He's gonna take good care of you and your Mom for a while. You all are gonna need some help. He's gonna see to it."

Lacy could hardly finish the sentence when his voice started to break. I could see his eyes watering up and I hugged him around the waist as hard as I could because it was looking like I'd never see him again, either. I couldn't stand the thought of it. He'd always been my best friend, even more than Jimmy.

"I'm not going if you're not going," I said.

"You have to. I'm too dern old to go, child."

"I ain't going nowhere with Hollis. He might have killed Daddy...don't you see, Lacy?"

Lacy got down on one knee like he'd never done before. "Do you think I'd let you go off with anybody who'd of hurt your daddy? No, sir. He's here to help."

"I ain't going without you. I ain't."

"You have to. It's going to be all right, Charlie. I wouldn't lie to you, now. I'll see you again one day."

"No you won't..."

Lacy reached out with one hand and pulled me to him, then patted me on the back with the other. He kept hold of me and I remembered all those times we had at the shop and the stories he told about those good people who help others he called music makers and how he always said he'd never lie to me.

I knew when he said he'd see me again that he'd just told me his very first lie.

I was so sad because I knew I had to go, almost like I was being pulled outside that cellar door by a wind I couldn't feel except it was moving me, so I let go of Lacy and ran up the steps faster than I'd ever run before to Hollis, who was standing up the street. He walked around the corner and I followed him to a car that was as big as the one Malcolm Boone drove but this one was blue. Before I got to it, I looked back at the house and saw Lacy wave goodbye from the basement shadows with his arm in that white shirt going slow back and forth.

He looked just like a ghost.

I finally turned and kept walking and got in that car with Hollis and he seemed calm as a crazy man would. I sat as far away from him against the door as he started telling me what he wanted me to do when we got to the jail. He took a last look at the trooper asleep in the police truck, started that big car up and we left as I peered back to where Lacy was, but the side of my house was blocked by a neighbor's fence. I waved even though I knew he couldn't see me.

I turned all the way around in the seat before we went down the foot of the mountain called Duncan Hill to see everything I could about the only place I'd ever lived in case one day I ever wanted to remember exactly what it looked like. In case I never came back, which I figured I never, ever would.

And that's when I saw something shine in the floorboard of the back seat. It was the sharp shine that comes from streetlight gleaming off the barrel of an oiled shotgun.

It looked just like the one that killed Daddy.

Even after seeing that double-barrel shotgun and the visions it gave me that lit my eyes on fire, I don't remember actually feeling scared on the ride to the jail. Not unless a person can get so scared they get frozen up and can't really think about anything and are so scared they don't even notice they're scared and pee in their britches and don't know they did it until they feel wet later.

I don't think I heard a word Hollis said, either. If he said anything at all after we drove off Duncan Hill. I do remember he parked the car in the back parking lot of town hall, got out, opened the back door and my whole body shook when I heard him grab that gun.

"I'm not gonna hurt anybody," he said. "This is just so they're gonna have to deal with me in a serious manner."

With that shotgun hanging down beside his good leg, Hollis walked around to the side of the car I was on and broke the action open. It looked like he was trying to show me that it was unloaded.

It was snowing again and I couldn't really see what he wanted me to, but he slammed the barrel back in line with the butt of the gun, nodded at me a couple of times and off he went toward the jailhouse.

He wasn't twenty yards when I had to open the passenger side door and throw up. He looked back but kept going. I watched him walk with that gimped-up leg and carrying that gun. It looked little in his hands.

Hollis didn't seem to be in any hurry at all about what he was about to do, whatever he was about to do. He kept leaning into the December wind and as he got closer to the jail, he hid the shotgun under his overcoat.

I suddenly prayed for all I was worth like I hadn't prayed since before Daddy died, that Mom would come walking out of there in one whole piece and me and her could leave Sunnyside because there wasn't any way to stay here now.

I knew since I'd been in the jail a bunch of times, that the cellblock was connected to the sheriff's office by a brick hallway with bars at both ends. Everyone in town knew there was no law awake in the wee hours of a Thursday morning in the dead of winter.

And anyone could find that out pretty quick if they ever called and needed help because it would usually take a good hour before some deputy would show up with sleep marks on his face.

The town had a dispatcher who was probably asleep, one patrol officer on duty who was somewhere else asleep and one jailer sitting in the jail asleep. Because they had Mom in there, there was also the part-time matron from the farm bureau who was probably in there asleep, too. They all slept as sound as the state police did working the way I had it figured.

I don't know exactly how Hollis busted in to get Momma out, but from what I could imagine sitting there in that still, cold car, he probably just walked in big and tall as a farm silo and stared with those black eyes. He probably pointed that gun and locked both the jailer and the matron in a cell without a word out of either one of them, and then he got Mom out using their keys. I doubt he even said anything.

If I had more courage, I could probably have done the same thing without too much difficulty. Prison bust-outs were uncommon in Sunnyside so I think the last thing that jailer expected when he saw Hollis at the door and let him in was seeing that shotgun pointed at him the next second.

I don't know how long I waited. Could've been an hour or a couple of minutes. It was long enough for me to real- ize my wet accident that happened earlier. I kept bracing every second for the sounds of gunshots when the wind would ease up. I do know it must've taken at least a few minutes because the windows fogged up and I had to wipe them a couple of times to see out.

The second time I wiped them, I saw Mom and Hollis walking, just plain walking, from the jailhouse to the car. She had his long coat on and it was blowing all around her legs. When he raised a hand up to point at the car, she ran toward it.

I wanted to get out but instead jumped into the back seat like I figured I was supposed to do. Mom got in and hugged me crying. She could hardly breathe she was crying so much. Her crying was so loud and she held me so hard it felt like my back was starting to break while Hollis put the shotgun in the trunk and we took off driving through town at a good clip until we hit Route 56. I thought for sure we'd wreck going through some of those icy curves.

"I'm so sorry, Charlie. I'm so sorry, baby," Mom kept saying.

I didn't know what to do with her in the shape she was in, so I just held her back and said, "It's okay, Momma. It's gonna be okay, Momma," as Hollis peered at the both of us back and forth.

I looked at the speedometer as it went over sixty and I kept holding Momma and realized that Lacy would've made a poor getaway driver. If he could've gone with us, he would probably be in the back seat with me. I wished he was, too, and not just missing him, I had a feeling we might be needing somebody as tough and smart as he was. Even if he didn't think he was brave, I knew different.

Hollis pulled off the side of the road about ten miles out

of town. "Hand me the license plates in that bag back there," he said to me. I rooted around in a green army duffel and pulled them out. They were Maine license plates. Hollis took them from me, got out and put them on. While he was working Momma hugged and hugged me.

We took off again and I looked at Hollis's wristwatch sometime during our getaway. It was almost three in the morning. I realized that I hadn't thought of Lacy in over an hour. It seemed like a terrible long time to not think of someone so important who you'd just found out you'd probably never see again.

I worried for him now, too. I couldn't imagine what he'd be telling the law come morning. Or my granddaddy. And I didn't know where he'd go 'cause it seemed like he didn't have nowhere to go anymore. He should have come with us because there was no way he was gonna stay up on Duncan Hill.

But I didn't think about all of that too long because I guess there were so many other things to think about.

Mom finally calmed and was still all teared up, but she laughed a little with a snort like she'd accidentally got pop up her nose or something. She asked me over and over if I were okay like she didn't believe me when I nodded, and she kept petting my head. Hard kind of petting, too, like a person would do to a bird dog that found its way home after being missing on the mountain for days.

Mom cleared room in the front seat for me to sit next to her so I climbed back over.

No one said anything as we began to pass town after town and Hollis kept the radio on and changed stations all the time trying to pick up better static from somewhere. I guess he did it to see if there'd be any news about what we'd done.

I think we hoped that it wouldn't be until the next morning when Mrs. French showed up at six with breakfast for the prisoners, that they'd find out she'd cooked one meal too many. We all looked behind us a lot those first hours just in case we were hoping wrong.

Mom put her arm around me pulling me to her tight and when her hand went limp on my shoulder, I knew she'd fallen asleep. And somewhere watching the yellow lines and blowing snow that swirled in the headlights, feeling the hum of that big car and every now and then looking up at Hollis's fierce eyes focused on the long road in front us, I fell asleep, too.

I already felt a long way from Sunnyside.

Chapter Fifteen

When I woke, the sun was high and Mom was still sleeping. I grabbed her arm to wake her up and Hollis put a hand
on mine.

"Let her sleep. She needs it," he said quiet.

I pulled my hand from his grip.

"Want something to drink?" he asked.

I ignored him and looked out the windshield and could
tell we were on a big highway now, heading through the hill
country of Pennsylvania. I saw a sign for Gettysburg, a place
I'd read about in my Lincoln books.

"Lacy made ham biscuits and I got a jug of orange juice,"
Hollis said.

I looked away and climbed over into the back seat as quiet
as I could. Momma moved and stretched out a little but
didn't open her eyes. I could see Hollis looking at me in the

rearview mirror. I looked at him back and for the first time, I kept staring until his gaze turned first.

Hollis poured himself a cup of coffee from a silver thermos bottle.

"Want some coffee, Charlie?"

I kept looking out the window, watching the pavement and white fields fly by that big Chevrolet. Momma only let me drink coffee to dunk sugar cookies in.

"We're heading to Maine. It's up north, near Canada," he said, in that usual voice that sounded like it came out of a cave even if he was trying to whisper. It was too deep to find comfort in, unless what was said came with some kind of expression or something. Which never happened.

"I know where Maine is," I said, even though I wasn't sure where it was exactly.

Even big and scary as Hollis was with all his scars and the rumors I'd heard, I wasn't scared of him anymore. I didn't like him but I wasn't scared of him. I knew Daddy was never afraid of him or he at least didn't let on. But there was something just under the cut-up and burned skin of Hollis Thrasher that no matter how cleaned up he got, he seemed to me like a big old house you never wanted to look into because you just knew there was something bad living in there.

I couldn't believe Mom and me were in that car with him. I couldn't believe what we'd all just done. I couldn't believe Lacy had allowed it and I couldn't believe Mom was next to Hollis sleeping like a lamb cradled up beside a wolf.

"I thought we might be heading to Mexico like you did a few months ago," I said.

"I told a couple of people that…wanted the word to spread. I told a lie to you but I couldn't let anyone know where I was going. I was in Maine getting things set up in case this day ever came, which it did. There was always the best hope me and Lacy had that they'd let your mom go."

"Lacy knew you were gonna do this?"

"If it came to it. He's known for a while," Hollis said.

"Momma, too?"

Hollis nodded.

"Malcolm?"

"No."

"And you're doing all this because…she's your old friend?"

"Yes."

"Why else?"

"She needed help, Charlie."

I didn't believe a word he said. He'd just told me he'd lied to me about going to Mexico. I got a bunch of courage all of a sudden for no reason just like I had when I whipped the Perkins boys.

"People said you been seeing Momma."

Hollis grimaced and looked at me quick in the mirror. "That ain't true."

"Why do they say it then?"

"I don't know."

"They say you were near the house when Daddy got shot."

"I asked your Mom if you all wanted a sack of wood I'd cut and split. I was at your neighbors, doing the same thing. I heard the shot. Never thought anything about it…just figured someone was shooting a crow or a groundhog in their garden."

"You hear Momma screaming?"

Hollis got real still, then took a sip of coffee. "I was walking through the woods on Foley's place when the gun went off."

"Did you tell the law that?"

Hollis shook his head again and took another sip.

"Why not?"

"I ain't got nothing to say to the law."

"Why?"

"We've had our run-ins is why."

I took a breath and rubbed my hand across the car seat. "Where'd you get this car?"

"I bought it from an old army buddy."

I wasn't sure I should believe that, either. The way I saw it, people who lie and bust people out of prison and have spent time in prison probably steal cars, too. I couldn't imagine how a man like Hollis could afford a car like this one but then I remembered that deputy talking about him selling the mountain.

"So, you wanted people to think we went to Mexico?" I asked.

"That's right. I left papers in the can behind my shack on the mountain where I burn trash. I burned things about property in Mexico, towns down there and so on. If they try, which I'm pretty sure they will, they'll find clues I left that we're heading west. I also checked out library books on Mexico and learning Spanish the last few months."

I tried to let all of that settle but it wouldn't.

"Why we going to Maine?" I asked.

"It's a place where we can all start over. It's a good place. Clean place. You'll see."

I thought about what he'd said and thought some more about Maine, a place I didn't know anything about, but I liked the sound of starting over, as long as Hollis wasn't starting over with us.

Starting over.

I wondered if Mom and me could really do that.

I hoped where we were going was like Sunnyside in a lot of ways but different in others. Same but different. I didn't know there was such a thing as just picking up and starting over clean like he was saying. I hadn't felt clean like that in a long time, ever since before I ever knew a person could feel clean like that. I did know the longer I was in that car with Hollis the dirtier I felt. You don't really realize the good feeling of being clean until you get dirtied up with something on your heart you can't get off you.

Hollis kept talking real low and quiet about how he'd picked out a house for Mom and me on the coast in a small town called Pawtuckaway, Maine. He said that where we were going wasn't far from the Canadian border, and an old friend he knew who was a good man but who'd spent time in prison before he'd found Jesus, had helped Hollis with the all the arrangements for me and Mom, like identification cards with different names on them and papers of different kinds he said we'd need. Hollis said you meet some good people in prison.

I'd never realized Hollis was so smart and could do all of

those things. All I'd ever seen him do before was bust up pallets or thumb for a ride. I never even knew he could say much of anything before now. I'd never heard him say more than a handful of words my whole life and now in the car he wouldn't stop talking in that steady, quiet voice full of pea gravel.

Hollis said the folks in Pawtuckaway wouldn't be a bunch of busybodies like the folks in Sunnyside because it was the sort of place people went to who didn't have hardly nowhere else to go. People like us, he said. He said most tended to respect a person's privacy and not ask a lot of questions.

"Part of all of us starting over up there is that we have to change our names," he said. "Your name now is Charles Jackson Cutter and your Mom's name is Emily Lane Cutter. She picked the names out herself."

"What's your name gonna be?"

"Tom, not Hollis anymore."

"Tom Thrasher?" I asked.

Hollis had long since finished his coffee, didn't say anything and started rooting around in a cooler for a bottle of pop. He found what he was looking for, uncapped it and handed it back to me but I didn't take it. He then kept it himself, took a big swig, cracked his window and lit a cigarette. Mom hated cigarettes.

"Is your name Tom Thrasher?" I asked again.

"No, my last name will be different. Still working on that...."

"Where're you gonna live?"

"I'm in trouble now, Charlie. I'll have to stay low for a while. A long while."

I looked over at Mom and thought she did look like an Emily and it was similar to her old name, Hadley, and my name was pretty much the same except for the "Jackson" and the "Cutter" part. Charles J. Cutter, I thought. It sounded like a pretty good name but not nearly as good as Charles W. York. I was gonna keep my old name no matter what Hollis said.

Hollis downed about half the bottle of Mountain Dew and asked again if I wanted one before he finished the cigarette and flicked the butt out the window.

I shook my head. I didn't want nothing from him.

All of that conversation about going to Maine and changing names took me for a big surprise and it all seemed pretty exciting, like something you'd read in a book or see at the Sunnyside theater downtown on a Saturday afternoon, but I knew we were doing wrong, too, not wrong like skipping school, but bad wrong.

I wondered how many policemen were after us and looked at Hollis or Tom or whatever his name was at that point, and something growing deep down bothered me about him being in the same car with Momma and me, just like it bothered me seeing him sitting in Dad's chair. Him busting her out of jail and everything.

Something about it made me start to hate him the nicer he was to me.

There was something different about getting help from Hollis as opposed to Lacy helping out like he did. It was a lot different.

But things had happened all so fast that I didn't have time to sort nothing out until now. I wondered what the police knew that I didn't about Hollis Thrasher. I started to believe right then that Hollis was the reason Dad was dead.

I wondered if he killed Dad to be with Momma.

I kept looking at the short hair on the back of his big neck and that thought made me feel ice cold all over seeing him sitting so close to Mom.

The only thing that made me feel better was that Lacy seemed to approve of the whole thing. And I didn't know anybody smarter than Lacy and I prayed that he was right.

After more miles of quiet, now going through some big mountain country like we had in Sunnyside, Hollis told me I could never again call myself Charles York. He then looked at me severe and said, "Never. Your name's Charles Cutter, now. Charles Cutter. Understand?"

"My name's Charles W. York."

I looked for his eyes in the rearview mirror but they stayed looking at the road.

"I'm just trying to tell you some things you need to know, Charlie, so your Mom doesn't get caught if we get pulled over or something. That's all. Like you can't ever tell anybody you ever lived in Virginia, either. We're telling everyone that we're from Greensboro, North Carolina. Your Mom picked that place because she said you've been there a few times to visit your uncle so you'd have a recollection of it."

The last time I'd seen Uncle Sonny was at Daddy's funeral. Aunt Henrietta wheeled Dad's only brother behind me and Mom at the gravesite. I didn't hardly recognize Uncle Sonny since I'd seen him last in Greensboro, and I'm not sure if he recognized me even though he was staring at me when I turned around to look at him. He looked a lot worse hunched up in his wheelchair with his oxygen bottle than the last time we'd traveled down to Greensboro for a weekend. Dad said Uncle Sonny was in poor health then. He told me that living hard had made an old man out of Uncle Sonny before he was even forty years old. Uncle Sonny never said anything to me at the funeral, but he did nod from his chair once. I was surprised Aunt Linda never came up to Mom after Dad's service was over. They had seemed like the best sort of friends always laughing and carrying on during those visits before Dad died. The four of them would stay up all night playing pinochle.

It was hard to remember old times about Uncle Sonny and Greensboro as Hollis kept talking about changing names and places and whatnot as we drove mile after mile heading north. I looked over at Mom. She looked so peaceful sleeping with her head against the window and with her hands together in her lap. She finally stirred awake when Hollis hit a big pothole and her head bounced a little bit.

Mom ran her hands through her long hair and then looked at me and then over at Hollis. He just nodded.

"Where are we?" she asked.

"About ninety miles from New York City," Hollis said.

Mom patted my hand. Hollis handed her his half-drank bottle of warm pop, which had to have gone flat by now.

She took a sip. She didn't even wipe off the top first like she did when she drank from one of my bottles.

"Want to stop soon?" Hollis asked her.

She nodded and put her arms around herself before she turned around and hugged me and kissed me on top of the head about ten times. I looked up at her and she looked so happy it made me happy. It warmed me all over and got the bad thoughts out of my head. I hadn't even realized when she was in jail how much I'd really missed her. She hadn't looked this happy since before Daddy died. I don't know if I'd ever seen her face that happy, ever.

For the first time that very second, even with Daddy gone and even though I still hadn't got a handle on being in a car with Hollis Thrasher with all of us on the run from the law, and her wearing his coat and drinking from his bottle, I finally felt things may just turn out all right for Mom and me.

Lacy would never steer me down a bad road with Hollis. He just wouldn't have done something like that, I kept trying to tell myself.

Maybe in this place called Pawtuckaway, Maine, in a small house on the ocean with the fishing boats in the harbor and ocean breezes and the good, hard-working people Hollis told me about on that drive, Mom and me could start over. I just kept wishing Daddy could start over with us.

We soon got off that big highway somewhere in New York and I wondered for a while if we were near the special school the Wilson twins were sent off to. I imagined they wore those Superman capes and red masks the whole way up there and that image made me grin those boys being the way they were. Whatever new school they were in, I'd bet they wore those capes right through the front doors on their first day.

Hollis drove through a town about twice the size of Sunnyside, and I read the name of the motel we stopped at from the big glowing sign out front. The Jetset Motel, the sign said. Clean beds. Low Rates. Truckers Welcome.

Hollis pulled in and parked way down the gravel strip where there were lots of doors to rooms but not many cars. He pulled on a Pittsburgh Pirates baseball cap low on his forehead, got out and limped slow to the office and in a couple of minutes came back toting a newspaper and keys to rooms 21 and 22.

He got the doors open to the two rooms and motioned Mom and me to go inside, which we did. I had to go to the bathroom pretty bad and once I quit searching for a pull light, I saw the switch on the wall and flipped it, did my business and when I came out Hollis had already unloaded Momma's suitcase in the room and two of my sacks of clothes.

"Where's Hollis at?" I asked.

Mom shivered and turned on the heater in the room before opening her suitcase. "He's next door, honey," she said.

I went to open the curtains but Mom told me with her eyes not to.

I thought about that sign out front about the bed being so

clean and knew there was no way to tell if it was or not, because there was so little light with only the one dim lamp in the room.

I'd been in a motel twice before that day with Mom and Dad when we went to the lake resort in Pipestem, West Virginia, and once to Virginia Beach. The room we were in now seemed about the same size and everything, except this one was so dark and the brown carpet stunk like wet cigarettes.

"Why we stopping here, Momma?" I asked.

"I have to change and we all need a good bath," she said.

Mom took off Hollis's coat. I saw she was still in that jailhouse dress and I thought about how I'd wet my pants earlier for the first time that I could ever remember doing and hoped no one had noticed and asked, "We gonna eat, too?"

"Hollis is going to run out and bring back cheeseburger baskets. How's that sound?"

"All right...."

I went to turn on the TV but Mom shook her head.

"I'll be out in a few minutes," she said. "Why don't you try to stretch out for a while, baby. Be good for you. We still have a long trip ahead."

She went in the bathroom and closed the door, and it seemed like forever before I heard the shower running. I turned the TV on when I knew she couldn't hear it and couldn't believe all of the channels and how clear the TV picture was compared to what we got from roof antennas in Sunnyside.

I sat on the bed and flipped and flipped channels and finally found the soap opera Mom used to like watching on late afternoons. I turned the volume way down and lay back. It did seem like a clean bed just like the sign said.

The newspaper Mom had asked Hollis to get was beside me so I picked it up and started looking for the funnies section, and I stopped turning pages on the third page and sat up.

There in that evening paper was a small picture of me from fourth grade, a picture of Mom from her wedding photo with Dad, and a military picture of Hollis Thrasher that I could hardly recognize being that he was smiling and had no deep lines in his face or scars or anything. I couldn't believe how much his face had changed from what it looked like now.

Under the pictures it said, Ex-Convict War Hero Breaks out Murderer from Virginia Jail.

I started breathing real fast and tried to read the small paragraph below it, but my hands were shaking the pages so bad I had to lay the whole thing on the bed.

I heard Mom's shower stop and I read the story how Hollis had strong-armed his way into the jail, broke Mom out of there and then kidnapped me. It also said he'd been a suspect in the deaths of his wife and baby who perished in a fire twelve years before.

It said that the FBI and State Police believed the three of us were heading toward Mexico and they'd arrested an eighty-three-year-old black man named Lacy Albert Coe, who police believed aided in the escape.

Mom pushed open the bathroom door with a big smile and I ran to her with the paper in my hands so scared I couldn't say a word. She had a towel wrapped around her and her expression went white when she saw my face and then our pictures.

She grabbed the paper out of my hands, read it quick and her face got angrier than I'd ever seen it my whole life. She threw the paper in the floor and made a terrible noise, and that's when I noticed that her hair was now short, even above her ears and sticking out everywhere. And it was blond.

She didn't even look like my Mom anymore.

I yelled and ran to the room door and opened it wanting to run away back to Lacy, and that's when she grabbed me around the waist, kicked the door shut and both of us went to the floor in a big heap. She kept hugging me until I calmed.

She finally stood and got her towel rearranged and pulled me over to the bed and I sat on the edge.

"That story is full of lies, Charlie. Lies."

"Hollis is a bad man, Momma!" I said.

"No."

"Yes, he is! He's a crazy killer! We got to get away from him."

"He's not crazy. He is not—"

"You always told me to stay away from him!"

"That's because—"

"He got us into this mess and Lacy in it, too. We got to get away…now!"

"No."

"Yes we are."

"No!"

"I think he killed Daddy!"

"Baby…no, baby."

"It says in the paper they still think he killed his own family, Momma."

"Charlie, the reason he was in a hospital is because of all of the terrible things he saw in that war, and then when he came home he saw more terrible things when his wife and little girl died. He did not kill them. He tried to save them and almost died…haven't you seen the burn marks on his neck and arms? He's placed himself in danger to help us, Charlie. Hollis is our friend."

"It says the FBI is after us and they've got Lacy."

I jumped about five feet at the knock on the door that connected our room to the one Hollis was in.

Mom jumped, too, and walked barefooted to the door. She said that she was in the bathroom and would be out in a minute.

She came back and hugged me again.

"Baby, Lacy is going to survive this, just like we are."

"You all shouldn't have gotten him messed up in this, Momma. They're gonna hurt him or kill him over it."

Mom shook her head.

"Don't you know nothing?" I yelled.

"Lacy knew exactly what he was getting himself into. He did this for you, baby. So you would have a chance to grow up like you should. He's going to tell the police that when he woke, you were gone and that's all he knows."

"He won't say that," I said.

"That's exactly what he's going to say."

"Lacy don't tell lies."

"Charlie—"

"He ain't like you, Momma. And they're gonna do something terrible to him. We got to go back and get him out of there."

"No. We can never go back."

What Mom had just said froze me solid. She stood and her head went back real far before she rubbed her eyes and took a peep out the curtains. She kept her back to me and said, "When we get to Maine, we're going to have a long talk and you'll understand why we can't go back. We cannot go back. I'm so sorry this has been so hard on you, and hard on Lacy, too. It breaks my heart, angel."

She finally closed the curtain, turned around and stared at me. "But right now, we need to go, and before we go, I have to cut your hair. We can't look like those pictures in the paper."

I took a breath as deep as I could but it didn't feel like it was going anywhere. I thought about my hair for a second and there wasn't much left since Lacy had gotten hold of it after Thanksgiving. But I didn't know what else to do but yell or cry about the whole mess. I'd already done all of that, and it just made me feel worse.

I was too scared for me, worried sick about Lacy and just plain wrung out to fuss anymore so I sat in the chair she pulled up in front of the bathroom mirror. She cut my hair so short I lost all the dark curls and I just had stubs poking up from the top of my head when she was finished.

I didn't think I could look any stupider unless she'd of shaved it all off like when I got lice one time in first grade, but Mom said it was a handsome haircut for a young man. I didn't care because I just felt like dying.

After I bathed and had the dry heaves in the shower, I put on new clothes and saw everything was loaded back up in the car. I figured that newspaper story had changed our plans to take a nap.

Momma was rushing around wearing a pair of dungarees and I couldn't remember ever seeing her in pants. It seemed like she was changing in all kinds of ways right before my eyes. And I didn't like it. I didn't like it at all.

We got back on the road and Mom passed out the cheeseburger baskets and tall bottles of Coke with paper straws poking out of them. It was one quiet meal. Nobody even asked for more ketchup or burped or anything. I guess the hunger left all of us once we read that news story. We threw away more food than we ate, which was highly unusual for folks like us who ate whatever was paid for whether we liked it or not.

That long, quiet meal where we all chewed slow not looking at each other began a long, quiet journey from the Jetset Motel to Maine as that day and the next and maybe part of the next blended into the days before it. We stopped when someone had to and kept gas in the car and crossed lots of state lines and took all our meals on the highway. I remember we passed scenery and people and things that I hadn't seen before almost like my car window was a movie screen, and Mom got in the back with me some and she told me to go up front some but I wouldn't. I'd sat beside Hollis Thrasher once and never would again.

Finally, one cloudy morning we went over a high bridge painted green with rust all over it. I looked far below at the river with ice up and down the banks and Mom looked back and told me we were in Maine. Her eyes were so happy when she told me. I'd already seen the sign. She smiled. I didn't. She finally let the smile slip away or it did it on its own. She turned around to look out her movie screen window, too, at the new land we were entering. It looked like another planet to me.

I'm not sure how long it took from that bridge to get to the Canadian border; I just know I didn't sleep much of the trip if any and I didn't have anything to say, either. Nobody did. Hollis even quit trying to find something on the radio once we passed a big town called Portland. The farther we went north and the colder it got and the less cars we'd see, the worse I felt alone with Mom and Hollis, watching the two of them in the front seat talking now and then in a hushed tone when I had my eyes closed and they'd share a cold drink or coffee sometimes just like she'd be doing with Daddy if he were alive. She smiled at him or looked concerned now and then just like she'd do with Dad. I hated Hollis Thrasher more and more the closer we got to our fate.

I started hoping the FBI would catch us. I think it was when Mom made and handed Hollis cheese crackers one by one.

I'd learned already on the trip that Hollis was not only calm all the time no matter what was going on, but he was smart—just not in the same way that Lacy and Dad were smart. I figured he messed up somewhere, and I figured Hollis thought the same thing the way he kept checking his mirrors behind us while he ate those cheese crackers.

After the whirlwind of what we did to get Mom out of jail, I just started thinking that people like us should be caught. While we were eating crackers and drinking pop, Dad was planted in the cold ground up on Angel's Rest with a crusty snow on his fake flowers and Lacy was sitting in that damp, dark jail.

Lacy had told me when a good man like John York dies, people think somebody should pay. I believed the same thing. Somebody should pay, and I was sure that somebody was in that car.

Mom and Hollis could run to Maine and live there if they wanted, at least for a while. But I made my mind up on some stretch of road that went on forever between tall, skinny pines and gray boulders that I was going to find my way back to Sunnyside somehow—by train or a bus because I'd been on both before and it wouldn't be too hard to do it I didn't think—but I wouldn't do that until I'd figured out who killed my dad and why he died like he did. My stomach told me I was with the person who'd killed him.

There was no accident.

I hoped it wasn't Momma with all my might as I kept looking at her and felt like throwing up, but I was going to find out if she pulled the trigger on that shotgun. If she did, I was gonna find out why she did it, even though I thought I knew the reason for that already after seeing the way she treated Hollis.

But I suspected more that Hollis killed Dad because a man like him was used to killing and would be good at it. And

I made up my mind in that back seat staring at his eyes in the rearview mirror that I was gonna get him arrested as soon as I was sure of it. This way justice would be served and Lacy could maybe get out of some of the trouble we got him in. Daddy could sleep in peace and me and Momma could go from this icy place back to Sunnyside—if they'd ever let us come back.

I wondered if the police were wrong about the gun, and the one Hollis had in the trunk was the actual gun that killed Dad. I thought Hollis may get to where we were going to and want Momma all to himself. My stomach started coming up in my throat. I yelled "pull over" so I could throw up.

As I leaned out of the car, I felt the cold air drying the sweat on my neck. I spit until it was all out of me and closed the door. Mom was turned around in her seat asking me if I was okay. She pulled my head toward her and wiped my face with a small towel she'd wet with water. After she was finished, she kissed me on the forehead and I leaned back in the seat as far as I could and tried to take in slow breaths. Hollis put the car in gear and looked into the rearview mirror. He was staring right through me. I wondered if those shiny, black eyes were the last thing my Dad ever saw.

Chapter Sixteen

"Those are the lobstermen I was telling you about," Hollis said, as the car jerked and then slid across ice 'til we hit dry pavement again. We were on a winding road that edged along the side of a cliff and I wanted him to be quiet and watch for the ice before he killed all of us.

We hit a clean stretch of road. I looked down below at the rocks and then out across the ocean and couldn't believe people were fishing for lobsters in those small boats in that choppy, dark water. As cold as it was, too. My face was practically stuck to the window looking out at all of the things in this place called Maine.

After climbing that hill, we went down the other side of it and in the low spots Hollis drove careful around clumps of seaweed washed up in the road. We passed a place called Smiley's Campground that was closed and sat on the edge of a beach half-covered in snow, and then through a place Hollis called Pawtuckaway Harbor. It looked like an old western town in the movies to me, except all of the buildings were white and on the other side of the road spread a huge ocean with foam blowing off the waves into the air.

There must have been a dozen or two wooden buildings filled with ice-cream parlors and restaurants with fancy signs, and stores that sold everything from nails to suntan lotion to the people from Boston and Canada who vacationed there in the summers, Hollis said. All of the buildings were boarded up as we drove by. Hollis said the whole town hibernated in winter like a black bear would on Angel's Rest.

"But wait until June," he said. "There'll be people everywhere. Tourists. Swimming and fishing and walking around. We'll come down here, too."

We went around a sharp curve and started up a big rocky knoll that had a bunch of nice houses lined up one after the other. Most of them were as empty as the town, and the snow piled up in the yards had to be taller than me.

"People who own these buy them to rent out to rich folks on vacation. They make a lot of money on them in the summer," he said.

Hollis kept talking and pointing and I looked at Mom because she hadn't said anything in ages. I saw tears in her eyes. They looked like happy tears though as she looked out the windows. I guess she hoped that we may be able to start over in this new place that was covered in snow with no people except lobster fishermen.

The whole place looked like a graveyard to me and the empty houses were tombstones.

"Where's our house?" Mom asked.

"We're coming up on it," Hollis said. "Close your eyes," he told both of us. "Don't open them until I say so."

Mom closed hers but I didn't.

The car finally stopped and I looked all around. About halfway out toward the horizon, there was a small piece of rocky land and on it sat a lighthouse. Everything else was a deep, dark blue in all directions but behind us.

"Where's me and Mom's house?" I asked.

Hollis pointed with his finger at the lighthouse.

I'd never seen a lighthouse before except in books. It was white with small windows at the very top and had a black, shiny lid on top of it. There was nothing between our car and it except for a thirty-foot rocky cliff and the ocean below.

"We're gonna live in a lighthouse?" I asked.

"For a while, Charlie," Hollis said. "See the big house next to it. That's gonna be your house. You and your mom will stay in the downstairs part, and I'll have a room upstairs."

I sat back in the seat when I heard news that I'd been fearing more than anything. He wasn't going away. Hollis looked at me in the rearview mirror.

"Just for a while...."

"You're not staying with us," I said.

Mom turned around and looked at me kind of biting her cheek. No one had said anything about Hollis living in the same house as Mom and me.

Nobody had said that.

"When I was up here getting things set up for you and your mom, I saw an advertisement where they were looking for someone to take care of the place. They took me and a few others on a tour of it, told us what kind of work involved in upkeep and so on and I just thought it may do for a while. Not forever, Charlie. We'll see how things go and if you and your mom like living there, you can probably stay as long as you want. If you don't want to live there, you can find a place just outside of town. Really pretty countryside around, too. Reminds me a lot of Virginia in the warmer months."

"I'm not gonna live in a lighthouse way out there with him, Momma," I said.

Mom was still looking at me and said, "We're just going to try it out. For a few days. If you don't like it, we'll move somewhere else. Just the two of us. I promise, sweetheart."

"How do we get over there?" I asked.

"We have our own boat to get back and forth," Hollis said. He leaned over Mom like a monster and pointed over her shoulder to an inlet. "It's a big, sturdy boat," he said. "I've been on it in rougher water than this."

I didn't like Hollis all leaned over Mom but looked where he was pointing at the boat. It was tied to an orange float. The boat was bigger than any I'd ever been on and had a place in the middle where everyone could get out of the weather. Hollis called it a whaler boat.

I kept watching that boat bob up and down and it scared me to where I started shaking all over that out of all the places Hollis would pick for us to live, he picked an island in the middle of nowhere where it would be just the three of us. I felt like a fox that had just found out it had a snare around its leg.

"Instead of a car to get back and forth, you'll have a boat now. It'll be fun," Mom said.

"You mean I'll have to get on that boat to go to school?" I asked.

"I'm going to home school you for a while, like some of the farm people in Sunnyside do with their children. You'll get up, and we'll go over lessons just like you used to do in school, but we're going to do it at home. And in the afternoons you can help Hollis with the chores and then have your own free time to fish and play and do all the things you love to do."

"I wish Lacy was up here," I said.

Mom looked at me all of a sudden like she was going to fall apart and a gloved hand that pecked on the outside of the window made me jump but not as bad as Mom did. Hollis rolled down his window and a gust of the coldest air I'd ever breathed rolled into the car and there was a woman standing there all bundled up. She looked to me kind of like a large ball of colored twine with straws for legs poking out of it. She had gray hair that was being held down from the wind by a knit cap and about the only thing I could see of her face were her eyes. They looked friendly. I wanted to leave and go with her to wherever she lived.

Hollis stuck out his hand and she took it with hers and he said, "Marie, this is my wife, Emily, and my son, Charles."

I couldn't breathe when Hollis called Mom his wife and

me his son. The lady looked at all of us smiling. You couldn't see the smile but you could tell by the way her eyes crinkled up in the corners.

"Nice to meet you, Mrs. Cutter. Charles," came out muffled from under a blue scarf.

Hollis grabbed his coat and got out of the car. He and the woman spoke for a minute before he opened the door and stuck his head in asking if we were ready to see our new house.

"I'm not your son," I said.

Hollis shivered and stared, and Mom looked like she was about to scream or die or something the way she had her face in both of her hands.

She finally got out and put on her pea coat, but I said I wasn't going anywhere, and that's when she got back in and with her face about a half inch from mine said, "I'm your mother, and I know you're upset…but you're going to do what I say. Now."

She hadn't talked to me like mothers tend to do when they get their feathers ruffled in a long time. Dad used to call it the warpath look and he always told me when you get it from a woman, to do just as told or worse was to follow. Much worse, he always told me. I wasn't scared of Mom like Dad used to be but figured I had no choice but to go.

I grabbed my coat and slung it on. Mom looked at me with the same look but nodded. We all got in Marie's station wagon, drove to where the boat was as the chains on her tires sounded like they were slapping that car to pieces. At the edge of another rocky rise, we got out and all grabbed a rail and walked down slick, stone steps to a concrete dock where Marie used a line to pull the boat over. We all stepped onto the rocking thing that smelled like dead fish when the wind blew a certain way.

The lady seemed out of place at first behind the silver steering wheel as we all crammed into the cabin. But she turned the key and pushed a button and worked two long levers. She drove that boat like she could do it blindfolded through the rocks until we were in open water. She talked the whole time to Hollis and Mom and pointed here and there for stuff I guess they needed to know about running a lighthouse.

I don't know about Mom and Hollis, but I didn't pay attention because I just felt like I was freezing to death and the most important thing, I was paying attention to how she had gotten the boat started and how she drove it. I was gonna need that boat soon, and it would just be me on it unless I could get Momma to leave, too. I did hear how Marie said she loved the lighthouse so much and she was the last person to live there. But she had to move out since her husband of forty years recently passed and she just couldn't bear to be there anymore for the pure lonesomeness of it all.

We went through a bunch of big waves that splashed over the front and a couple of minutes after we'd left one dock, we came to another dock, this one smaller and it was made of dark timbers and lined with old tires that had icy green slime on them. The boat edged right in next to the tires and Hollis limped out and tied off the front and back to rusted hooks.

He helped the lady out even though it was clear to me by now that a strong woman like her didn't need help. Then he helped Mom and reached for me when I was trying to keep my boots from getting wet from the saltwater sloshing around in the boat. I pulled away and got out on my own.

We all walked in a line up a path cleared through the snow to the lighthouse. There was an iron rail along the path but the snow was so high in some spots the rail was covered over. I looked up at the lighthouse and it was so tall, it looked like the closer we got that it was going to fall over and squash all of us.

I couldn't look up at that big tower long because it made me dizzy and cold air kept seeping down the front of my coat. I'd never felt so cold as walking up that hill, and before the lady could even turn the key to the house, I thought my face had froze solid.

We went in, all of them stomping their feet on a mat made out of rope glued together. I tried to wipe my nose but couldn't really feel it. My first thought was, besides Malcolm's house, this house was the biggest house I'd ever seen. It was warm inside, and to me, that was the only good thing about it.

Mom looked around slow, so slow at the huge room and the big stone fireplaces everywhere. I don't think she was hearing one word that lady was saying.

The floors were wide pine like we had in our house in Sunnyside, but in this house most of the walls were covered in pine boards, too. Even some of the high ceilings were covered in thin boards joined real close together and painted white. All the wood floors looked oiled and bright and shiny looking, and I saw Mom bend over and quickly smell the back of a padded chair when the woman had turned away.

Mom ran a hand against each stick of furniture she passed, and to me it looked like the same sort of things we had in our old house but everything looked older and heavier in this one. And there was a lot more of it.

She walked up to Hollis and grabbed his coat sleeve real gentle like she used to grab Dad. And that's when I yelled as loud as I could in the middle of that huge wooden room with the high ceilings.

"I'm going home!"

It just shot right out of me.

The lady showing Hollis and Mom around quit talking. All of them looked at me and then Mom grabbed me by the hand and led me into the kitchen.

"Charlie, you can't do this, not right now. Please, honey. We're going to have a long, good talk when Marie leaves and if you don't want to stay here, we won't stay here. Okay? We'll get on that boat and me and you will find a place to live."

"I'm not staying out here with Hollis, Momma. Why's he have to live here with us? Why can't it just be me and you?"

Mom leaned down. "We need him," she said.

"I don't."

Mom breathed deep and closed her eyes tight for a long minute before she opened them again. It looked like she'd been praying.

"It's going to be all right, Charlie. It's just all too much for you right now and I understand that, but we're going to talk and talk and get it all worked out. Please, please behave as best you can."

I was standing there lost and scared as I could be in that lighthouse in Maine when just a day or more before I was in my house in Sunnyside with Lacy. I wanted to go back right now…with or without Mom.

Mom suddenly picked me up and I thought she was going to give me a whipping in another room. But she held me like she did when I was younger and didn't weigh near as much. She struggled to hold me and kissed my cheek and then put me down. The lady with the nice eyes peeped her head in and said she was going.

"I'll be back with our things in about an hour," Hollis said.

I decided right then I was going back, too, and I was gonna say something to Marie when Hollis couldn't hear.

"I'm going, too," I said.

Mom squeezed my hand, shook her head and then smiled and nodded at the two of them, and after they left, she kept a tight grip on me as we walked all through that big house one room at a time. Mom walked so slow it was like she'd never been in a house before.

There was that living room the size of two or three normal living rooms with the big oval rug covering most of the floor, two big downstairs bedrooms, a bathroom, and a small room.

kitchen had white cabinets and a white-painted floor pretty good slope to it and the whole thing looked ugh for three cooks to cook at once. Beside it there ffice that had two desks and a green, tall radio one of them, and lots of papers that had to do er and tides. Must have been a dozen bulletin boards with stuff pinned up on them all over the walls. Pictures of ships and shipwrecks. It was packed with all sorts of cabinets and thick books and electronic stuff like Dad's old office of the shop. I was most interested in that room because when I saw that radio I knew that was how I could call for help because I didn't see any telephones anywhere. But Mom just took a quick look at that room and that was enough for her. She was more interested in the other small room off the kitchen that had a washing machine in it. She gave that machine and room a careful look over and I couldn't believe out of everything in that house, she'd care so much about a dang washing machine.

After seeing all of the downstairs but the two big bedrooms, Mom pointed out which room would be hers and she told me how the one next to it would be mine, just like our house in Sunnyside. They had a lot of windows and the floors creaked. Mom smelled both beds and both passed her sniff test but I'm not sure by how much.

She sat on hers and then we both sat on mine for a second. It didn't give in too bad. I looked at the two dark wooden dressers in my room. I didn't have enough clothes to even fill a drawer, I thought.

We sat there for a couple of minutes quiet and took our coats. Then we walked up the steep, narrow stairc I was surprised the upstairs wasn't roomier like the stairs. There was only one small bedroom with a l ing and a blue bathroom that just had a sink, toilet shower. It didn't look to me that Hollis could ev all the way under that ceiling or fit in that sh took a close look at the grout work and sneered at the green and black in places.

"This is where Hollis will be staying. Not downstairs with us. Downstairs is our house. Upstairs is his house. Kind of like an apartment building."

"Where's he gonna eat?" I asked.

"He'll be able to use the kitchen and I'll cook enough for all of us," Mom said.

"But he'll take his meals up here, right?"

We were standing in his bedroom and Mom took steps to the one window. She pulled away inside wooden shutters, looked out over the ocean with her hands on her hips like she stood so much of the time. All of a sudden, Hollis's room felt like it didn't have any air in it.

"You sure Hollis didn't have something to do with Dad dying?" I asked.

Mom kept her back turned from me for a few moments and closed the shutters and it was dark again. She turned around and went down on her knees in front of me. She was all teary-eyed again like she seemed to be about half the trip and then I started crying seeing her eyes all watery. I'd never cried so much in my life as I had the last two days even when I'd get whippings, and I just wished my eyes would quit doing it because they were so swollen up I looked like the Perkins boys had given me a pounding.

"No, baby," she said looking right into my eyes and hugged me again. I'd never gotten so many hugs, either. I was hugged out, too.

Mom looked like she was about to fall over from exhaustion and led me downstairs. After we put our coats back on and went out to peek into all the outbuildings and the light-house, we ended up in my bedroom where we both laid down in our coats for a minute trying to warm up. She held me tight in front of her like we were spoons in a drawer.

Mom kept saying, "Shhh…shhh," whenever I tried to ask her more questions and she pulled a blanket over the both of us. I'm not sure when it happened, but I finally fell asleep.

When I woke, it was nighttime and there was a small, hot fire burning in the fireplace across the room from my bed. I could tell the wood was good and seasoned the way it was so lit up and didn't smoke. It scared me thinking that Hollis may have lit it while I was sleeping. That scared me bad.

I heard Mom and Hollis talking quiet in the living room. I listened to the waves against the rocks outside my window and them talking and could also hear that washing machine going full blast.

I got up and had to go to the bathroom but when I got to the door, I stopped.

Hollis and Mom were both sitting on the ends of a long, blue couch talking about something in front of the fireplace that was made of rocks the size of boulders.

I heard my name a couple of times but couldn't make out enough of what they were saying because of the wind out-side and the washing machine going.

I saw that both of them looked worried and tired, but in a happy way it seemed and I couldn't stand it. They didn't look at each other like that when I was around. Hollis never looked at Momma at all if I were around.

They looked a lot like Mom and Dad used to look sitting on a couch having a conversation at night. I stood there until I couldn't hold it anymore, went into the bathroom and passed some water, as Lacy always called it, and walked back in.

Both turned and looked at me and Mom stood. She was wearing the robe she wore in Sunnyside. I guessed Lacy had packed it for her.

"I thought he was staying upstairs," I said.

Hollis stood and it seemed like he filled the whole room when he turned square toward me.

"I am, Charlie, already have all my stuff up there. I'm heading up now. Me and your mom were talking about taking care of the lighthouse. I'll see you in the morning. Good night, everybody."

Hollis made sure the smoky glass doors were closed on all of the fireplaces including the one in my room, checked the dampers, and then checked the woodstove and the furnace setting, then all the doors before he walked upstairs kind of dragging that bum leg. Basically he did all the things Dad and Lacy used to do before they'd retire for the night. I waited until he was all the way to the top and heard the door close at the top of the stairs.

"You want to watch TV?" Mom asked. "We pick up a couple of stations."

"You all were talking about me. I heard you."

"Yes, we were," Mom said. "Come here, baby."

I walked over and sat in a puffy chair that smelled like dust. It was at the end of a dark coffee table that looked like it had been made of split railroad ties.

"After you get used to living in the house with Hollis upstairs, just like Lacy would do if he lived here, and you meet some friends and the weather warms up and you can do all of the things you love to do, I really think you'll like it here. It'll just take time. Some things take time."

"How will I make friends? Ain't gonna be nobody out here but us."

"People love to see lighthouses. They take pictures of them and paint them. And people will come out in nice weather and picnic and fish off of the rocks. People your age. You can fish with them and show them around."

"Nice weather's a long way off, Momma. I don't want to be out here another day."

"Once we get settled in, we'll go into town every week and do things and watch movies and we're going to do a lot of traveling. Just me and you but we'll meet lots of people. You wait and see."

Mom finished what she said and kept looking me in the eyes.

"We're going to have a great Christmas in a couple days. Our first Christmas here and me and you are going to decorate the house and I'm going to make pumpkin pies and we're going to get a tree."

She finished talking about Christmas and I wasn't sure what day of the month it was anymore, but knew it had to be coming up quick. Mom smiled and took a deep breath still looking at me, got up and fixed me a bowl of beans and franks she had on the stove. She carried the bowl back in with a plate of buttered slices of loaf bread and put it all on the coffee table.

"Let's find something on TV," she said.

I sat down and ate a little as Mom tried to get the TV going but she dropped the rabbit ears and couldn't pick up anything.

"We'll ask Hollis about it in the morning," she said. "He had it working fine earlier."

I quit eating and jumped up and walked in front of the old floor-model set. I wiggled the rabbit ears and then checked that the ribbon cable was under the screws in the back like Dad had taught me to do a long time ago. One of the wires had pulled loose and I used my thumbnail as a screwdriver like Dad said a man could do if he was in a pinch for proper tools.

I found a station but it was coming in in a funny language, moved the rabbit ears around some more and then picked up a station that Mom said was out of Caribou, Maine.

I wanted to say that it was pretty obvious we didn't need Hollis to fix the TV, but decided my actions had said enough about that. So I walked back to finish the beans and franks. We both sat quiet and watched the rest of *Gunsmoke*.

After it was over and Matt Dillon had locked up all the bandits and Festus and Doc finished bickering about something and Matt stood with Miss Kitty in the Longbranch Saloon, I sat back and watched the dying fire like Mom was doing.

She pulled my head into her lap and started telling me over and over how lucky she was to have me and how happy she was that we were together again because I meant more to her than anything or anyone else in the whole wide world.

She told me how sorry she was for all the things I'd had to go through the past few months but one day soon I'd come to love living in Pawtuckaway, Maine.

"I don't want Hollis to call you his wife and me his son anymore," I said.

"Honey, he said that because remember part of starting over is that we have to act like a family around other people. It's just acting. That's all. It makes us look…normal to other people."

"I don't want to act," I said.

"I know you don't, baby. Believe me, I don't, either, but sometimes in life you just have to."

"Why's he trying to act like he's my dad? Why couldn't he be like an uncle or a friend like he says he is?"

"It's easier like this. We fit in better to other people as a family and—"

"Do you love him, Momma?"

Mom's hands froze rubbing my head. She pulled me up slow and looked at me but didn't say anything.

"Why did you ask that?" she finally said.

"People talked in Sunnyside saying you and Hollis were doing stuff behind Daddy's back."

"That's not true, Charlie."

"So you don't love him?"

"I care about Hollis. I've known him a long time and he's always been a good friend. He's a very special person to me."

"You care about him like you cared about Daddy?"

She shook her head.

I kept looking at her.

"You loved Daddy, didn't you?"

"Yes, baby," she said. "And you don't have to act like Hollis is your dad when we're here. Just when someone else is around. And if this just doesn't work out, we'll go somewhere else. Okay?"

"I don't like this, Momma."

"I know."

"Dad wouldn't like it, either."

We both looked at the fire a minute more before Mom patted me on the back and stood. She used one finger to wipe under her eyes.

"Did you put your dad's picture up yet?" she asked.

I shook my head.

"Let's go find it," she said. "And then we're going to get a good night's sleep and tomorrow is going to be a great day. It's going to be the biggest adventure. You wait and see."

"This house is too big," I said, listening to the wind and all the strange noises of a new house.

"Did you bring your Abe Lincoln books?"

"They're somewhere...."

Mom looked around. "Maybe you'll let your mom sleep with you tonight like when you were little, if you don't mind. I never liked sleeping by myself in a new house the first night."

All of a sudden it hit me what she'd just done a minute before. "I don't mind, Momma," I finally said, but part of me minded a great deal and I felt all cold and damp and sick to my stomach again.

I don't think Momma had any idea the terrible thing I'd

just seen. She'd spun that diamond ring and wedding band on her finger when I asked if she cared about Hollis. She spun that diamond around and around slow the whole time she answered me, and I couldn't take my eyes off of what she was doing. The only other times Mom would spin that ring was when I'd ask her questions about why Daddy died.

Daddy had taught me a long time ago that the real truth is hard to find in what people say, but their hands and eyes always tell you.

Momma's fingers spinning that shiny ring had just told me Dad was dead because of Hollis Thrasher.

Chapter Seventeen

꧂

There were no voices of other people, no sounds of cars or neighbors or anything. Not even a dog barking. Just the constant sound of the wind and the rumble when the furnace kicked on. I yelled for Mom a couple of times and when no one answered back, I pulled back a heavy curtain and saw that the whaler boat was gone.

Goose bumps spread across my arms and back.

That house out in the middle of the ocean felt way too far from the rest of the world. I stood in the living room wearing my red union suit that first morning in Maine and all I wanted to do was go back to bed and wake up in Sunnyside with Dad and Mom and Lacy and find out that all of this had just been a terrible nightmare.

I went into the kitchen and looked at the clock on the stove that said it was after eleven. I'd never slept so late.

Never. I then saw the note hung up by a magnet on the re-frigerator like Mom used to do in our house in Sunnyside. It said that she'd went to the market in town with Marie and would be back soon and that Hollis was in the machine room off the lighthouse trying to fix one of the generators.

It was just me and Hollis.

I went directly to the radio room and sat looking at all the knobs and switches trying to figure out what I'd need to turn on to call the police when I needed to. I knew I would soon.

I turned one knob and it made a loud squawking noise that made my hair stand up. It wouldn't stop making the noise so I turned it off, backed into the kitchen, looked out the windows for Hollis and saw the plate on top of a stove eye. I took off the other plate covering it and smelled the pile of scrambled eggs with toast and strips of bacon Mom liked to pepper too heavy, Dad always said.

It wasn't nearly as big a breakfast as Lacy always made, but I ate a piece of bacon, grabbed the plate and a fork and walked around the main room and noticed all of the things I didn't notice the day before when we'd first gotten there. Everything in that house smelled and looked like the stuff real old people kept out.

When my plate was empty and I finished looking at the wood carved ducks and the driftwood hanging here and there, I ended up in front of the dark stairway that led up to Hollis's room.

I peeped out the windows again and still didn't see any-body, and knew I'd hear the boat coming so I went up the steps one slow one at a time.

I got about halfway up when I realized maybe Hollis had come back in from the generator room and was now in his bedroom. I stopped and held my breath.

"Hollis?"

I didn't hear anything and stared at the closed door at the top of the stairs. I knew why I wanted to go up there, it was more than simple curiosity like I did when I went into Lacy's room one time snooping around. I did that just to see what an old feller like him would keep on top of his dresser and nightstand.

With Hollis it was different, just like I'd always wondered what was in that tarpapered shack of his up on the mountain. I needed to know if that shotgun was in his room.

I thought for a minute about what I was about to do and listened some more before I decided to go on up. I turned the small brass knob and opened the door and swung my head around, and there was his bed made up with a green wool blanket and folded quilts on top, just like it looked yesterday except this time there were sheets under the blanket.

Except for that and the white pillowcase on the pillow, nothing was different except for a small picture that sat in a frame on top of the nightstand. I walked over to look at it.

I could see pretty well with the light coming through the dirty windowpanes at the head of the bed, but the picture wasn't in good condition the way it was faded and the edges were worn off. I pulled a chain on the bed light.

It was a photo of a baby in a blanket.

I looked at the baby a while longer and didn't see anything else of interest until I thought about seeing what was in his dresser and closet. I heard footsteps downstairs.

I shot out of that room and it was a good thing I did because when I got to the top of the stairs, Hollis was standing below me lit up like he was on stage at the end of that dark staircase.

I froze and couldn't say a thing. I was so scared I actually felt like I was shrinking.

He had on a knit cap and his long army coat. In his good hand that had a glove on it, he held a red pipe wrench.

"Charlie, just wanted to see if you were up. A man's coming over from the mainland to help with the generator, but I could use your help, too, after you get dressed.

"Please," he added.

All I could do was nod while standing there in my union suit and socks. He nodded back and I heard his army boots walk through the kitchen and out the back door.

I started running down those steps but only got halfway and stopped, and then ran back up to his room, turned off the light and bent over beside his bed. I saw something wrapped up in a quilt under there. I grabbed the biggest end of it, and found out like I'd dreaded that it was that shotgun.

About the time I got myself together and washed my face and got dressed, I heard the boat coming, and then another one that sounded different...smaller with a whiny engine, and Mom soon walked through the kitchen door toting two armfuls of groceries. She kicked the door shut.

"How'd you sleep, baby?" she asked.

"Who's in the other boat?" I asked.

"The man who's going to fix the generator."

I looked outside at the docked boat with the small engine hanging off the back. I couldn't believe anybody would go out on big water on such a little metal boat. Then I saw our boat going fast back to shore. There were two people in it.

Mom put down the groceries and tried to shake off a chill. "My gosh it's so cold here." She took a couple steps toward me. "Are you all right?"

"Yes, ma'am."

She looked me over closer.

"Who's in our boat?" I asked.

"Hollis is taking Marie back over to the mainland. He picked her up this morning so she could take me over in the boat and show me around town."

"So she was in the boat with you coming over just now?"

Mom nodded.

"When you get it figured out will you show me how to drive it?" I said.

"Hollis will when it warms up one day soon. He'll show both of us." She stepped back into the kitchen.

"I don't want him to show me, I want you to."

"Okay, honey."

"Does it look hard to drive?"

"Well, I'm not ready to go out by myself, and you're not, either. Listen, I know we're just getting settled in, but I want us to go ahead and get started on your school work. I need to find out where you're at in your lessons."

I had other things I needed to do, like learn how to use that boat and the radio, and get rid of that gun.

"But it's almost Christmas," I said.

"I know. But we're going to start today. Tomorrow and Christmas and through the weekend will just be fun time. No school."

Mom finished stocking the refrigerator, took off her coat and walked to a big oak chest that looked like something a pirate would keep plundered loot in. She opened the squeaky lid and pulled out my schoolbooks and writing tablets.

I couldn't believe it when I saw them and wished Lacy hadn't packed that school stuff because I knew how stern Mom was about children getting a proper education. Especially her child. There was no sense in me learning anything anyway, because I was leaving soon. Mom didn't know that though and she wasn't gonna know until I was long gone if it looked like she wasn't going to go with me. I'd been trying to build a good raft since Daddy died. Now I had a boat.

Mom was putting the books in order on the table and poured herself a cup of coffee. She'd gone to college at James Madison to be a teacher a long time ago, but Dad had never let her work for money because it wouldn't be right for the wife of John York to work. So Mom volunteered at the school, teaching painting and drawing classes, and she helped at the library and basically worked all of those years teaching but never got paid for it.

Once we both sat down at the dining table, her at the head and me at the next chair, she got started and she did sound just like all the other teachers I ever had as she went over things with a long finger pointing at this and that on a page.

We went through each book and worked on numbers and spelling and the names of all the states and where they were and finally, she had me read a short story about a boy and an elephant and write a page report about it.

It took me about an hour to read the story and another hour to write a page. About the time she was going over it marking it all up with a red pen, Hollis walked in with an icy wind that followed him straight from the North Pole. He looked like a mountain of dark clothes coming through the door, except for his face that looked like a beet with a cap on it. I noticed that he was growing a mustache that went all of the way down to his jaw. As mean and dark as he looked usual, I couldn't figure why he'd want to look even meaner, which that dark mustache made him look.

"How's school?" he asked.

Mom said, "Fine."

"The electrician said the Coast Guard should be coming out within the next two weeks to go over a few things."

"Are they going to let us know when they're coming?" Mom asked.

"I don't know," Hollis said.

Mom looked nervous and drummed her fingers on the table. It was the best news I'd heard since we'd gotten here.

Mom had told me when we went to bed the night before how dire important it was to get started off on the right foot because if we could do that, we'd all be fine in the long run.

She'd told me, too, that for a while, I'd have to keep my hair short and all of us wouldn't go to town at the same time. She said that Hollis figured it would make it more unlikely that we'd get caught if, for a while, people didn't see the three of us together. He thought anyone who'd read the story about us or seen our pictures in a newspaper wouldn't put it together as easy that we were fugitives if we weren't all there to look at at the same time. He said it was important, too, at least for a few months, to always keep caps on and heavy clothes like we had around Marie. And if anyone started asking personal questions, to change the subject to something else. Mom said we were going to have meetings about our story to make sure we all say the same thing. She gave me a bunch of examples on how to answer a question without really telling the truth. I was learning that Mom was a lot better at lying than I thought she was.

But she said that Hollis doubted our pictures or even the story of the jail bust-out got in any newspapers up this far north. Too small in the whole scheme of things going on in the world, Mom said. At least they all hoped so. And Hollis was going to go by the post office now and then to see if we were on a FBI poster pinned up and if we were, he'd take it down. But if word did get this far, she said we'd have to move to Canada or some other place and we'd be leaving in a hurry. She told me I had to realize that, at any time, we may have to leave.

I just let her talk and talk that night and never said a word.

"You need help outside?" Mom suddenly asked Hollis.

He nodded standing near the door still stone still. "Whenever he's through with his book work."

"I'm in school," I said.

"We're through for the day. Best student I've ever had,"

Mom said as she gave me a hard hug. "Now go help Tom, Charlie."

I still wasn't used to hearing Hollis called "Tom." The name just didn't fit him. He looked exactly like a Hollis.

"You sure you're all right?" Mom asked.

I nodded even though I was feeling a long way from being all right.

"That's okay if the boy doesn't feel like it. He can help me tomorrow," Hollis or Tom said.

"I'm not a boy," I said, and that was a fact because I was getting almost as tall as Mom.

"Of course you're not. You're a handsome young man," Mom said. "Listen, we're all in this together, and we're going to have to help each other. Get your warm clothes on."

Mom prodded me up and Hollis stood for a minute longer. I just looked at nothing in particular and couldn't imagine living in that house, getting up and doing school-work with Mom, and then helping Hollis run the lighthouse until I found out the truth about Daddy's death. I didn't want to help Hollis do anything but pack his stuff so he would leave or get the FBI to put him in jail.

After he went back out the door to the lighthouse, I wanted to tell Mom about that shotgun under the bed but knew I'd get in trouble for going up there so I didn't. But then a second later I just turned around because it was coming out anyway and said, "Hollis has a shotgun under his bed."

Mom nodded. "What else does he have up there?" she asked.

Mom was pretty smart about getting things out of me but

I could plain see through what she was doing dangling out a noose for me to stick my head in it.

"I don't know."

"Why were you in his room looking under his bed?"

"I thought I heard a noise up there when I got up so I went up there to see what it was."

"You did...."

"Yes, ma'am."

"What was the noise?"

She caught me off guard for a second and I shrugged.

"Did you go through his things?" Mom asked.

"No."

"Are you sure?"

"I didn't go through his drawers or nothing. I just looked under the bed."

Mom took a deep breath. "I'll ask him to lock the gun up somewhere else."

"We don't need any guns out here. I don't want him to have a gun under his bed or anywhere else. He don't need no gun!"

"I'll tell him and it will be gone. I promise," she said. "Okay, baby?"

"I want us to see him get rid of it."

Mom nodded her head. "Okay."

"Who's in that picture in his room?"

"I don't know. I haven't been in his room."

"It's a picture of a baby. He's got it framed but the picture looks all worn out."

"We'll go up there this one time," she said. "But not again

unless Tom invites us up or we need to go up there with his permission, understand?"

I nodded and Mom stood and grabbed my hand and both of us walked up the stairs to Hollis's room. She bent down and looked at the picture and smiled.

"That was his baby girl, Sarah."

"She the one that died in that fire at his old house on the mountain?"

"It was such an awful thing. Was just awful." Mom looked at the picture a few more moments and then said, "Come on, honey. We shouldn't be up here."

"What caused the fire," I asked.

"They never were sure—but it started from the fireplace. Hollis…Tom was walking home from being downtown one night and saw his house burning. By the time he got to it, he tried to save them but it was too late. Come on, you need to go out and help Tom and this evening we're going to start getting ready for Christmas."

"Seems like he'd frame a better picture than that one all torn up like it is."

"Well, it looks like a picture he'd keep in his wallet. He lost almost everything in that fire. Could be the only picture he has of her, I don't know."

When we got down to the bottom of the stairs, Mom grabbed my coat from one of the iron hooks that ran along the wall next to the kitchen. She started to help me put it on but I took it from her because I didn't need help. Then I put on the gloves and the hat with earflaps she'd picked up for me and when I opened that kitchen door, I again couldn't believe how cold it was outside. That wind blew right through me in a thousand places.

I ducked my head into my shoulders and walked as fast as I could through the crunchy snow to the white brick generator room attached to the bottom of the lighthouse. Mom had shown the room to me the day before after we peeped up into the lighthouse. She'd told me I could walk up the winding staircase to the top to take a look but I didn't want to go. I think she thought I was scared to climb up there, but I just didn't want to go up and look out and see how far we were from the people who didn't have to live in a lighthouse.

When I opened the door of the generator room, Hollis and the electrician were both on their knees looking at the noisy motors. They both had their backs to me and I saw the metal toolbox that was laying there. It looked a lot like the green metal toolbox Dad used to have and that I'd carried into every house in Sunnyside that had a TV.

I bent down and started looking at it and poked a finger in.

"Hey, leave those tools alone!" the man said in a voice so loud I thought he must've thought I couldn't hear very good.

I stood up fast and backed away and the man turned back to look at the generator. Then Hollis stood and he had a real strange look on his face like he had an itch that he couldn't get to.

"Charlie, ask your Mom for a rag and bring it to me. Please."

I didn't want to do anything for him and dreaded facing

that wind again, but I walked outside and was about to shut the door when I heard Hollis tell the electrician, "Mister, don't ever speak to my son again in that tone of voice."

I kept that thick wooden door cracked just a little and put my ear up to it.

The man said, "I didn't mean anything. I just didn't want him messing with my tools."

Then Hollis said, "I'll tell him to stay out of them, but I'm telling you not to speak to him again like you just did. I won't stand for it."

I stood a few moments longer and didn't hear anything else but the metal on metal sound of tools doing stuff, so I closed the door the rest of the way until it latched, then ran to the house, fell down once and then got up and threw open the kitchen door.

"Are you all right?" Mom asked.

I looked under the kitchen sink and pulled out a dust rag hanging over a can of wax spray. When I stood up, Mom was standing there.

"What do you need, honey?"

"Hollis needs a rag."

She took the dusting rag from me. "You're all out of breath. And it's Tom. Tom needs a rag."

Mom opened the broom closet and pulled out a clean rag, shook it and handed it to me. By the time I got back out to the engine room the electric man was leaving. He nodded at me walking out the door and stared at me with small eyes sitting above a big red beard.

"You got it?" Hollis asked me.

I walked over and handed the rag to him and he began wiping his hands. I couldn't believe he'd be sweating in that cold room but I saw the beads just under his cap.

"We got something else to do," he said. "Need to get up to the crow's nest and show you around a little bit."

"Where's that?"

"Top of the lighthouse."

"I don't want to go up there," I said.

He kept wiping grease off his hands. "I don't, either. I never did like heights. Never did like them."

"Why you want to live in a lighthouse if you don't like heights?"

Hollis shrugged. "That's a good question. I have to go up there, though. I was hoping you'd go up there with me. I know how you used to help your dad with electrical things and I need to check the lens. Part of my job."

"You don't need me," I said.

Hollis draped the rag over a pipe. "Have you been up?" he asked.

I shook my head.

"Well, if you don't want to go that's okay. I'll see you and your mom later. Sun gets low quick up here and I don't want to be up there in the dark."

He put his gloves back on and prodded me on the shoulder with one hand and we went out the door and he latched it so the wind wouldn't blow it open.

I squinted to see my eyes were tearing up so fast from the gusts. I started walking toward the house and before I passed the wood shed, I turned around and saw Hollis making his way through the snow path and scrubby pines at the bottom of the lighthouse. I decided to follow him.

He opened the door and started to shut it behind him when I pushed it open. We both went in and stomped our feet and looked up that spiral black staircase. He pulled a cigarette out of the pack with his teeth and lit it with a silver lighter. He took a shiver and I did, too. He then flipped a switch and bare bulbs placed about every twelve feet came on all the way to the top. He only took one or two puffs looking up and then squished out the ashes with his glove fingers and stuck what was left of the cigarette in his coat pocket.

He pointed to a red switch and turned it off. "When you come in here, turn this off. The light works automatic on a timer, but just to be safe, turn this off to make sure it doesn't come on when you're in here. So turn it off, then turn it back on when you leave."

I nodded my head. Hollis looked up.

"Guess I'd better get to it," he said, and started climbing slow with his bad leg.

He never looked back and I watched him get halfway to the top and then I started up the stairs. I wasn't scared of heights, at least I didn't think I was. I didn't like being in there with him, though. But I was going up for some reason.

Chapter Eighteen

⚜

I caught up to him before he was all the way to the top. He stopped on a small metal grate that seemed shaky the way it would move when we moved. Hollis pulled off his coat, then pulled out a handkerchief and wiped his face before throwing the coat over one arm and heading up the rest of the way.

The spirals got smaller and, at the very top, turned into a regular set of wood stairs that were narrower than the rest of the staircase. Both of us stopped before we went up them and looked down.

"Long way, ain't it?" Hollis said.

"Doesn't scare me."

"Does me," he said. "My balance isn't what it used to be."

I couldn't believe Hollis would be scared of anything as he went up first. I followed him to the very top where there was a circle of metal grate around a shiny lamp the size of two canning tubs. The glass was so thick and looked like it had giant bee honeycomb in it and the whole thing looked like it weighed more than a car.

"Don't ever look at it in here when it's on," Hollis said. "It'll blind you. Remember to throw that switch at the bottom."

I thought that was good advice because I probably would be tempted to look at it just for a second.

As I looked at that lens and then out all of the glass windows surrounding it, Hollis opened a metal locker and pulled out spray bottles and some more rags, but he said these were special rags, real soft and clean. I pulled my hand out of a glove to feel one of them.

"Need to wipe down the lens and the windows," he said. "Very important so ships can see the light way off."

Hollis checked the rag and then wiped the big oval lens. He then walked to one of the windows and looked out across the ocean.

"You get the inside ones and I'll get the outside ones from the catwalk," he said. "You ever cleaned a window?"

I nodded that I had even though I hadn't and looked at the two dirty glass panes he pointed to. And then I looked at what he'd just called a catwalk.

"You scared of going out there?" I asked.

"I've never been comfortable high up," he said pulling on his coat. "But it's got to be done. Fog's supposed to be setting in tonight when the wind lays. Ships need to be able to see the light. Very important these windows stay clean."

Hollis undid a bolt latch and opened the small wooden door. A gust hit me like someone was pushing me backward.

I was scared about going out there when that happened, and especially once I saw the narrow metal grate circle around the outside of the light. I walked to the door and looked down at the ocean under my feet moving toward the shore in huge swells that never stopped. Another gust blew and I felt the lighthouse move in the wind. Every gust it moved a little or it seemed like it.

Hollis bent over and stepped out with his back to the windows and I took a couple of careful steps out and saw Hollis had a hold of the back of my coat. That scared me—him having hold of me like that—so I grabbed the metal railing and looked back at him.

"Pretty windy," he yelled.

"Yeah," I yelled back.

I held on to the black painted rail with a death grip and finally he let go of me and motioned for me to go back inside. I didn't let go of the rail until he'd let go of me. I thought that minute we stood out there was longer than either of us could stand it.

"Go back in. Too cold," he yelled.

I let go of the rail with one hand and grabbed the door with the other.

He looked like he was going back in, too, but when I walked through the door he closed it behind me. I stood inside and watched him inch his way to the dirty windows. He pulled out the spray bottle with cleaner and antifreeze in it from his coat pocket and had a rag in his other hand. He sprayed the windows and wiped them down quick.

"Whew," he said, coming in and shutting that door a few minutes later.

His face where it wasn't scarred and burned was dark red.

"That's enough for today. The rest of them aren't bad and we'll get them tomorrow. It's supposed to warm up to around thirty, tomorrow."

We both stood there and he moved around a lot on his one good leg and swung his arms back and forth and made all kinds of noises trying to warm up.

"Don't ever go out there by yourself," he said. "Especially in bad weather. Always tell your mom or me if you're coming up here."

"I'd never come up here," I said.

Hollis put the bottle and rags back in the locker.

"You might on a nice spring day with a friend or something to take in the view. Whales out there, Charlie. All kinds of them. You can sit up here and watch them, Marie told me."

"What do they do?" I asked.

"They swim around. I'm not sure what all they do to be honest. You'll see all kinds of things, though. Jellyfish and stingrays and birds and all kinds of fish. Being up here is kind of like being up on top of Angel's Rest."

"You been all the way up to the top of the mountain?" I asked.

"A few times," he said. "Used to grouse hunt up there around the holidays."

"Did you go to the top of Widow's Watch?"

"Yep. Climbed up there once."

"I thought you were scared of heights," I said.

"I was a lot younger then. But climbing a mountain is a lot different to me than climbing up into a tower like this in the middle of the ocean, you know?"

He looked at me a minute with those eyes and then we both looked out across the water and I could see the town a mile away covered in snow and cars and trucks going wherever they were going. The whole place looked like a toy set.

"Why don't you like living near people?" I asked.

Hollis was still breathing hard and pulled out his handkerchief to wipe his nose.

"I like people," he said.

"But this place is like your place sitting alone up on the mountain."

Hollis nodded. "I guess it is."

"I like living near people. So does Mom."

Hollis looked down the stairwell. "You ready to go back down. Bet your mom's got your supper on the stove by now."

"What did you do up on that mountain by yourself?" I asked.

Hollis took a deep breath and put a gloved hand on top of the metal cap over the light housing. "I made things. Carved things. I tried to make a good fiddle for a long time but never could get one to sound right."

"You play a fiddle?"

"I used to before I hurt my hand in the war. Played the guitar and banjo, too. Fingers won't work right now though."

"What else did you make?"

"I carved ducks and just anything I could think of that I could take to flea markets and sell. Made a little money. Not much."

"So you just stayed in there by yourself and carved?"

"I…it wasn't so much toward the end that I didn't want to be around people. It was more like I knew they didn't want to be around me."

"Why didn't they want to be around you?" I asked.

"Well, people started shying away from me when I got out of the hospital, and then they said that I had something to do with the fire…know you've heard about all that. Sure you've heard some pretty bad things about me, Charlie. Things that aren't true. It just got to be where I'd rather be by myself, I guess. Less trouble for everybody that way, but I wish I'd have never done it, spending so much time alone that is. Isn't good to get too comfortable in the quiet. Start needing it after a while or something. Let's head on down."

"I heard you killed some men in a pool hall."

"I hit a man and he fell hard against a concrete floor…it hurt him bad. I didn't kill him."

"Did you mean to hurt him?"

"I was drunk, Charlie. I don't even know what we were fighting over."

"They threw you in prison for getting in a fight?"

"Like I said, he got hurt pretty bad when his head hit that floor, and I'd already had a couple problems with the law by that time. Little things, I guess, but they started adding up."

"When did you decide to get all cleaned up and come up here looking for a place for me and Mom?"

"I didn't plan on coming up here at first to find a place for you and your mom."

"You didn't?"

"I was looking for a place for me."

Hollis looked at me and I looked at him. We just kept looking at each other. Finally he said, "I've been trying to get away from my problems for a long time. That's what I was doing…I wanted to go somewhere new and start over, but when I got up here, I realized all my problems had followed me. You know what I'm saying?"

"No," I said.

"My problem was the man I saw in the mirror every morning. That's a bad thing when that happens, Charlie."

"Why didn't you like what you saw in the mirror?" I asked.

"Well, put it this way. I wanted things to be different."

"So what made you come back to help Mom?"

"I needed to do something for somebody else for a change, I guess. Something like that."

I looked him as hard in the eye as I could even though it was just the two of us up there. I was pretty shaky but I knew Hollis would never catch me going down those stairs and I already had one foot on them. I could feel my voice tightening up.

"'Cause you care for Momma?"

"I care for your mom."

"Did you care for my dad, too?"

Hollis went from moving around to standing still. "I liked your dad. I hate what happened to him, Charlie. Always respected your dad."

"But you care for Mom more...."

"Well, your mom needed help after your dad died. That day you saw me leaving with the suitcase in Sunnyside, I wasn't planning on coming back. I was leaving that town and everyone I'd ever known. But after I walked you home and went back to catch the bus, Lacy came down and had a little talk with me. He's a sharp feller, Lacy. He sat beside me on that bench and told me a man every day has the choice of acting out of strength or weakness. He said both things are inside of every man. Like good and bad. They're in there, too, he said."

Hollis finished talking and we both stood for a minute in the cold draft of that lighthouse.

"What else did he say?"

"That's about it and he got back in your dad's truck and pulled away."

I grabbed the rail and took one step down. "Why were you seeing Momma late at the library before Dad got killed?"

"I wasn't seeing her. I'd stop in now and then. We'd talk. She's about the only real friend I've had in that town for years. I ran everyone else off who cared about me in one way or another."

"Police wanted to ask you questions about Daddy getting killed."

Hollis went to reach for me and I took another step.

"They got a warrant for you. That's why you left."

"They didn't have a warrant for me when I left."

"They got one right after you did."

"Charlie, I don't know what you're thinking or what you've heard, but I didn't kill your dad."

"I didn't say you killed him," I barely got out.

"Well, I didn't."

"You didn't have nothing to do with him dying?"

"It was an accident."

"That ain't what I asked...."

"Charlie, your Dad wasn't killed. He died in an accident."

"That ain't what the police said."

"That's what it was, Charlie."

"Someone pointed a gun at him and shot him."

Hollis looked like I'd kicked him where it hurt all of a sudden. He took off a glove and then pulled off his cap. He ran one hand through his hair pushing it away from his face before he put the cap back on.

He started to say something and then stopped. For the first time, I could tell he was nervous and all pent up with something he couldn't get out. He didn't have that usual hard look about him. He looked out the window for a second and when he turned around he reached for me and I took off running down the stairs as fast as I could go.

Mom grabbed my arm as I shot through the kitchen door. I tore away from her and heard her fall in a big thud behind me but I didn't look back.

"Charlie!"

I ran up the dark steps to Hollis's room, locked the door and threw open every drawer until I found what I'd hoped I'd find. His money roll that I'd seen him pull from his pocket on the trip to Maine.

I grabbed the wad and stuffed it in my coat pocket when

I heard someone coming up the stairs. Mom pounded and kicked on the door.

"Open the door, Charlie…open up, baby," she said.

I opened the door and she looked scared at my hands before looking at my eyes. She was crying.

"What's wrong, sweetheart?" she asked.

I heard the heavy footsteps coming across the floor downstairs and pushed Mom out of the way. She had me by the back of my coat, yelling for me to stop and I was halfway down when Hollis stepped in front of me. I kept going.

"Charlie, listen…." he said.

He didn't try to grab me as I ran into him hard with my hands out in front of me, knocking him backward. I got to the kitchen door and had a hard time getting it open as Mom screamed for me to come back.

The knob finally turned and I yanked the door open so hard the glass broke and that's when I felt Hollis's hand on my shoulder. I turned around and hit him as hard as I could in the face and took off down the path to the dock. I didn't realize it until I tried to unhook the lines to the boat that my whole right arm was numb from the blow and wouldn't work.

I pulled off both gloves and fought with the knot and looked back toward the house and saw Hollis limping down the hill.

"Wait a minute, Charlie!" he yelled.

The one hand that wasn't numb felt like it was freezing as I finally got one line undone and ran to the other one. I slipped and fell on the ice, got up and by the time I was at the timber that held the line tight, Hollis was standing a few feet from me.

"Where you going?" he asked.

I turned and got the line undone and jumped into the boat. I fought with the cabin door just like I'd done with the kitchen door and felt the weight of the boat shift. I looked over my shoulder as I got the cabin door open and Hollis was walking up the back of the boat toward me. I threw the latch on the door. I went to turn when he held up a gloved hand holding a piece of yellow foam that had a key dangling from it.

I looked at the bare keyhole in the ignition.

I was breathing so fast I felt light-headed and thought I was gonna fall down. I looked out over the water. The sky was turning dark and lights were coming on in town less than a mile from me. I slid one of the windows open and started screaming for help.

The boat shifted again and I thought Hollis was coming at me but it was Mom. She pressed her face to the window-pane and opened the door. I thought I'd locked it and backed away from both of them and just busted out crying and screaming. She tried to hold me but I pushed her and then we both fell. I saw Hollis was now standing on the dock. I crawled out of the cabin, jumped out of the boat and ran toward the house. My lungs and throat burned like they had gasoline in them. I could hear Hollis's feet crunching the snow behind me.

I got to the house and the door was open. I fell on the glass, got up and locked the door and went into the radio room and started throwing on all kinds of switches. There was a loud racket and I turned some knobs and grabbed the microphone stand. I pressed both buttons at the bottom down and yelled for help in it.

I could hear Hollis pushing and pulling on the kitchen door. More glass broke and that stomp-dragging sound of him walking came into the house.

"This is the lighthouse. I need the police. Someone get the police! This is Charlie—" I screamed into the microphone.

Hollis jerked it out of my hand and I went to run and he pushed me back into a chair. The side of his head near his eye was bleeding down his face.

"This is Pawtuckaway P.D. Identify yourself."

I froze looking at Hollis and he looked at me and just kept shaking his head.

"Please identify yourself."

Mom walked around the corner and leaned against the wall. She wasn't wearing a coat and looked frozen. She finally wrapped her arms around herself.

"Charlie…what's going on?"

"He's called the police," Hollis said.

I pushed the chair back as far as I could from them and stared at the radio.

"What's happened?" she asked. She walked toward me slow. "What happened?"

"Please identify yourself caller and state the emergency."

Mom looked at the radio, then at Hollis and started crying.

"Charlie, what have you done?" she said in a terrible loud voice.

"Can you hear me, Light?"

Mom's legs went out from under her slow as she slid down

the side of the wall. She just kept looking at me crying, shaking her head.

"Pawtuckaway Light, we're going to send a boat out to your location, copy?"

Hollis pulled the microphone up to his mouth.

"This is Tom Cutter, the new keeper at Pawtuckaway Light. We had a minor scare out here but we're fine now. We don't need any assistance. Thank you."

I jumped up to grab the microphone and Hollis kept me back with one arm. There was a long silence in the room except for Momma crying.

"Shore patrol is on the way."

"That's not needed," Hollis said.

"They're out now and will be at your location in a couple of minutes."

Hollis dropped the microphone down to his side like it weighed a ton. He put it back on the desk and flipped off the switches on the radio.

"What're we gonna do?" Mom asked him.

Hollis shook his head, pulled open a curtain and looked out across the water. I could see the sky was almost black. The sound of us all breathing heavy and Mom sniffing filled the room.

"There's a boat pulling out of the harbor. We have to go. Now," Hollis said.

Hollis grabbed Mom's hand and helped her up.

"Why did you call the police!" Mom screamed at me.

I pointed at Hollis. "He killed Daddy, Momma. He killed him."

"We don't have time for this," Hollis said. "We need to go!"

Mom grabbed me by one arm. I tried to pull away and the harder I tried the harder she held onto me. She yanked me into the living room and threw me into a big padded chair and shook me back and forth by my shoulders.

"You were in on it, too, weren't you, Momma."

She slapped me and got on her knees between my legs and then grabbed both my hands. Her eyes were wild.

"Hollis didn't kill your father. The gun was in your hands when it went off, Charlie. It was in your hands."

I couldn't move.

"It was in your hands, baby…"

Chapter Nineteen

Mom cried soft from somewhere deep inside her and I'd stopped struggling. My arms and legs felt numb and I couldn't breathe. It felt like I'd been alone in this long, long, dark hallway and all of a sudden a doorway at the very end I wasn't sure was there began opening up. I thought I was gonna get sick and tried to pull away but Momma wouldn't let me.

"You pointed the gun at your dad because he was beating me, dragging me around the kitchen by my hair. You tried to stop him. He threw you out of the room once and you came back in and you tried to hit him to get him off of me. He threw you out in the yard and when you came back in and grabbed him again, he hit you hard. And then he grabbed me again. You can't remember because it was such a horrible thing. You were traumatized and still are by it. I couldn't find a way to tell you…you pushed that day so far from your memory. You're just a little boy…I was afraid to tell you the truth, Charlie. I was afraid of what it would do to you and what would happen to you if I did. I lost my husband. I couldn't lose you. Do you understand that? I just couldn't. It was the only thing I knew to—"

"I didn't do it, Momma…I didn't—"

"Charlie, the shotgun was in your hands but it was an accident. It was an accident, just like we've been telling you over and over and over. It was an accident!"

Mom stopped talking and took a deep breath and wrapped me in her arms. I couldn't say anything as a hurricane of bad visions came into my head. She'd just told me pieces of the exact same dreams I'd had about a gun and Daddy laying dead in the floor. Him yelling and hitting her. Hitting me. And then I felt myself holding that gun.

That evening came rushing back with all the pieces put together like I wasn't in a lighthouse anymore but back in Sunnyside on that day.

I saw Dad with Mom's hair all balled up in one hand, smacking her across the face and head with the other, as she was on her knees screaming at him to stop. And I did try to stop him. I tried three times and finally after he hit me that last time, I remember running into their bedroom and getting the shotgun out of their closet. I went back in and pointed it at him just like he'd always taught me to do to scare away somebody who'd ever try to hurt Momma. I could remember seeing his face change when he turned and saw me standing there, that gun shaking so bad in my hands that I could hardly hold it and I couldn't say one word. I couldn't speak. He finally let go of Mom and put his head in his hands and collapsed into a chair and cried and it was a terrible low sound. I'd seen Dad hurt before but never seen him cry. He slumped over with his head between his knees. Then he stood all of a sudden and walked to Mom and helped her up, then walked to me with his eyes closed tight.

He opened them up a little when he got close to me, wiped his face on his sleeve, and pinched the top of his nose with one hand covering up his eyes. With the other hand, he grabbed the very end of the gun barrel.

A loud noise exploded in that kitchen. The gun flew out of my hands, Daddy fell back into the kitchen table before he hit the ground holding his stomach and there was blood on the floor and the walls and cabinets, and then my knees just went out from under me and I hit the floor, too, and Mom ran to him, trying to stop the bleeding from his belly with her apron.

I inched my way across on my hands and knees and was crying and telling him I was sorry and I didn't mean to shoot him and he just laid there shaking his head back and forth. He looked down at his stomach and then at me and Mom and real soft said, "I'm sorry." He could barely get it out and then he said I'm sorry again and again. And then he told us to tell the police that he was cleaning his gun and it went off and we never saw what happened. He told me to get his cleaning kit, which I ran and did. He then told me to get it out and put it on the table. I did. He said he was going to tell the police that he'd accidentally shot himself, but he never got a chance to say anything else to nobody but us. I remembered Mom jumping up and grabbing the phone and she kept trying to dial the hospital but her hands were all bloody and she couldn't get her fingers to work right so I dialed it and told them that Daddy was shot. After I called for help, I went back by his side next to Mom, who was holding and kissing his head, and he had quit moving and his eyes were open but they didn't cry or blink anymore. I remember walking out of the room, getting on the couch and throwing up all over it before I sat there and started watching TV as Mom let out the longest wail that just wouldn't stop.

"We gotta do something," Hollis suddenly said.

The sound of his voice brought me out that awful memory, and Mom unwrapped her arms from me and kissed my forehead. She turned and looked at Hollis, who was looking out one curtain.

"They're pulling up to the dock," he said.

Mom let out a huge breath and stood. Her shoulders slumped down and her fingers dug at her pants.

"I didn't shoot Daddy on purpose, Mommy. I could never do such a thing. I could never do it, I don't care what he'd do."

Mom turned back around and pulled me tight against her. "Shhh...shhh. I know, baby. I know."

"I could've never shot him on purpose."

"Shhh...Charlie, when he grabbed the gun, it went off."

"I must've had my finger on the trigger or near it or something caught on it when he pulled the end of the barrel away from—"

"Shhh. I know! No one was more surprised than you

when it went off. You didn't do it on purpose, baby. Listen to me," she said grabbing my face. "We all know that. We've all known it all along."

"Who's we?" I asked.

"Your dad, Lacy, me, Hollis, and I'm sure Malcolm knew."

I looked over at Hollis, then at Mom.

"Why was Dad so mad, Momma? He never done nothing like that before...."

"They're coming up the path!" Hollis said.

Mom moved her ice-cold hands to my cheeks and looked right into my eyes. "We've come too far to get caught now. We've come too far, do you understand?"

A loud knock at the door.

Hollis paced back and forth. "Goddamn it," he said in a quiet voice.

"Police department."

Mom kept holding my face tight before she finally let go of me. She stood and wiped her eyes and Hollis stood still, like he didn't know what to do. Mom ran to him and yanking the inside of her shirt out, wet the end of it, grabbed his head and used her shirt to wipe the blood off his face where I'd hit him.

"Police department. Open up."

Mom tried to tuck in her shirt but it still looked a mess.

Hollis looked at the door, then at Mom and me and pulled both hands out of his gloves. He opened the door and stood in front of it.

Where I was sitting I was staring right into Hollis's back, which took up the whole doorway. Two policemen with heavy, shiny coats and fur hats on stepped around Hollis, stomping their boots. I could see they both had guns poking down from one side of their long coats and they didn't have gloves on.

"How we doing this evening?" the shorter of them finally said.

Mom smiled and sniffed. But nobody said anything back to them.

"You folks doing okay?" he asked again.

"We're fine," Hollis said.

The skinnier, taller policeman walked around Hollis toward me.

"Are you the one who called us on the radio?"

I was still sitting back in the chair and didn't know what to say.

"He—" Mom started to say, before the man turned quickly toward her.

"I'm talking to him."

He turned back toward me and bent down. "Did you call us?"

I nodded.

"What's your name?"

"I'm Charlie—"

"I'm Tom Cutter, this is my wife, Emily, and my son Charlie," Hollis interrupted in a calm, loud voice.

The policeman who was in front of me bent down never turning away from me. "Hi, Charlie," he said. "My name is Officer Gagnon. What can we help you with?"

I looked over at Mom and her eyes were wide as the bottom of a jelly glass.

"The boy got a little scared—" Hollis started saying.

The policeman who was bent down stood up quick. "Let's let Charlie talk."

I looked at Mom and Hollis and both policemen and everybody was looking at me.

"I thought I saw a ghost," I said.

Officer Gagnon looked at the other policeman and then pulled up a stool, which he sat on, then his face got really serious.

"Where?" he asked.

"In the lighthouse."

"I see. What did it look like?"

"It looked like a ghost," I said.

"Was it a man ghost or a woman ghost?"

"It was a boy ghost."

"A boy ghost...."

I nodded.

"What did it do?"

"It was following me."

I watched the policeman look me over, then he patted me on the leg and motioned for Hollis and Mom to go over to the dining table. I watched as both officers stood on different sides of Hollis and asked questions. It looked like Mom did most of the talking. I caught some of it, like Mom saying we'd moved from Greensboro, North Carolina, because she and Hollis were both artists, she was a painter and he was a sculptor and they wanted to...she said they wanted to "broaden my horizons" before I entered high school. She said that we were only planning to be there a couple of years. Somewhere in their conversation when my mind was still going over and trying to get away from that terrible night in Sunnyside, they all ended up sitting at the dining room table drinking coffee and one of the officers called me back over.

I went and stood beside Mom. Hollis got up and I slid in beside her. Officer Gagnon pushed away his fur hat on the table that was between me and him so he could see me better.

"You like living out here with your mom and dad?" he asked.

I just sat and my leg started bouncing up and down. I felt Mom's hand rest on my thigh.

"Charlie, your mom tells me you have a big imagination and that's a good thing. But I've known the people all of my life who were taking care of this lighthouse before you and your family, and I've never once heard about a ghost."

I nodded.

"There aren't any ghosts."

My leg was still going up and down and I stared at him. He never took his eyes off of me.

"Well, it was good to meet you all. If you ever need us, you know how to get hold of us," he said, getting up. "Come here, Charlie," he said.

He put his fur hat back on and walked toward the kitchen door. When I walked up to him he kneeled down and said quiet, "If you ever need us, for anything, you call. Okay. We're only a couple minutes away. If you ever need to talk about something, anything. Maybe something you'd want to talk about when your parents aren't around...you call."

"Okay," I said.

"That a promise?"

"Yes, sir."

"Are you feeling better now?"

I nodded my head.

He stood and both officers were now at the door. They nodded and opened it to leave when the tall one turned around. "How'd the glass get broken in the kitchen again?" he asked.

"Charlie was trying to get back into the house and he was…excited and broke the glass to get the door open," Hollis said.

"I see," he said.

The officer continued to look at Hollis. "Is that how you got the cut above your eye?"

Hollis walked closer to the officer, shaking his head. "I got that trying to catch up with him. I didn't know what was going on. He came in running scared…I fell trying to catch up to him."

"Ahhh…" The officer nodded. It looked like he was studying all of the old scars on Hollis's face. "Can I have a word with you outside, Mrs. Cutter?"

Mom looked surprised and went and got her coat. She tried to button it up but her hands were shaking so she gave up and wrapped it around herself. She walked out with both officers and I looked at Hollis, who had the same look he had on his face that time at the shop when I'd yelled that he'd killed the missing Wilson twins. I ran to the bathroom and got sick in that old rusty stained toilet bowl, and when I came out Mom and Hollis were both sitting at the table.

"Come here, baby," Mom said.

I shook my head. "Why was Daddy so mad that day, Momma?"

Mom stood and walked across the big oval living room rug toward me. Her fingers started spinning that ring.

I ran into my bedroom and locked the door.

"Open up, Charlie."

"No."

I backed up to the bed and sat and watched the old painted doorknob work back and forth.

"I did something that he found out about…and it hurt him. It hurt him badly."

"You did something bad?"

"No," she said. "It wasn't bad I don't think, but it hurt him. It made him very angry. I never meant to hurt him. I'd never intentionally hurt him."

I grabbed the pillow, held it in front of me and unlocked the door. I pulled it open and she was crying. I looked around for Hollis and heard his footsteps going up the stairs.

"What'd you do to Daddy?"

"I can't tell you now, Charlie. But you'll learn some day when you're older and will be able to understand, but not now. But I want you…I need you to forgive me. To trust that I wouldn't intentionally do anything bad to your father."

"You sure it wasn't bad?"

"Sometimes adults do things which aren't bad that hurt other people. I don't want you to think bad things about your dad, either, for getting so upset. That's the only time he ever raised a hand to me. We have to go on now, Charlie. Your dad would want us to go on."

"Was Dad mad at Hollis?"

"No. He was mad at me."

"Was he mad at me, too?"

"No, baby. Your dad loved you more than anything in the whole world."

"Did Daddy love you?"

Mom nodded and looked sad. "He did."

"I wish he was here. I wish you'd of never hurt him and he never found out and was beating on you like he was."

"I know," she said.

"I wish I'd never tried to scare him away from you with that gun."

"I know."

"I didn't mean to shoot him, Momma. I just wanted him to stop hitting on you."

"Charlie, we have to start over now."

"But how we gonna do that?"

"We've been starting over," she said. "It just doesn't seem like it. But it will, baby. It will."

Chapter Twenty

It didn't seem like Christmas morning to me seeing Mom mopping the whole house wearing her thick blue robe. She was straining so hard against that mop handle it looked like she was trying to get the brown linoleum off of the bathroom floor. I waited until her back was turned and ran to the stairwell going up to Hollis's room. I knew he was outside doing something in the shack because I heard a circle saw whining and hammering coming from there.

I crept up the stairs as quiet as I could and got his small squeaky door open. I'd seen something two days before in one of his drawers just before Momma came in as I was ransacking trying to find his wad of money. It was a small photo album. After I'd thrown it on the floor with a bunch of other stuff from Hollis's drawer before I ran past

Momma, I'd seen a picture of me fly across the floor. At least it looked like me.

I got to the top of the staircase and took a good ten seconds to close the door so Mom wouldn't hear. I went in Hollis's room and started opening and closing drawers until I found the album. It was all put back together and covered in stained black leather and had a forest scene carved into it. The whole thing looked old and in pretty bad shape. Probably worse since I'd slung it across his room. I sort of felt bad over what I'd done, and sat it gentle on the bed.

I started flipping through old pictures of people I didn't know and came to the middle and there were old yellowed clips from the Sunnyside newspaper. One of them was about the funeral of his wife and daughter and there were several that were about him in the war. The last two were birth announcements. I didn't pay much attention to them until I saw my name.

One of them was my birth announcement.

Charles William York it said, born to John and Hadley York. I couldn't believe it and took it to the window to make sure what I was reading. When I stood up, a bunch of pictures spilled onto the floor. School pictures of me and there was another picture of a kid who looked just like me only a little different.

I started bending down to pick them up when there was a movement in the corner of my eye. It was Momma leaning against the door. She was resting her face in one hand and her eyes were all watery.

She stood there and I just stood there, her looking at me

until I finally looked at the mess I'd made. I knew I was in for it being up here and didn't know what to do.

"I thought we talked about this," Mom finally said.

I was expecting a whole lot worse than that and she didn't look mad, just sad or something. She walked over and sat beside me on the bed looking all around the room.

"What's Hollis doing with pictures of me, Momma?"

Mom looked down at the pictures on the floor. She picked them up and tried to shuffle them like cards into a deck.

"He's got something from the newspaper when I was born, too."

Mom didn't say anything and flipped through the book. I handed her the old black and white picture of the kid in a checkered shirt.

"Who's this?" I asked.

Mom held it and her hand must have been shaking because the picture was.

"Is that me?"

Mom gathered up the rest of the pictures and put them in the album.

"Where'd you find this?"

I pointed at the drawer.

Mom placed it back and pushed the drawer back in slow. Then she pushed the other ones in I'd opened before she looked around the room.

"Who was that in that picture?"

"That's a picture of Hollis when he was younger," Mom said. "Let's go downstairs. We have no right to be up here."

I couldn't believe how much I looked like Hollis when he was a kid and just stood there.

"Right now," Mom said again at the door. Her voice was shaky. I knew I didn't have to mind her quite yet.

"Why's he have all those pictures of me?"

"People always give school pictures of their kids to their friends."

She motioned me to go and started to say something else and then she turned and walked down the steps. Halfway down she stopped. "Never go in his room again, Charlie."

I was behind her and nodded.

"I mean it. You do it again and you're going to be punished. We have to respect each other's privacy in this house. Understand?"

"Yes, ma'am."

"Never again."

Her voice was strong again. "Yes, Momma," I said.

She turned and when we got to the living room, I opened one of the curtains above a roll-top desk and looked out. The sun was coming up blazing and it was clear except for flurries circling around in the air.

"Merry Christmas," Mom said.

I closed the curtain and turned around. She now had both hands on her hips and was smiling a little bit.

"Merry Christmas," I said back.

I felt a chill standing there next to the window in my long johns and walked over to the big stone fireplace. I chunked a couple more logs on the iron grate and turned with my back flap to it and looked at the Christmas tree. I still had no idea why Hollis would keep those pictures and stuff. I thought and thought about it, standing there. I turned back toward the tree.

It was the littlest Christmas tree I'd ever seen, especially sitting in such a grand room as this one. Mom said it was the best we could do on short notice and besides that, she just liked it. She told me even though it was scrawny, it may be the prettiest Christmas tree she'd ever seen.

Mom had picked it out the day before from a small bunch of bent-over pines on the windy side of the lighthouse. Hollis chopped it down. I watched the both of them through the window in my bedroom where I stayed the whole day because I was so terrible sick and worn out I didn't want to eat and couldn't hardly move or anything, but I don't think they saw me.

I got too warm on the one side and turned my front to the fire for a minute before I knelt down beside the tree. There were a lot of presents under it and I saw most of the wrapped packages had my name on them. I even saw the ones Lacy had gotten for me in Sunnyside but I'd never opened.

"When do you want to open presents?" Mom asked, now way across the house scrubbing in the kitchen.

I looked up and saw where Hollis had fixed the broken window. Mom kept scrubbing and I knew when she got in those scrubbing moods before the end of the day she'd probably be scrubbing on me, too.

She came over and moved the short blond hair back from her forehead as she walked in wearing wooly slippers. "Did you hear me?" she said.

"Whenever you want to."

Mom went to the record player, pulled out a Christmas record from the shelf above it and put it on. Although it was scratched a little bit, it was really nice hearing that music. I'd never realized how bad that house needed music until I heard it. I knew right then that big houses need music more than little ones.

Mom asked me if I was warm enough and then she got down beside me and grinned so big she looked funny.

"Hollis coming, too?" I asked.

"Call him Tom, honey. No. This is our Christmas. He's out working in the wood shack."

I looked under the tree. "Does he have any presents?"

"I picked him up a pair of heavy work gloves, he's outside so much. I wrote on the card that it's from both of us."

I sat thinking about everything, especially thinking about Dad, and then Mom jumped up all of a sudden. "I forgot to get the cider. I heated up some nice cider we could have with cinnamon while we open presents."

She went back in the kitchen and I walked over past the big bookshelf filled with books that were so old some of them made noises like they talked when I'd open them. I peeped out the one window where I could see the shack, which was about fifty feet from the house and lighthouse. All of the buildings formed a big triangle on the white slope leading down to the water that faced the mainland. I could see a yellow light in the shack just like his shack up on the mountain. Smoke came up from a stovepipe in the tin roof.

Mom walked in with the two mugs of cider and sat like

an Indian. She handed me the biggest mug and I watched the steam come off the top of it.

"Very hot," Mom said, grinning.

I'd missed Mom's cider and I don't think I'd ever seen her so happy. She looked a lot happier than me and that wasn't the way it was supposed to be on Christmas. I was the happiest, usually.

"I'm gonna fix you your favorite breakfast after we open presents. French toast and sausage with a big pot of hot chocolate."

All of that sounded good to me because I was hollowed-out hungry. I couldn't keep anything down the day before because my mind was thinking about all that had happened and been said. I felt better in a lot of ways finally knowing what had happened to Daddy on that day, but it made my belly hurt terrible wishing I could take back what I'd done. If I could just take it back. It was a terrible pain when I knew what I'd done, a whole lot worse than when I didn't, but I knew I didn't shoot him on purpose. I knew that for sure. That didn't change anything, though. He was still gone. And the worse thing was he was never coming back. Ever. After all of those months of him being gone, that hit me in a bottom place with nowhere else to go and I think that's where the worst aching came from. It really, finally, set in and I'd never felt so lonesome.

"Open one," Mom said.

I looked up at her blowing on her mug. "Is Hollis gonna eat breakfast with us?" I asked.

She shook her head. "Honey, Christmas is a time for families to be together. I wasn't going to invite him to join us. Unless you want to."

"Has he had breakfast?" I asked.

Mom shrugged and took a loud sip.

"What's he doing out in the shack on Christmas?"

"I don't know. I think he may be fixing it up. He said something about moving out there so we'd have more space."

"He'll freeze in that shack," I said.

"It has a woodstove in it."

I knew that was true but also knew the wind blew through that shack like there weren't even walls.

"Have you been in there yet?" I asked.

"I peeped in the door with you that day we looked at the whole—"

About that time the record really stuck on the third song so Mom put the needle on the song after it, but it was worse so she started the record back at the beginning on "Silent Night."

"Which one do you want to open first?" she asked.

I looked them over real good and took all of the ones with my name on them and made a pile. It hit me once I got all mine together that there weren't but two left under the tree. One of them was the present Mom got Hollis, and the other was one that he had gotten her. I realized I hadn't gotten anybody anything.

"Go ahead, angel," she said, grinning.

"Hollis may as well come in, too, 'cause he has a present," I said.

"Well go get him if you want."

I went to my bedroom and put on my overalls and boots and grabbed my dad's big wool coat and the hat with flaps and my gloves. It didn't take me long to crunch my way through the snow to the shack. I opened the door and saw where he'd moved most of the lumber and shingles and paint cans that were piled everywhere to one side of the room. He had his back to me framing some kind of wall.

"Whatcha doing?" I asked.

Hollis turned around and I couldn't believe he didn't have a coat on. Just overalls with a big turtleneck sweater under it.

"Merry Christmas," he said.

"Merry Christmas...."

"I figured I'd make my living quarters out here so you and your mom can have more space in the house. I'm used to living in a small place."

"Kind of like your house up on the mountain?"

Hollis didn't say anything after I said that. I looked at the outside walls made out of plywood that had cracks in them everywhere where daylight was peeking in. Wind was finding those cracks, too.

"Gonna be cold out here," I said.

"Not bad with the stove. It's a good stove."

I pulled a hand from my glove and put it near the top of the green potbellied stove and could tell it was going good. Then I breathed and noticed I could still see my breath.

"Mom wants you to come in and open presents with us," I said.

"Well, that's nice of her, but you all go ahead and enjoy your Christmas. I have things to do out here."

"She's gonna make breakfast."

"I'm not hungry."

"You're not?"

Hollis shook his head.

"You have a present under the tree, too. Mom says you should come in and open it while we're all there opening presents."

"I have a present?"

I nodded my head and he scratched his chin and undid a nail bag he had around his waist.

"Well, let's go see what it is, but first me and you have something to do."

Hollis checked the stove real good and turned the draft down and then he walked to the corner and pulled his coat off of something leaning in the corner.

It was that shotgun.

He put on his coat and buttoned it up. "We're gonna throw that gun out in the ocean. Your Mom says we don't need it around here...nothing to hunt out on this rock I can see anyway, so thought we'd just get rid of it."

I didn't nod or say anything but I did back up as he picked it up and broke it down into two separate pieces. Then he took a big hammer and busted the wood off of the butt end that he handed to me. I stuck a hand out and took it, the trigger housing rested in my hand. He carried the barrel end. We tromped down to the where the waves were breaking over rocks on the side of the island facing nothing but water as far as I could see.

He stepped slow out to the rocks farthest out and ended up standing on a big one that jutted out tall at the very end. He turned around.

"Come on out but be careful."

I did what he said and after a minute stood beside him. "Nice day, today," he said, closing his eyes and tilting his head up toward the sun. "Nice to have good weather on Christmas."

I looked at the ocean. The wind had layed and the water looked peaceful. Then I closed my eyes like Hollis did and tilted my head up at the sun, too. Then for some reason I looked back toward the house. I saw a curtain move and knew Momma had been watching us. Hollis held up the two barrels attached together.

"You wanna go first?"

I shook my head.

"Here goes, then," he said.

Hollis wound back like a baseball pitcher with the tip of the barrels almost touching the ground. He flung it over his shoulder with a loud grunt. It looked like it flew end over end for a half minute or more, reflecting the sun before it hit the water with no splash. Almost like the ocean opened up to eat it.

"Your turn," he said.

I took my glove off and got a good grip on it and looked at the trigger in my hand. I did what Hollis did and threw it as hard as I could. It didn't go near as far but it went a long way before it got swallowed up by the ocean, too.

We didn't say anything after that and Hollis finally turned to go to the house and I followed behind him. We went in, both hung our coats on the big iron hooks near the kitchen and then both of us went and stood in front of the fireplace with our backs to the fire.

"Merry Christmas," Mom said.

"Merry Christmas," Hollis said back.

Me and Mom sat around the small tree and Hollis tried to sit like we were doing but gave up trying—I guess being as big as he was with his bum leg not cooperating—so he pulled a stool over and sat on it. It looked like it about broke when he did.

Mom got the record started again and brought both of us cider and then she nodded at me. I started opening up the ones I knew were clothes first that had Lacy's handwriting on the packages. I got a sweater like I got last Christmas, except this one was black and heavier and bigger, and a pair of leather boots with rubber soles that Mom made me try on that were way too big but she said I'd grow into them. Mom said she'd asked Lacy to order those from a mail-order place and he wrapped them for me. I had two more presents left and couldn't figure out what they were because they were in boxes and rattled not like clothes do when you shake them. I saw one of them was in Mom's handwriting and one wasn't. I guessed that one was from Hollis.

I opened Mom's present first and it was a pair of black binoculars that she said would be fun to use to look out over the ocean. I looked them over real good and thanked her. I figured she didn't know that there were two pairs of them in the radio room already but it was good to have my own set, I figured.

"You all open your presents," I said.

Mom nodded and I handed her the present from Hollis and handed him the present from us. He opened the gloves and liked them. But I noticed he had trouble with the one hand that wouldn't work quite right as he tried to get his fingers in the glove.

"I've been needing a good pair of gloves," he said and thanked us both.

Mom carefully unwrapped the newspaper from around her gift and it was a cookbook that had on the front, "Old Maine Chowder Recipes."

"Thank you, Tom," Mom said. She seemed to like her present and smiled and thumbed through the book.

"Chowder is big in Maine," Hollis said shy and quiet-like that seemed kind of odd for him.

There was one present left and I went ahead and tore into it when both of them were focused on the cook-book. I pulled out the box and it had twine wrapped around it. Hollis handed me his pocketknife and I cut the string and opened it up. Inside was a piece of wood. It was about a foot long and I couldn't figure out what it was until I held it up. Once I did, I saw that it was a carving of Abe Lincoln. He had on his big beaver pelt hat and had a crumpled bow tie and everything just like in pictures. He was standing on a knot of wood and had one hand holding a roll of papers and his other hand was up near his heart.

"Your Mom told me you liked Abe Lincoln so I tried to whittle you one," Hollis said.

I just kept looking at it and nodded. It looked just like Abe from all sides.

"Still needs paint though. Didn't have enough time to paint it but we'll get it in good shape."

"I like it the way it is," I said.

"Okeydoke," he said.

It got quiet all of a sudden except for the singing on the record.

Hollis said, "Man needs a good pocketknife, too, up here in Maine." He then nodded at his pocketknife that I'd just used to cut the twine.

"That was my grandpa's knife but I'd like you to have it. He used to whittle me toys with it. It's a good one, just gotta run it across a whetstone now and then and keep a little oil on it."

I already had a three-blade Uncle Henry in my pocket that Dad had given me but I didn't say anything. I looked at the blades on Hollis's knife and noticed how all of them were much thinner and worn than the blades on my new knife Dad had given me. I figured I'd use Hollis's knife to whittle and Dad's to carry around to peel apples and stuff. I folded up the blade I'd used to cut the twine and put my new knife in one pocket with my Dad's knife in the other.

"Let's have a big breakfast," Mom said.

She started to get up and then Hollis stood. "Wait a minute. I think I got something else. Something for Charlie," he said.

Hollis walked over to his coat and pulled out a small package wrapped in brown paper tied with another string. He handed it to me and I felt the weight of it.

I pulled the twine bow and pulled away the paper. It was an old silver pocket watch with a long chain. It looked all shined up. I held it in my hand and popped the top of it like I'd done a hundred other times in the shop while Lacy would tell me stories. The picture of him and Mrs. Coe wasn't in there.

"Lacy told me to give it to you on Christmas."

I kept looking at the inside of it.

"That's where the picture of you and your wife or your kids will go someday," Mom said.

I just kept looking at that watch. I pulled it up to my nose. It smelled like pipe tobacco.

"I wished Lacy was here," I said.

"Me, too," Mom said. She looked at me for a moment and then turned to go into the kitchen almost like she'd smelled something burning on the stove.

"You think he's still in jail?"

She stopped and walked back a step. "I don't know, angel."

"You think they may have let him go 'cause he didn't do nothing?"

She walked back over to me, held her hand down and I let her look at Lacy's watch. She handled it and smelled it, too.

"Do you think he might not be in there, Momma?"

"Lacy is a very, very smart man. I don't know where he is, but I believe he's okay. I'm sure Malcolm has been doing all he can do to help him."

"He didn't help you, Momma."

"Yes, he did."

I looked at her the way she said that strong like she did, but I didn't see where Malcolm helped anybody except he kept smiling at everybody and talking into the TV cameras but that didn't help nothing.

"Lacy's so old. He won't make it in there and nobody cares about him but us. We got to do something."

"Honey, Lacy did what he did, for us. We can't go back, baby. That would take away everything he did for us, and not help him. It would really hurt Lacy if after all he did, it was for nothing."

"Hollis got you out of jail and it weren't too hard. He could get Lacy out, too. I'd help him."

I looked at Hollis and his expression didn't change. Just his eyes, which turned from me to mom.

"We can't," Mom said.

I started getting aggravated at Momma like I had the past months. "Why couldn't Lacy have come with us?" I asked.

"Honey, Lacy wanted to stay in Sunnyside."

"Even if he'd go to jail?"

Mom nodded.

"Why?"

"I'm sure he had reasons."

"Did he know he was gonna go to jail for helping us?"

Mom nodded again.

I started getting a big frog in my throat. "Do you think he might be having a nice Christmas even if he's in jail?"

"I hope so," Mom said.

I started getting more messed up inside because I could tell Momma was getting messed up inside, too. I stood up and went to go to my room.

"You all get cleaned up," Mom said. "We'll eat in a minute." She turned to go into the kitchen but I followed her and grabbed the back of her robe.

"Did Lacy leave a note or anything?" I asked.

Momma looked startled for a second. "Not that I know of, angel." Then Momma looked at Hollis so I did, too, but he shook his head.

"He didn't leave a card or nothing?" I asked.

"No...."

"Do you think he might send us a letter one day or something?"

Mom's face broke right in two and it looked like she was gonna start crying all of a sudden. She bent down and found a frying pan and started pulling stuff out of the refrigerator. "He may, Charlie."

"Can I write him a letter?"

She turned around. "Yes, baby."

"Will he get it if I write it?"

"I'll do my best to make sure he will," she said.

I decided not to go to my room after that and it got quiet for a long time as me and Hollis got washed up for breakfast. It stayed quiet all the way through the meal.

When we finished, Mom said she couldn't believe we almost went through a loaf of bread. I didn't know we'd ate that much French toast but I knew I ate more than Hollis. I know because I counted how many slices he had. I didn't eat more than Daddy used to eat, though. He could eat more French toast than me and Hollis put together even if he wasn't near as big as him.

After the big Christmas breakfast, I went in my room and wrote Lacy a letter. I'd never wrote a real letter to nobody before. Mom asked me if I wanted help with it but I shook my head and kept writing. I told Lacy at the end of it that I was gonna see him again one day, just like he told me right before I left Sunnyside.

That was the first of many letters I wrote to Lacy, but he never did write back.

Chapter Twenty-One

Mom was right that over time I'd learn to like living in Maine, and that I'd find friends and would even learn to care about Hollis. I never thought I'd ever treat him like a father, but over the next five years the roles we played in the village or around the occasional visitor to our small island started to become the real roles we played at home. He did become like a father to me, and we got along with little effort once I gave him a chance. I had many struggles to sort out at that time, and I'm sure he knew that by the wide paths and second and third chances he always gave me. I could tell more every day that he genuinely cared about me. I knew from the beginning of our long trip north how much he cared for Mom.

And I learned much about him. Hollis was the sort of person it took years to know, as he rarely said anything. But over time he told me how he got wounded in Korea and came home a mental and physical mess to his first wife and daughter while trying to resume his life in Sunnyside. Hollis said he was decorated with medals but didn't deserve them. He never did tell me what happened to him in Korea, but he said he changed over there and when he returned home, he began to slip away.

Hollis attempted to take his own life after the war and was admitted to a mental hospital. He told me that he felt numb all of the time and didn't have the urge to live anymore, and that he believed his wife and daughter would be better off without him. The world would be better off without him. He never said what haunted him, but it sounded like even though he left those old battlefields, their ghosts never left him. But he finally learned to live with them, I believe.

In the hospital, Hollis was given shock treatments and after six months was sent home, but he soon drifted into rage and depression and got in scrapes with the police after he began self-medicating each morning with a whiskey bottle.

Hollis said he was downtown drinking one night when a fire took his young family and the house he had built himself before the war. He saw the flames on the mountain as he stumbled on his walk home.

After his family was buried, Hollis roamed the country for a couple of years. He spent time in prison for a beer hall assault that led to an assault charge on a police officer who had the unfortunate task of trying to arrest him. After he was released, Hollis eventually came back to Sunnyside, where he lived in a one-room shack on the mountain. He began retreating inside of himself. He got too used to the quiet, he said, and then began to depend on it. That is, until he helped us escape our lives in Sunnyside.

Hollis never did move into the shack like he had planned on doing that first Christmas in the lighthouse. And slowly over my teenage years, he made it down one step at a time from his tiny upstairs room into Mom's bedroom. I remember the first early morning I saw him come from her room, but it wasn't a big event, as I'd been noticing other things they may have thought I didn't see or hear. Nothing was spoken about his move before or after, not by me, Mom or Hollis. No explanations and no apologies. Mom's room simply became their room from that day on.

During that time I thickened out and grew much more than I ever imagined I would, and around my sixteenth birthday, I went into the downstairs bathroom where Hollis was shaving. I knocked and pushed open the door, stood behind him to get something and when I looked into the mirror, I saw my face behind his and for the first time, I truly realized we were not only about the same height and had the same hair, but we had the same exact eyes.

Dark, shiny eyes.

The same eyes that had haunted me from the first day I ever looked into them. I guess that's why they scared me so much when I was younger. It was something I'd suspected for a long time, probably ever since I found his photo album and the secret things he tried to keep there. I was practically looking at myself when I looked at Hollis Thrasher.

* * *

An hour later on that same early fall morning, I paced and shivered near a wooden bench that had bits of fishing bait carved into it. I waited and waited on that craggy hill for the bus to begin my sophomore year of high school after being home schooled by Mom for five years. She told me I was ready. She called it my first day back in the world, and I'd never seen her so happy and scared at the same time.

I heard the faint blast of an air horn and looked across the Atlantic Ocean and saw her arm waving. The Boston whaler had almost made it back to the lighthouse. I then turned back toward the bluffs and the tiny fishing town with its white Cape Cod houses and tall pines breaking up the sky.

I checked the pocket watch in my hand. The bus was three minutes late. I stood and then sat, stood again and sat again, and every so often read who loved who according to the markings on that bench in Pawtuckaway, Maine.

I pulled up the collar of my sweater and rubbed my hands up and down my brown corduroy pants. My favorite pants. I'd tried to age my boots the night before, but they still looked too new so I scuffed the soles of each one against the toe and heel of the other. I didn't wear Dad's old coat as I'd outgrown it a year before, but Hollis gave me his army jacket that I'd always admired.

The bus finally made its sharp turn on the coastal road and came down the hill in my direction just like it had in my dreams.

My legs weren't shaky but my stomach told me as it always

had that this was a big moment. I looked at all of the faces in the dirty windows as they all looked at me. The door finally opened.

I went up the steps and stood near the driver.

"Pop a squat," he said.

I had no idea what "pop a squat" meant.

"Find a seat," he said, seeing my blank look.

I nodded and walked down the aisle, and tried to find a comforting face as all of their eyes looked me over from top to bottom. I noted that either the bench seats were all filled, or the seats that were half-filled were determined to stay that way.

I made it all the way to the back of the bus where there was nowhere else to go except out the emergency back door. I thought about it for a moment, but turned around.

The driver was looking at me in a big rearview mirror and raised a hand for me to sit.

"You can sit here if you want," a girl with glasses and puffy cheeks said. I'd seen her a few times the past couple of years in town but we'd never spoken.

She scooted over wearing a thick coat that seemed much too hot for the weather. I sat next to her, placed my lunch sack on my lap and felt like I'd passed some great test.

The bus did a half circle and began rolling back up the hill and the quiet turned instantly into a roar of twenty people all talking at the same time. All except for me and the girl next to me. It had been so long since I'd heard so many different voices. So many. I realized how much I'd missed being around people, terrifying as it was.

As the bus made its way through the old fishing town,

we slowed near a chain-link fence that surrounded a ball field. There were kids of all ages outside playing, and I guessed the fence was put there to keep an outfielder with sun in his eyes from running right into the ocean while trying to catch a pop fly.

"Are you one of the lighthouse people?" the girl asked.

"What?"

"The lighthouse people. Are you one of them?"

I turned and she looked genuinely curious as she leaned closer and scrunched up the glasses on her nose. I cleared my throat but only got out a nod.

"I've always wondered who'd want to live way out on the ocean in a lighthouse."

"People like me, I reckon."

"You talk funny," she said.

"You talk funny to me, too," I said back.

We pulled up to the square clapboard schoolhouse surrounded by the ball field and the doors of the bus opened. Everyone jumped up from the benches like the last one off lost some sort of game.

When I stood from my seat, the sack lunch in my lap fell on the floor and the apple, ham sandwiches and a bag of leftover breakfast biscuits with blueberry preserves on them rolled to different places.

The girl who had been nice to me picked up most everything and I picked up the rest among all of the moving feet.

"What's your name?" she asked.

I'd hated answering that question for most of the last five years, but for the first time, I actually thought I could say it without feeling like a liar. I wiped off the mud and gravels from the lunch Mom had made for me.

"Charles J. Cutter," I said.

Epilogue

March 12, 2002

She didn't show up for church services, and a concerned friend found her in my old bedroom that she'd long ago converted into a painting studio. Mom had been sick for over a year, but to me her death still came suddenly. I guess that's the way death is, whether it's expected or not. It catches you not quite ready whether you're at bedside or a thousand miles away.

The town funeral director told me when I drove up to see her that Mom's hands were covered in oil paints of different colors. It made me smile as we tended to her final arrangements. Mom was always happiest her last years when she had paint on her hands.

Three days later, I buried her in a cemetery beside Hollis as was her request, both of their graves overlooking the ocean and the lighthouse, which had been their home since I was a kid.

I was humbled by the number of people who came to fare her well on that snowy March day. I never realized Mom had made so many friends up and down the Maine coast since I'd left home twenty-five years before. I wondered if any of them knew her secrets as they paid their respects.

After our children fell asleep on the long drive home from Mom's funeral to our home in Boston, I told my wife how Mom, Hollis and I came to be people who lived alone out on the ocean in a lighthouse. "The lighthouse people," as a girl on a school bus once described us. With Dad and Lacy, Hollis, and now Mom gone, I believed I could finally tell Jen their story. I needed to tell it.

I began by telling her that I was born and raised in a small town called Sunnyside in the Appalachian Mountains of Southwest Virginia, that my birth name was Charles William York, and the mountain in our town was named Angel's Rest because Mom told me angels waited on the summit to come down and help those in need of God's assistance. And then I began telling her about the horrible, tragic death of a great man who I thought was my father and the trouble that soon began, and I described the old, scarred angel who walked with a limp, smoked a pipe and carried a fine watch, who went through so much to help my mom, Hollis and me survive a tragedy.

I told her about the truths of my past, some of which had taken me almost forty-six years to discover. It was a long drive, but it was a long story.

* * *

One evening after the town library closed, Mom went to check on her former high school boyfriend, who no one had seen or heard from in weeks. Hollis didn't want her to see the way he lived and the man he'd become, but she insisted and entered. Before the evening was over, the old flames they still carried for each other combined with their loneliness took them too far. A son was produced from that one night who was named Charles William York.

John York, who I also consider my father because he gave me such love and raised me as a little boy, and taught me so many important things about growing up and being a man, found out when I was eleven years old that I wasn't his son, after he'd gone to a specialist in a nearby city. He and Mom wanted to have another child but were having a hard time conceiving. Dad found out that not only could he never have children, there was no way that he could have ever fathered a child. It was impossible, the doctor had told him.

On that horrible day when I accidentally shot my father, he'd just learned that I wasn't his son. Mom told me everything when she was sick in the hospital with cancer a few months before she died. She told me many, many things those last few months visiting with her.

I've long since stopped trying to put together the reasons why what happened, happened. My father didn't deserve to die so young and violently after discovering a truth that hurt him so badly it turned into rage.

As Mom always said, he was such a good man. I'll never

forget what my Dad said to me before he died on that kitchen floor. He said, "You're my son."

I didn't know what that really meant, then.

After the accident, Mom and I tried to somehow go on with our lives but someone was going to pay for Dad's death. Justice did demand it.

Mom was afraid on that day that I would pay forever for her one night of "sin," not her. She'd lost her husband, but she was terrified that she was going to lose her only son to scandal and a juvenile prison. At best, she believed I'd be shunned and feared by everyone as the boy who shot his own father. She feared I'd never be able to go on and survive the horror of that day, especially when my conscious mind had blocked out what happened.

From the first lies Mom told, things spiraled out of her control, starting with the simple lie that Dad had accidentally shot himself while cleaning his gun.

It is what he told us to tell the police.

People in town didn't hate my mother or me, and I don't blame them now for the way they treated us. Small towns are really big families, and that whole town loved my dad so much, and they knew something was not right about his death. They smelled a secret.

Mom tried to protect me not only from the criminal justice system, but also from the truth that I wasn't actually the son of her husband, something I wasn't ready to hear. Living in a small town, there is sometimes a great price to pay when such things are revealed.

She wanted to tell me when I was older and maybe would

understand. She told me much during that last year of her life, like the rumors of Hollis seeing her at the library after closing time were true. Mom told me Hollis would come down to see me while hiding behind a book on the days I'd accompany her there, and he'd ask how I was doing in school when everyone left. She said he'd been keeping a close eye on me since I was born, including the day when he had stopped by our house on Angel's Rest to ask about me moments before my dad came home from his fateful doctor's appointment.

So in late 1967, as Hollis, my mother and I traveled the highways into Maine, the one thing I did notice was a genuine caring between Hollis and my mom. I didn't like that of course and feared both of them at that time, but I did like to see her smile again and none of that made sense to me. I couldn't understand what connection she had to this strange, dangerous loner named Hollis Thrasher.

I know now that she'd been in love with him all of those years, and from what I've come to understand, married my dad after Hollis hastily married another young woman during one of their breakups before he went off to war. Mom said they were all so young and much more kids than adults. She always said Hollis was a much different person before going off to war than the man that came home. But deep inside, he was always the same.

"Just without the grin," she'd say.

In Sunnyside, my mom ended up marrying a man she respected and cared for, a man who was good to us and worked hard to provide for us, but she'd never been in love with him.

She'd been acting long before we went to Maine. She'd been acting ever since she got married and then became pregnant with Hollis's child.

She raised the son of her one true love in life, and that was a secret she could never share with anyone until the accident, and then she had to tell someone and she told everything to the wisest man she knew. If for no other reason, she couldn't tell anyone else. Mom drove to Town Heights and sat down with Lacy Coe.

My mother didn't know what to expect when she told Lacy what happened because he and my dad were so close. She told me she received understanding.

I asked her why Lacy put himself in so much danger to help us. Mom told me how Lacy would travel from black church to black church in the late 1940s and early 1950s, telling his simple stories about good and evil, strength and weakness. She said he was warned to cease with the stories because according to some in Sunnyside, he was "stirring up the niggers."

Lacy kept telling his stories.

A few weeks after being threatened, Lacy was found in the middle of a dirt road with his hands tied, he was semi-conscious, with wounds on his back and a deep laceration across the base of his neck. He'd been whipped and almost dragged to death and was told if he ever told another story to anyone, he would be killed. Lacy begged for his life and became a quiet man.

Mom told me it was my dad who found Lacy that day and took him to the hospital, and she also told me my dad believed that the man I knew as my grandfather was one of the men who hurt Lacy. She said Dad and Granddad never got along once Dad became a young man, and she said Dad was protective of me whenever I was around him. Dad didn't want Granddad's hate spilling into me like he had tried to spill into him.

So after weeks in a hospital, Lacy did quit telling his stories, and slowly he became an old man and over the years ended up loafing downtown. I asked how it happened that Lacy ended up spending his days at the store, and Mom said he just walked in on a hot day and took a seat in the chair beside Dad's office. Dad didn't ask him to move on like other store owners did, so Lacy came in the next day and the next until months and years went by and Dad began picking him up before work.

Mom told me Lacy never spoke in public again, but he did tell his stories to a small boy who climbed up on his lap wanting to hear them. Mom said the men who almost killed Lacy shut him up, but not completely.

I missed Lacy terribly after we fled north to our small island. I wrote him a letter every day from that first Christmas until March 1968 when Mom finally found the courage to tell me that he had died.

I still write to him occasionally.

The lives my mom, Hollis and I led on our island in Maine were simple but difficult ones to get used to. The up-keep of the lighthouse didn't take much energy or time once we got used to the routines. There were so many hours in the day to fill. I became a decent fly fisherman and also began writing stories. First, setting Lacy's tales to paper so I'd remember them, and then my own.

Mom began painting seascapes and she and I took many trips together to see different places. We sold her work and Hollis's carvings to the shops in Bar Harbor and Freeport several times a year.

Hollis turned the woodshed into a carpentry shop, where he would go alone for hours every day and carve his things. He even finally learned how to craft stringed instruments, and that's what he focused on until he died from a heart attack in 1989. Hollis built handmade violins, which were sold all over the world.

In a very big way, Hollis saved Mom and me, and we likewise saved him from himself. Hollis would forever be a loner carrying all of his scars. He needed that lighthouse, just like he needed his shack up on Angel's Rest, but taking care of the both of us gave him a reason to live. We gave him a reason to be strong. I do think toward the end, Hollis Thrasher found a way to live with the man he saw in the mirror each morning.

I traveled to Sunnyside with my family a few weeks after Mom passed away. I had to go, almost like I was being called back there. Once we left the interstate and got on those curvy mountain roads, I rolled down the window and took in the smells from cool breezes and looked at the never-ending hills that led up to long blue ridgelines. It was almost springtime. I slowed down driving. You just slow down in places like Sunnyside.

But driving into town, I was surprised that so much had

changed. I saw a huge discount store near the middle school where a cornfield had been. I remembered hiding in the muddy, stobby rows while skipping school that terrible year Dad died.

The Tastee-Freez had closed but there were a couple of chain fast-food restaurants. As we drove down Main Street, I saw how almost all of the old businesses I remembered were gone.

The buildings were still there, but there was little life in them. The town looked like it was in a period of transition. My Dad's old radio and TV shop was now empty, and it looked like the last business to occupy that space was a used furniture store.

All in all, I remembered how wonderful a place Sunny-side was in the 1960s. It could have been such a great place to grow up. Tragedy and ugliness live in places and people everywhere I've learned. They live in me. It wouldn't be a real town if Sunnyside didn't have its fair share of dark se-crets, its villains and its victims. Its heroes. Even with every-thing, Sunnyside was still a very warm place to me. I felt at home here, more than anywhere else.

It looked much different in my memory than now, but I thought it would find its place again. Maybe Sunnyside was trying to start over, too. If I've learned to believe in any-thing, I believe in starting over.

I don't know what happened to Jimmy and Alvin or the Wilson twins or Mary Elouise or the old friends I had be-fore the accident. I've wondered many times where life had taken Jimmy. Something told me he was doing okay and would never end up like his father.

I drove by Malcolm Boone's estate and it looked so much smaller than it did when I was as a kid. I remember hating him when I first found out that they'd found my mom guilty of murder. We'd put so much trust and hope that he could convince a jury of her peers that she didn't shoot her husband. But after time, I realized even the great Malcolm Boone couldn't defend her. Mom was a lost, young, confused mother who was willing to go to jail to protect me from truths she believed would damage me forever.

Malcolm knew what happened. Mom never told him, but she told me that she could tell he knew. Like Mom, I believe at a point Malcolm felt that we'd crossed a point of no return with our story. Even if she ended up changing it, now no one would believe it.

I tried to add up in my head how old Malcolm would probably be now as I drove by. Somewhere in his early eighties, maybe. I figured he was probably in a card game somewhere.

The place I wanted to see last before my family and I drove up on Angel's Rest was Lacy's old lot on Old Tannery Road. The remains of his house were long cleared away and someone had built a much larger brick house where his small cinderblock home had stood. As we drove by, children played in the yard.

I didn't go by my old house on Duncan Hill. I'm not sure of all the reasons why, but I thought it better to leave that one place in my memories.

Going up the mountain, I saw how all of the roads were now paved and a developer had put in a large subdivision beyond the reservoir. Hollis's old house was now someone's backyard. His tiny shack was gone. The many secrets hidden in that mountain, I thought.

I continued to drive by the living that afternoon, but my one stop was to visit with the dead. My road-worn daughters were curious why I'd taken them to this little town in the Appalachian Mountains. They were in a hurry to begin their vacation in Florida. I told them that I had distant relatives in Sunnyside and had spent some time there when I was young.

"We won't be long," I said.

I pulled over at the graveyard on Angel's Rest. My father's grave and the others around it bearing the York last name were still being tended to. After talking with him about many, many things and showing my two little girls his marker and telling them what a great man he was, it began getting dark and I stood to look for the resting place of the best friend I've ever had.

It didn't take long to find Lacy's grave. I walked through the iron gate that separated the white graves from the black graves and found his small tombstone. It made me feel good seeing that his wife and young child lay beside him.

I knelt down and read that Lacy had passed away only two weeks after Mom, Hollis and I had fled Virginia. I'd known that since Mom told me a long time ago, but it did feel differently reading the date carved into a small piece of rock.

Mom had broke the news of Lacy's death to me a few weeks after she found out herself while researching what had happened to him during our second month in Maine.

She ended up finding his obituary. Mom never got a chance to mail the letters I wrote to Lacy. She gave them back to me before she died.

Those emotional times and all that he gave to help us go on must've been too much for him. I figured he knew it would be all along. Lacy died in jail. A large part of me believes he died in peace, there. He died brave, something men carrying hate and ropes just couldn't take from him in the end.

I still don't know for certain if Ethan York, the man who I believed to be my grandfather, was one of the men who torched Lacy's house or terrorized him. Mom said Ethan York was a powerful man in Sunnyside, and he used to be one of those men. But I don't know who hurt Lacy. The answers to those questions have probably been buried on the mountain for a long time, now.

Ethan and my mother fought a brutal battle over my custody, a battle I never knew was going on until he tried to take me from Lacy one night. Mom believed that if I were taken from her control and into the arms of my dad's extended family, she'd never be able to get me back with all of the charges and forces against her. They did, after all, believe she was a murderer, as I did at times. Once arrested, her only hope in keeping her son was an old, tired, wise black man who she knew I would listen to.

As I sat beside Lacy's grave, all of the stories he told me as a boy, the high and low notes of living that he loved to weave into the longest tales between puffs on his pipe, began filling my memory. I wished he were still around so I could introduce him to my family and tell him that I was beginning to appreciate the music as he always called it, of living and dying. Of choosing strength over weakness, because as he told Hollis, both reside in every heart.

Lacy always told me his stories were true and I still believed him, and then I remembered how the only lie he ever told me was that he'd see me again one day.

I smelled the cool mountain air and suddenly realized that he may not have lied after all, because if there is a place where the music makers go once they leave this world, he is surely there with the company of my two fathers and mother, and maybe they'd let me in, too, once my song ends.

But maybe he just knew that someday I'd return to visit with him here. I'd have to come back.

I sat for a long time on the kept grass Lacy's body had been feeding for almost forty years. I looked out over the valley of my boyhood, and for the first time, I believed I had a good story to tell him. A story about a troubled kid who eventually overcame a tragedy because of the selfless acts of his mother, a wise old man and a battered war hero.

I saw my two daughters playing under a wild apple tree and called them over. They ran toward me dodging the gray stones that carved up the ridgeline. I pointed to a marker and told them that this was the resting place of my best friend.

I looked down at their blond hair as Lacy and Hadley studied the dates with their fingers, and my oldest daughter recognized that she had the same name as he did. After they ran back to the car and the comfort of their mother, and as the night wind began singing down the ridges of Angel's Rest, I told Lacy I now understood some of the meanings of all of those great stories he told me.

I also told him that I'd recently begun telling a few of them to my daughters, and at the end they'd ask me if the stories were true. I'd tell them that a wise old mountain man who'd spun those tales between puffs on his pipe assured me that all of them were.

The mountain was now dark and the lights of the town were coming on below me. I patted Lacy's grave like he used to pat my hand, pulled a small bundle of letters from my jacket and placed them on his stone.

I stood to walk forever out of that Angel's Rest graveyard of my past, but something told me I'd be back someday to visit with him again.